"My heart will be heavy when I steal your spirit," Geronimo told Man Killer, looking with regret at the captive he would be forced by duty to slay.

"Geronimo!" An Apache approached. "Our warriors come with a white-eyes."

Into sight came a small party on horseback. One of them was a ruggedly handsome man on a large black and white paint, with eagle feathers braided into the mane and tail. He was clad in a Lakotah-made buckskin shirt, yellow-striped blue cavalry pants, rough-out boots, and large-roweled Mexican spurs. A single eagle feather stuck on the right side of his headband. Around his waist he wore a double-rig holster with twin mother-of-pearl Colt Peacemaker .45 revolvers, with an eagle, biting and gripping a serpent, carved into each butt. A large bone-handled Bowie knife rested in a fringed and beaded sheath behind the left holster.

Geronimo saw him, too. He said simply, "Colt."

Chris Colt had come into the camp of the most feared Indian in the West to somehow save Man Killer's life. More likely he would join him in agonizing death. . . .

WARRIOR

by

Don Bendell

Ⓞ
A SIGNET BOOK

SIGNET
Published by the Penguin Group
Penguin Books USA Inc., 375 Hudson Street,
New York, New York 10014, U.S.A.
Penguin Books Ltd, 27 Wrights Lane,
London W8 5TZ, England
Penguin Books Australia Ltd, Ringwood,
Victoria, Australia
Penguin Books Canada Ltd, 10 Alcorn Avenue,
Toronto, Ontario, Canada M4V 3B2
Penguin Books (N.Z.) Ltd, 182-190 Wairau Road,
Auckland 10, New Zealand

Penguin Books Ltd, Registered Offices:
Harmondsworth, Middlesex, England

First published by Signet, an imprint of Dutton Signet,
a division of Penguin Books USA Inc.

First Printing, March, 1995
10 9 8 7 6 5 4 3 2 1

This book is dedicated to Chief Joseph, Looking Glass, White Bird, Sitting Bull, Crazy Horse, Geronimo, Cochise, Mangas Coloradas, Quannah Parker, Tecumseh, Sequoyah, Gall, Black Kettle, Ouray, Naiche, Red Cloud, Rain-In-The-Face, Victorio, Manuelito, Powhatan, Osceola, Washakie, Nana, Sacajawea, Captain Jack, Red Jacket, Black Elk, Bloody Knife, Buffalo Calf Road Woman, Pocahantas, White Bull, Too-Hoo-Hool-Zote, and many other chiefs, warriors, and noble women, not listed here, their sons and daughters, and theirs and theirs, and those with white, black, yellow, and brown skin who have believed in those of the red skin. The red that flowed through your veins, poured into this land we call America, and hallowed the ground, consecrating it with pride, dignity, family values, and the spirit of the warrior. The courage, nobility, and principles of the American Indian, the Native American, have been imitated and duplicated by warriors all over the world, those who want to stand for something great.

Warrior from the City Tribe

A warrior from the City Tribe
Who's living at the white man's side,
Who hasn't felt his father's pride,
Or changed to white, although he's tried,

Who's never thought of sun dance times,
Or children's games, or shaman's rhymes;
He's never tasted buffalo hump,
Or rode a horse with spotted rump.

He steals no ponies, counts no coup,
Yet hides from long-knives dressed in blue.
He watches smokes from tall square hills.
He says no prayers to cure his ills.

He never speaks to Father Sun,
Or shoots a bow or white-eye's gun.
Forgetting that his skin is red,
His heart is now what's really dead.

So, if you join the city clan,
And live upon their asphalt land,
Do not forget your tribal ways:
A warrior always fasts and prays.

And always walk with head held high,
Like braves who live up in the sky;
And if you wear the white-eye's suits,
Remember, Son, your proud red roots.

—DON BENDELL
from *Songs of the Warrior*

"When they will not give a doit to relieve a lame beggar, they will lay out ten to see a dead Indian."

The Tempest
—WILLIAM SHAKESPEARE

Chapter 1

>>>>>>>>>>>>>>>>>

The Warrior

The coyote stopped in midstride. He turned his head and his ears perked up, twisting left and right. It was instinctive for him not to stand still very long. His head went up slightly and the little back nostrils started flaring as he tested the wind. The hot, dry, acrid heat was like the inside of a dutch oven loaded with coals, but to the coyote, it was something uncomfortable that forced his tongue out to pant heavily.

There was movement, and he spotted a scorpion moving across the desert sand. His attention went back to sniffing the wind.

Suddenly, it shifted again, and he waited. The smell would return. His mind instinctively catalogued the various smells wafting through his nostrils. Cacti, old urine from a desert bighorn sheep, very faint odors from a decaying mule deer carcass five miles distant, horses, buzzards; blood, feces, death; gun oil, vomit, gunpowder, leather, steel, and other man smells. Those were danger smells, and he wanted to run, but the scents of blood, urine, feces, and death attracted him so he moved closer, following the smell, his senses ever keener, more alert.

He traveled fast, but only a few feet at a time, his eyes, ears, and nose checking all about him with each halt to ensure there was no enemy nearby. The coyote bitch was one-quarter mile out to the south, but her eyes had been on him and knew he had a scent. All these thinking processes were simply instinct, and that was how they hunted. The two always hunted in pairs and had greater success that way, sometimes one jumping a quarry that would run in abject fear, then circling back close to the other mate, who would pick up the chase, while the first one rested. Jackrabbits and kangaroo rats aside, these hunters, however, preferred finding carrion when it was available. Even though the man smell signaled danger, they had eaten that meat once before, and it sated their appetites. He smelled vulture, so there was carrion from where the smells were originating. There was also fresh blood.

Three Chiricahua Apache lay dead a distance behind the coyote in the hot sun, and a fourth, the youngest, now lay near death, blood slowly seeping from his right thigh and running fairly freely from the bullet hole

through his right side. He was only in his fif-
teenth summer and was beginning to prove
himself a real man with his band, though he
knew he would now make the spirit walk
and meet Usen, but first he had to put dying
and pain out of his mind and concentrate on
killing this strong-heart enemy, who had
struck down his friends. This warrior he
faced, from a northern nation, was mighty—
the best he had ever seen or faced.

The wounded young man was named
Strong Rope, and he had only one thing in
mind: He had to defeat this enemy and
maybe steal some of his powerful spirit medicine, so it would help him in his journey to
and through the afterworld. He wished his
band's shaman was here to bless him and
help him on his journey, but Geronimo was
many days' walk away with the rest of the
band. The white-eyes thought Geronimo was
a chief, but Naiche was the chief, though Geronimo's name was on the tongues of every
white, black, red man, and Mexican in the
southwest.

Strong Rope saw little bugs fly around in
front of his eyes, but there were no bugs
here, just sand fleas in some places. He felt
panic, but he tried to push it from his mind.
This was like the time the horse fell with him
in the rocks near the Mimbres Mountains,
where Victorio had grown up. His side had

been torn open in a bloody gash, with much pain in his stomach. He still felt pain sometimes when he had to void waste from his body. As he lost blood then, he had started seeing little bugs flying around in front of his eyes. Soon after that, he would get weak and everything would get light, then black, and he would sleep when he didn't want to. Geronimo healed him then, but he was not here now.

The northern Indian looked totally different from Strong Rope. Strong Rope with a square jaw and round face, wore high-top leather moccasins, which were pulled up to protect against cactus needles. His body was short and very stocky. He wore a faded brown breechcloth and an ammunition belt with bullets for his brass-studded Henry carbine, and a sheath and knife on the right hip. He also wore an old cavalry shirt that had faded to a very light blue, almost white, by hour after hour in the hot sun. His black hair was parted in the middle and hung straight down, a wide, brown bandanna headband holding it in place.

The northern Indian, on the other hand, was tall and lean with high cheekbones and a hawklike nose. He was very muscular, his muscles rawhide tough but not bunchy. His hair was parted in the middle also, with a small pompadour in front and was braided in two pigtails, which were both wrapped and braided with long strips of beaver fur. He wore a beaded leather headband and a single bald eagle tail father hanging at an angle from the back of his head. He wore a conch shell and a bone hair pipe choker necklace around his neck and a red shirt with large white polka dots all over it. He also wore a leather beaded armband just above each rock-hard bicep. He wore faded yellow-striped, blue cavalry trousers and colored porcupine quill-decorated soft sole moccasins. On his waist he wore a well-used and well-worn brown gunbelt and holster with a walnut-handled standard Colt .45 Peacemaker revolver, and he carried a second, as a belly gun, tucked into the front of his belt, which had all the loops filled with .45 bullets. On his left hip was a large bowie knife in a quilled sheath. In his hand he carried a Winchester .44 carbine with brass studs and a hawk feather and eagle feather decorating it. It had a leather sling. He also wore a leather pouch, or parfleche, around his shoulders that was filled with .44s for the rifle, some beef jerky, and other "necessaries." An empty canteen lay over another shoulder.

The northern warrior lay flat on his belly behind a small rock, the last Apache lying wounded in a jumble of rocks fifty meters to his front. He decided to crawl forward to the next rock, which was even smaller, only about one foot in diameter. It would not shield every bit of his body. Some parts would be exposed to the Apache's rifle fire, but the man figured he was a warrior, not someone who sat in a tepee, making buffalo hump stew.

The warrior went ahead on his knees and elbows, his left elbow scraping against a prickly pear cactus. The needles penetrated the skin of his arm, but he paid no attention. He could not afford to. There was pain, but it was ignored. He scrambled until he was safely behind the cover of the small rock.

Intelligent eyes scouring the jumble of rocks, the warrior hoped the Apache lay dead among them and wondered why his scramble forward had drawn no rifle fire. He risked rolling over on his back while he gasped for breath. He had been out of water for some time now, and the blazing sun over the Mexican desert was sapping his strength. One of the Apaches, earlier sniping at him, had shot a hole through his canteen. The warrior had quickly whittled a small stick into a plug and cut a small piece of leather to act as a gasket around the plug. He had pounded it into the hole with the butt of his pistol and kept the canteen with him, until he could get to water again.

He looked up at the blue cloudless sky, and off in the distance a little saw more vultures flying in to feed on the carcasses of the dead Apaches. Quite a distance off, he could still see the buzzards, like little dots, circling around and feeding on the last of the Apache ponies. When he saw how much trouble he was in without water, he chased off his big black Appaloosa horse, Hawk. The sixteen-hands-tall horse with the white blanketed rump, covered with black spots, kept returning, but the man knew he could not burden the horse with his weight. The gelding's stomach was already sunken from the beginnings of dehydration. He kept waving the horse off, and it finally understood that it had to leave and get help.

Like the warrior, the big horse was straight from the band and animal husbandry program of the famous Chief Joseph of the Nez Perce. In fact, the tribal leader had named this warrior Man Killer several years earlier, ending his childhood name of Ezekiel, when the warrior was just a young teenager.

Saved by the legendary cavalry chief of scouts, Chris Colt, nephew of the famous gun maker, Man Killer had been captured by some bad hombres and tortured. His younger brother was even killed by the men, who had stolen a horse herd that the two boys had been watching. During that period Man

Killer's legendary sidekick had been blinded after being struck by a grizzly bear. Man Killer had to be Chris Colt's eyes while the pair crossed the wilds of Montana and Idaho, along the Snake River. When various criminal elements heard the news that the mighty Chris Colt was blind and escorted only by a little Indian boy, they swarmed to the area like so many packs of coyotes. The young Man Killer, then named Ezekiel, did all the seeing for Colt and helped fight off numerous outlaws, hence earning his name from a grateful Chief Joseph.

Man Killer, a scout, generally worked for Chris Colt and lived at, as part owner, Colt's Coyote Run ranch in Colorado. But now he was working as a scout for Crook against the renegade Geronimo and his band with Al Sieber, the famous mountain man, working as his principal chief of scouts. There were 193 Apache scouts and three chiefs of scouts, but Colt had not been offered the job because it was well known that Colt wanted to see fair and humane treatment for all American Indians. It also had not been working out well for Man Killer since he was a Nez Perce and just about all the other scouts were Apache; also he was almost like a younger brother of Chris Colt.

Educated by Christian missionaries and exceptionally smart, he could hold his own in conversation with any American who could speak English. Being American Indian, however, especially from the band of Chief Joseph, one of America's most celebrated orators at the time, Man Killer would sometimes change his speech pattern and speak more poetically, which was the nature of many red men.

Man Killer now rolled back over and looked at the group of boulders. There was no movement. Like the Nez Perce and many other nations, the Apache had infinite patience in situations like this, so a lack of movement from the rock was not going to cause Man Killer to charge forward blindly.

Strong Rope opened his eyes and shook his head to make the bugs go away from his vision. He was getting weaker and weaker and would have to soon confront the enemy.

Because Man Killer was considered an outsider, Al Sieber had sent him alone on the trail of the four Apaches who were a small scouting party sent out from Geronimo's main group. The young warrior didn't even flinch. He had been against much greater odds before and had survived, even trumped-up murder charges in a white man's justice system. He had followed the four Apaches for five days before they spotted him, and the route kept taking them farther south in a meandering course.

The desert was forbidding and unforgiving, filled with rocky canyons, flood-carved arroyos, and steep-sided mesas. There were desert bighorns, mule deer, sidewinders, scorpions, colorful but deadly Gila monsters, and coyotes. Cacti grew here and there, and some seemed to wait to ambush any intruders into the fiery domain who escaped the other dangers. It was almost as if the cactus plants could sometimes shoot their needles. More than one time during the journey, Man Killer had to pull painful needles out of his legs and feet.

Man Killer was Nez Perce and a warrior of the mountains and what Colt called the high lonesome. But he could see the beauty of the desert; the rich colors of the changing skies, the different soils, the sharp contrasts of bright green and the different shades of flowers and cacti against the dull colors of rock and sand, but here and there, rock formations and cliffs with wildly varying colors and tints. He understood how some nations such as the Apache, the Modoc, the Navajo, Hopi, Zunis, and others could appreciate the desert, but he longed for the snow-capped peaks, trees, giant rocky cliffs, plunging streams, and all the dangers of the mountains. He did understand the feelings of the others, though, figuring their feelings toward the desert must be like his toward the mountains.

Man Killer was ready to approach the rocks and take his chances with the wounded brave. Earlier, he had finally been spotted by the four warriors, so they had set up an ambush for him in a rocky gulch, and the running fight began.

Man Killer easily outdistanced their war ponies with his long-legged Appaloosa, but most people did not realize that the Apache would run a horse until it died and could continue running on foot until the horse they pursued also dropped from exhaustion. Man Killer knew enough to pace Hawk and kept him going at a fast trot most of the time, but he also knew what they were doing. The terrain offered fewer and fewer hiding places, so he tried desperately to think of a plan. He was angry with himself for having been discovered by the four, and he was growing angrier because they now had him on the run.

When he had finally decided that he had to make a stand, it was almost too late, for himself and his horse. He saw ahead of him, a couple of miles out in the flat Mexican desert, an area of dunes, which was unusual, but sometimes found in North American desert regions. Man Killer suddenly urged Hawk into a full-out sprint, which puzzled the

Apaches, whose ponies were now dead, the Indians following on foot.

Soon the big horse and rider disappeared behind the dunes. Slightly over ten minutes later, they entered the dunes area, following the tracks of the loping horse. When they topped out on the first hill, they immediately spotted the line of tracks down the slope of the dune they were on and back up the next dune, disappearing over the crest.

They followed the tracks, the force of gravity causing them to run down the hill a little faster than they had been.

Suddenly, the ground in front of them exploded upward, as Man Killer jumped up, a blanket and a thin covering of sand flying off him. He held a Colt .45 Peacemaker in each hand, and both weapons started stabbing flame as bullets poured into the bodies of the four Apaches. The last one over the dune and the most coordinated, Strong Rope, quickly analyzed the situation and retreated farther over the dune, ignoring the first of his wounds.

The withering fire was too much for the others, but Man Killer was concerned. He knew he had let one escape, and he had too much respect for the Apaches to stick around. Two gravely wounded warriors somehow made it over the dunes, as well, but he did not worry. He knew they would not last long. The scout put his two hands to his mouth and gave the whistle of a red-tailed hawk, and seconds later Hawk cantered over the top of the far dune and ran up to his master.

Man Killer grabbed the saddle as the horse slowed slightly and trotted by him. He swung up on the mount's back and touched his heels to the horse's flanks, galloping out of the dunes.

Within fifteen minutes Man Killer saw that his horse had been too long without water. He sent him away, hoping the horse would head for the last military fort, Camp Bowie at Apache Pass in Arizona. Once there, at least the horse would have a chance to survive, and if Man Killer was lucky, someone would recognize the horse and maybe a patrol would go out on his trail. Thinking this, the Nez Perce laughed at himself. He was an Indian. No patrol would be sent out. No matter what, Man Killer decided, without being burdened by scout or saddle, the horse might make it to water.

He had sent the horse away several times with shouts of "Go home! Go home!"

And finally the big mount had listened and headed north, finally disappearing from sight.

Man Killer decided he would have to defeat the surviving Apache and trust to God to save him from the desert. Many in Joseph's Wallowa Valley band, including Joseph himself, had been raised and educated with Christian missionaries. Like his father Old Joseph, Chief Joseph had turned back to tribal spiritual beliefs, but Man Killer had remained a Christian in his thinking.

He went forward on his belly, pushing a two-foot-wide rock in front of him. Slowly, carefully, Man Killer crawled toward the hideout of Strong Rope, always keeping the heavy rock to his front, hoping to protect the vital areas of his body. He was so exhausted by the time he reached the rocks, Man Killer had to roll over again and just pant. He felt he could no longer sweat, his body was so dry and drained.

Finally, catching his breath and fighting exhaustion, he rolled over and jumped up, scrambling into the circle of rocks, a gun in each hand. Strong Rope lay on his back, unconscious, arms out spread, blood seeping from his wound and mixing with the hot, gray soil.

Man Killer immediately opened his parfleche and produced clean dry cloth, then started treating the wounds of the young Chiricahua. He amazed himself and thought how much Chris Colt had affected his way of thinking. It was not his way to let this enemy live, this warrior near twenty summers, just like himself, but his way of thinking had been altered even by Chief Joseph. During the seventeen-hundred-mile retreat of the Nez Perce, their famous leader, acting on the advice of Chris Colt, would not kill, torture, or take prisoner wounded American soldiers, take scalps or mutilate dead enemy, harm civilians, or bother settlers in any way. In fact, during the retreat, with the cavalry closing in, the Nez Perce entered one Montana town and bought supplies, treating the townspeople with friendliness and respect. In the meantime, the U.S. cavalry, pursuing them on several occasions, attacked the Nez Perce village, killing women and children. American newspapers picked up on this curious phenomenon, and public opinion, for the first time in U.S. history, was on the side of the red man and against the white military.

The young Apache had lost a lot of blood and was very near death, it seemed. The scout looked all around, trying to locate a distant spot to head toward that might hold water and shelter, but all he saw was heat waves, sand, rocks, and cacti.

Strong Rope awakened, but kept his eyes closed, half awake and half unconscious. He knew that the enemy was touching him and doing something to his wounds. His mind drifted back into the blackness, and he remembered standing at a pile of small stones as a young boy. He and the other boys in his band were placed at two piles of stones, half the boys at one pile and half at the other. Each Apache boy would pick up a stone from the pile, throw it at another boy, then wait until another threw one and hit him. He had three bleeding cuts on his face from rocks and a swelling eye, plus a bruise over his left rib cage and another on his right shoulder. The idea was to keep hitting one another with rocks to learn to withstand pain. A boy could quit or yell out if he wanted to, but it was shameful. The boys kept hurting each other this way, until only Strong Rope, who was one of the youngest there, still stood by the rock pile, blood seeping from many cuts.

He could conquer pain with his mind, and he knew he had to now so as to vanquish this mighty warrior and steal some of the man's powerful medicine. His eyes opened and his hand closed around the bone handle of his steel knife. It came out of the sheath and his upper body pushed up off the ground. Man Killer, kneeling over him, drew one of his pistols and struck the Apache's raised knife arm with the barrel, severely bruising the radius bone and nerves in the forearm. Strong Rope dropped the knife like a hot poker, but he grabbed for Man Killer's

24

face, wanting to gouge his enemy's eyes with his thumbs.

The Nez Perce grabbed the Apache warrior's wrists with his powerful hands and pinned the weakened warrior back against the ground. He held the struggling brave there for a second, his mind searching for a solution. Man Killer looked down at the Apache's wounds and nodded with his head. Strong Rope looked at the fresh bandages on his wounds and immediately stopped struggling.

Man Killer got off of his chest and again attended to the injuries. Using the international sign language of Indian nations, Man Killer placed the heel of his hand against his lips, as if letting water run from his cupped palm into his mouth, indicating water.

Strong Rope looked around and pointed toward the farthest mountains to the west. They looked devoid of trees, just some hills, rocks, and mesas in between. The scout nodded and the Apache suddenly passed out again. Man Killer continued to bandage the wounds, then stood, slinging the warrior over both his shoulders, and started walking toward the far purple and blue mountain range.

The words of Chris Colt kept echoing through Man Killer's brain: "If you have a long journey to make, Little Brother, and you feel you cannot make it, just take the first few steps, and the end will look that much closer."

As he passed along the corridors of blinding sun rays and heat, he did not see the almond-shaped black eyes staring at him from beneath a creosote bush one hundred yards to the south. The eyes looked at the long black braids wrapped with beaver fur, and the man pictured that scalp hanging from his side. He would follow this strange warrior. His right hand came up and signaled the others to follow as well. They followed, not because the man was chief; he was not. Naiche, son of Cochise, was the chief, but he always deferred to this man, because he was not only a mighty shaman but a brilliant tactician, too. This man, the one they called Geronimo, was really the leader of these renegades, and they would all follow him into the bowels of Hell. In fact, on this day they had. Geronimo squinted against the sun's glare and saw Man Killer fall for the first time with his heavy burden. The young scout rose to his feet though and kept on toward the far-off mountains.

His head pounded with pain, and it hurt to swallow. His mouth felt as if it had been stuffed with dry oak leaves and he had to swallow them with no saliva. Man Killer stooped and picked up a small pebble, placing it in his mouth to keep the saliva flowing.

His legs and back ached already from the heavy burden, but he kept walking, his mind picturing the long, flowing golden locks and hypnotic laughing eyes of Jennifer Banta, the woman he loved: the white woman. He thought of their first meeting when she had wandered off from her ranch a little southwest of Westcliffe back in Colorado.

It was an unusual way for a teenaged boy and girl to become acquainted. Man Killer and Chris Colt were scouting ahead of a cavalry patrol sent to escort them to Fort Union in New Mexico, where they were to scout for the Ninth Cavalry against the Mimbres renegade Victorio. That's when Man Killer spotted her tracks for the first time.

It was close to noon when Chris and Man Killer found the tracks due east of Music Pass. From the eastern side of the valley, the two scouts could look at the path taken through the tall mountain grass toward the big range. At first, the trail headed toward Medano Pass but turned toward nearby Music Pass.

This was one significant way a tracker could catch up to a quarry being pursued. A scout had not only to read a track, but put a story to it—use powers of reason and figure out where the person or animal is ultimately headed.

Man Killer said to Colt, "You saw the tracks where a small horse left the ranch house back there?"

Colt said, "Yes, and I saw where the young lady dismounted, then got back on."

Man Killer said, "She stopped her horse to pick some pretty mountain flowers. How many girls do that?"

Colt answered, "Some, I'm sure."

Man Killer said, "And the Utes started following her. Right here, she stopped and looked back and saw them coming and ran toward that pass."

Colt said, "Music Pass."

The leg- and arm-weary Man Killer carrying the heavy Apache across the deep sand remembered how easily he vaulted onto the saddle atop the big Appaloosa. Chris had spoke to him again, knowing the young man was going to go off to save a fair maiden.

Colt added, "Man Killer, you know that I cannot come with you. I have committed to scout for Lieutenant Wiggin's patrol. I cannot just leave, or their point will be unprotected."

Man Killer said, "I know this, Great Scout, but you know I must go and try to save her?"

"I know it. Take care, my friend. You'll do

the right thing. I'll be taking the cavalry across Raton Pass. I told you how to get there."

"I'll find you."

Colt smiled and nodded, reaching into his scabbard and pulling out his twelve-gauge Colt revolving shotgun. He tossed it to Man Killer, who smiled, wheeled his big horse, Hawk, and headed toward the unseen girl and some of the powerful Ute warriors they had fought the day before.

Chris turned War Bonnet, his big black-and-white pinto, toward New Mexico and went on with his job. He was somewhat worried about Man Killer, but he viewed him as a man and warrior, not a boy, which he might have done had Man Killer been white. He also saw the concern on the Nez Perce's face when he read the story told by the tracks of the young ranch girl. Chris chuckled as he thought of Man Killer's impression of her stopping her horse just to pick some flowers. It had apparently really impressed him, and Colt didn't have the heart to tell him that many sensitive young ladies had done the same thing. The chief of scouts always yearned for action, especially coming to the aid of someone in need. He, however, had a patrol of cavalry troops following him who could be wiped out if Colt went off to save one person and missed a big war party that was setting up an ambush. He had to be loyal to his commitment, but he was glad Man Killer could go after her. The odds were tremendously against the young man, but he was a protégé of Chris Colt. That put him far ahead of the game.

Chris Colt stayed in sight for a good while, while Man Killer pushed quickly across the narrow valley. He could easily see his buckskin-clad hero as Colt rode south down the green valley, but soon Man Killer had to ride into the trees at the base of Music Pass. The girl had galloped while the Utes kept their ponies to a steady trot. The whole time, Man Killer tried to think of what Chris Colt would do in this situation. He knew that the woman's horse would tire out a lot sooner, and the Utes would eventually catch up.

This had been a few years earlier, and now Man Killer was more experienced pursuing the small war party from Geronimo's band, but in just that short period of time, he had gained a lot of confidence. His mind went back to that first meeting with Jennifer, and it at least made him smile as his weary feet moved one after the other through the blistering sand. It was one of those major successes that had given him the confidence he now had. He kept after the beautiful young lady he could envision but hadn't yet seen.

He kept on and admired the fact that the young woman had pushed her horse into a stream running parallel to the trail, but the Utes were not fooled. They kept on the trail, over Music Pass, and Man Killer noticed that, every so often, they would send one man to the stream to ensure she was still climbing up the cold watercourse. Dudes and dime novels tried to indicate that one could lose a tracker by simply riding up the middle of a stream, but any good scout knew how to find rocks in the clear water that had been scarred by a scraping horseshoe or an overturned rock. With the young lady, the Utes were so close, they could tell she was still in the water by the mud flowing downhill through the fast, clear water.

Man Killer kept trying to figure out what Colt would do in his position, and he finally concluded that the big scout would simply push on and deal with rescuing the woman when the time came. He was learning from the chief of scouts and his other hero, his former chief, Joseph, to be patient and take problems as they came.

He had no problem following the Utes, as he was fairly certain they would stay on the trail over the pass. He wondered if she would, at some point, try to circle and make it back to her ranch. He knew that the warriors hoped for that, and they would let the natural terrain funnel her right back to them. Man Killer also wondered if the girl, or woman, had been missed. For some reason, he felt that she was his age, and he had already developed a special bond with her, in his mind.

Man Killer rode higher and higher toward the clear blue sky above the Sangre de Cristo range. Somewhere, not far beyond him, rode a frightened young woman, a young woman who liked to stop her horse just to pick some pretty flowers. Between the young Nez Perce man and the young woman was a war party of Utes with a thirst for blood. Man Killer knew that Chris Colt would be able to save the woman. No matter what happened, somehow, someway, the mighty Colt would win, and the girl would be saved. How would he measure up to the test of his manhood, he wondered. Would he measure up as a mighty warrior?

Man Killer, alternating between a fast trot and a slow canter, knew that he was slowly catching up. He looked down at his left index finger and held it up while he trotted down into the massive San Luis Valley. Around the end of it was wrapped a long golden hair. He had picked it up off some long grass stems a few feet from the spot where the young woman had picked the flowers. She had long, golden hair and tiny feet. The depth of her foot tracks, and those of her horse when she was mounted and when he had no rider, showed the young tracker that she didn't weigh very much. He also estimated her height to be slightly over five feet, because of the length of her stride coupled with her boot size. These were all simple things that almost any tracker would know just by reading sign, but Man Killer, like Colt, could see much more.

Man Killer plodded on, but realized he was slightly smiling, so in love was he with this gorgeous golden creature from a totally alien world, a civilization which had, ofttimes, been anything but caring toward his own people. But he could not help himself. He heard a noise behind him and started to turn and draw, but his mind wandered off again, back in time.

Man Killer, love-struck by simply reading tracks, took off after the young lady and the party of Ute warriors who also followed her. He found her and ran her down in a chase, ending up staring at a girl who was the most beautiful creature he had ever seen. Man Killer finally got to see her face-to-face, and she turned out to be every bit as beautiful as he had imagined. He led her away from the

Ute war party, but the trail would not take long for them to find.

They ran for just a few minutes, and already she felt as though she could not take another breath in the thin air, when he stopped and hid her among some boulders. He had been carrying the Colt revolving shotgun and handed it to her, as well as his walnut-handled Colt .45 Peacemaker. Her eyes widened with fear again, as he stood preparing to leave.

Man Killer said, "Stay here and hide. If they find you, shoot and shoot. Do not give up. That is a shotgun. Wait until they are close."

She said, "Please don't leave me. How can you? You gave me all your weapons."

He smiled softly and said, "You need them more than me. I will come back. Do not be frightened, pretty one."

He was away in a flash, and Jennifer watched him move quietly down the mountainside. Man Killer ran quickly through the undergrowth to the spot where the two landed when they fell off their horses earlier, when he first saw her.

Jennifer watched the handsome young Indian and admired the breadth of his shoulders, and the long, flowing black hair as he streaked down the mountainside. She was amazed that he said he was a friend and that he gave her both his guns, leaving him with nothing other than a knife to protect himself. He may be an Indian, she thought, but he was the most handsome man she had ever seen. In fact, the sight of him took her breath away again.

Man Killer pulled a knife out and suddenly slashed his arm. Blood ran down the arm, and Man Killer scraped some off and flicked it onto the path the Utes took. He then ran down the side of the mountain until he was out of sight.

She let out a whimper watching this, but stared at his actions with amazement. He had actually cut his arm so he could create a blood trail and lead them away from her. What courage, she thought, what incredible daring, and he had done it to save her life. Now she wondered where he had gone.

Man Killer came to full consciousness again as he trudged along leg- and arm-weary beyond belief. He knew what he had done with the blood trail was a courageous act, and that is what he expected of himself, but was he now being brave or simply foolish. Should he not drop his enemy and leave the brave to his own fate? Man Killer thought back to that day in the Sangre de Cristo range and one of his early successes. He did not give up then. He pictured Jennifer fright-

ened and alone waiting for him to reappear,
and indeed she had been.

She waited. The dark woods got quiet.
Then she started hearing birds and insects.
Far off, there was the sound of a red-headed
woodpecker tapping on a hollow tree. He
was gone, and an hour passed. Jennifer got
more frightened with each passing minute.
He was bleeding heavily from his large biceps, she thought, and wondered if he might
have fainted down the mountain somewhere.
Her grandfather was one of the early settlers
in this area, homesteading along the Arkansas River. She knew from the family what
would happen to a pretty young lady captured by the Utes. What had happened to the
handsome young Indian, she thought. If he
was dead, she would never forgive herself, or
forget him.

There was movement to her right front.
Without a sound the war party suddenly appeared. Three of them walked in front,
studying the ground, leading their ponies.
With their war paint and the looks on their
faces, they frightened her a great deal. The
last man in the war party led the handsome
Indian's Appaloosa. Jennifer noticed that it
was a large horse and not an Indian mustang. It was also saddled with a cavalryman's

McLellan saddle and a blue-and-yellow-trimmed cavalry blanket.

The three warriors in front found the spots of blood and got excited, pointing them out to the chief. The entire war party followed the blood trail down the mountainside. She feared for Man Killer. She had a feeling that he alone could protect her. His coolness and quick thinking were remarkable. What in the world had happened to him, she wondered.

The war party disappeared down the mountain, slowly and carefully following his blood trail. Where was he?

Man Killer popped up not ten feet in front of her out of the thick, green undergrowth. She stifled a scream, and he grinned, giving her a shushing gesture. His wounded arm was bandaged with a strip of cloth, and she wondered where it had come from. As he ran up to her, she noticed tiny lace around the edges of the white bandage. She lifted the edge of her cotton dress and saw that a strip of her petticoat had been cut away with a razor-sharp knife. She looked into Man Killer's laughing brown eyes. He had cut it away before, without her knowing it and had already been planning then to cut himself and leave a blood trail.

The two stared into each other's eyes for several seconds. Volumes of love poetry and

many stanzas of romantic ballads were sung
with those looks.

Man Killer looked at the bandage on the
arm of the lifeless-seeming Apache, and the
sight brought him back to the present. As
Man Killer trudged step after step across the
hot sand, he looked at the golden rays of
sunlight streaking down and thought of the
long, yellow tresses of Jennifer Banta. They
looked as though golden honey had been
poured all over her head and slowly dripped
off the ends of each hair, melting in the blistering sun.

Like now, his bravery then was beyond
that of others, when he had cut his arm and
left the blood trail for the Utes to follow,
carrying them away from the young beauty.
He had safely returned to her hiding place in
the Sangre de Cristo Mountains and led her
away, with the Utes in distant pursuit. After
that, they made their way across Medano
Pass, and finally out into the Great Sand
Dunes, where giant dunes over five hundred
feet high had piled up sand against the western slope of the steep range. There, Man
Killer hid the blonde and used her boots
with sticks in them to make a phony trail,
then buried them in the sand. He finally
made his stand against the warriors.

It reminded him forcefully of his current

predicament. Wounded many times over, Man Killer fought bravely against all the warriors, finally defeating the last with a desperate knife thrust as he was beginning to faint.

Jennifer, now madly in love with her muscular red hero, treated his wounds, made a travois, and transported him back over Medano Pass to her ranch.

After that, Man Killer was treated by a doctor at Jennifer Banta's ranch house, and he met her father, Chancy Banta, a slight, cantankerous, but wonderful, leather-skinned, white-haired cowboy with an ever-present twinkle in his eye.

As he weakly placed one foot in front of the other across the Hades-like Mexican desert, Man Killer wondered if Jennifer Banta's boots were still buried where he had left them in the Great Sand Dunes. He pictured some white man, maybe a prospector, finding the boots upside down in the sand and thinking someone was buried underneath them, maybe falling headfirst out of them. This struck the warrior funny, and he started laughing hysterically as he continued toward the far-off mountains.

Behind him, many eyes watched and many ears listened as this strange and courageous northern warrior laughed aloud when he was so near death. It was hard for some to understand but all who watched and listened respected the warrior, for these watchers and listeners were warriors, too.

People, especially warriors, and animals sense when someone stares at them. Even the average person will occasionally experience this when they suddenly feel someone behind them, staring. Turning around, the person, many times, will actually see someone there. Almost delirious from lack of water, Man Killer wheeled and fell, but kept looking behind him. Something moved, and he knew someone was there.

He thought it might be a big miner wearing Jennifer's tiny boots, and he started laughing again. It dawned on him he was in more danger, and he shook his head, trying to make himself think clearly. He sensed someone behind a saguaro cactus to his rear, and he took careful aim at it, but decided not to shoot and holstered his gun.

Geronimo, still behind the cactus, let out his breath. This young man was maybe of the Pierced Noses, he thought. He was not an Apache, but this young one was a warrior indeed. He also handled a short gun like the white-eyes and that, too, surprised Geronimo. Geronimo carried a short gun, holster, and belt, but usually only when showing off for cameras. He decorated the gunbelt and holster with numerous pieces of silver and hammered-out dished silver coins, but for warfare he preferred a rifle.

Man Killer hoisted the limp Apache, turned back toward his destination, and took three more steps, finally spotting something to give him hope. Still carrying his heavy burden, he almost ran to the small, squat barrel cactus. Geronimo wondered if the brave would spot this and know about it.

Man Killer lay Strong Rope down gently by the cactus and pulled his big bowie knife out of his sheath. He slashed off the top of the cactus and pulled a green, wet, spongelike pulpy substance from within. He opened Strong Rope's mouth and squeezed water into it. The Apache's eyes fluttered, and then opened. He looked up at Man Killer and gave him a weak smile. The Nez Perce reached his hand into the cactus stump and scooped out water, drinking it with relish. Strong Rope accepted more water, then looked off to his left and smiled. Man Killer turned his head and saw a whole line of Apache warriors walking toward him, weapons pointing his way, Geronimo walking in front of them all, a carbine carried at the ready on an angle across his body.

He stood and wheeled, going for his guns, and the blood rushed from his head. Lights started flashing before his eyes, and suddenly there was blackness, cool, soothing blackness.

Man Killer saw trees all about, and it was hot, but this place was different. There were strange animals jumping along from his left to his right, and they were like giant rabbits, but each had a long tail.

Somewhere in the trees he could hear Jennifer crying and pleading, "Man Killer, save me, please?"

He was in blackness again, but he felt Jennifer rubbing a cool, wet rag on his forehead. Water poured between his thin lips, and he swallowed it, savoring the sweet coolness running down his throat.

Man Killer struggled through the veil of blackness and realized he had long been unconscious. It was not a strong realization, but rather a slowing, growing awareness. He slowly recognized smells, burning mesquite, pine needles, leather, corn, sweet bread, a woman. His eyes wanted to open, but he felt himself slipping back into the blackness again. He wanted to see Jennifer again, however, so he decided to leave the comfortable blackness and make his eyes open. He looked up into a pair of black eyes. His head was on the lap of an Apache warrior. No, he thought, it was an Apache woman, then he thought again, no it was an Apache woman dressed like a warrior. Her eyes were smiling and she gave him some more water.

"You have been a long time in the land of many dreams, Pierced Nose," she said. "How are you called?"

He said, "I am Man Killer of the Nez Perce. Who are you?"

"I am called Lozen."

Man Killer sat up suddenly and his head swam. He said, "Lozen, the famous warrior woman who fights with Geronimo?"

"You know of my name?" she asked, genuinely surprised.

"All who follow the trail of words about the Apache know of Lozen, the warrior woman," he said.

"This is true?"

Man Killer replied, "This is true. Where am I?" He did not thank her for his care, as that was not the Indian way. Gratitude was always understood.

Lozen replied. "The rancheria of Geronimo."

Man Killer was surprised, saying, "Why do I live?"

She said, "No one questions Geronimo. He is wise."

As if it were a given signal, none other than Geronimo himself entered the wickiup and looked down at Man Killer.

Man Killer said, "You are Geronimo, a mighty enemy and a great leader. I am Man Killer of the Nez Perce."

Geronimo said, "And you were a scout who led the buffalo soldiers against Victorio and his people."

Man Killer smiled and said, "Victorio was a great warrior and hard to defeat."

Geronimo asked, "You are the brother to the great scout called Colt?"

Man Killer replied, "I am proud to be the brother of Wamble Uncha as the Lakotah call him. I live in his lodges, and we ride on the same lands side by side."

Geronimo said, "He is not here now."

Man Killer said, "He is at his lodge with his woman and children. He has two children now, a son and a daughter."

"You scout for Al Sieber?"

"Yes."

Geronimo grinned and said, "They send you alone after my warriors because you are not Apache or Navajo."

Man Killer smiled. He said, "Why am I not walking the spirit trail now, Geronimo?"

"It was not your time. You carried Strong Rope on your shoulders and cared for his wounds. Why did you not kill him and go?"

Man Killer said, "I do not make war on men who cannot fight me back, or women, or children." He glanced over at Lozen and said, "Except maybe some women who fight as good as any man."

Geronimo said, "I do not think I understand this, but maybe so."

Lozen said, "How many wives do you have?"

Man Killer said, "I have none."

Boldly, she said to Geronimo. "This one could make me work among the wickiups with the other women and make babies."

Man Killer blushed a deep red, and Geronimo left the wickiup, grinning.

No sooner did Geronimo leave than Lozen stared into Man Killer's eyes and quickly removed her clothing, standing before him totally naked.

Man Killer looked away and said, "Lozen could only be the woman of a mighty shaman like Geronimo."

She moved down to him and dropped upon her knees directly in front of him. Her hand went up under the tanned antelope hide covering his own nakedness. His breath caught, and he looked away from her, not speaking.

She said, "Or the mighty warrior Man Killer. Why do you not look upon the body of Lozen? Do you not want to lay with me?"

Man Killer gulped and said, "Yes, very much." He sat up with a look like an excited little boy, continuing, "But Lozen, my heart is

45

with another woman. When my thoughts are
of her, my heart sings."

Lozen was angry. She snapped, "She is of
the Pierced Nose?"

Man Killer said, "No, she is of the white-
eyes."

Lozen spat at his feet and stormed out of
the wickiup, her clothes in hand. He struggled to his feet then to the door, watching the
naked woman warrior as she stormed past
several men. One pointed at her and held his
bow, making some phallic joke with it to two
others who laughed. She stopped, picked up
a rock, and slugged the brave squarely in the
face with it, sending him reeling over a bush
onto his back. The others laughed at him as
she walked into the brush.

Man Killer went back to the fur bed and
lay down, his head spinning. He sat up and
drank several gourds full of water from an
earthen pot and felt a little better. His eyes
closed, and he was instantly asleep, his
dreams of a beautiful blond maiden, green
grass, and high mountain lakes.

Lozen rode out from the rancheria and
thought of killing more white-eyes and Mexicans. She usually kept more to herself and
had even been photographed by white-eyes
only one time, while many in Geronimo's
band had had their pictures made many
times. From then on, she decided, she would

not again make her feelings known to another man. She would show them how a woman could fight.

At the end of the second day of resting, Geronimo entered the wickiup of Man Killer and said, "Come."

Man Killer, feeling much better and stronger now, followed the legendary Apache across the rancheria. They came to another wickiup at the end of the village and Geronimo showed the scout the way in. The shaman left and Man Killer entered. Inside, Strong Rope sat up and looked at the Nez Perce. He stuck out his hand, and the two shook, holding on to each other's forearms. They spoke for several hours and Man Killer found he respected the young warrior.

He was surprised to find out that people were pretty much the same all over. Living among the whites, he had seen it, just as he had in the lodges of the Nez Perce. There were those who were brave and those who were not, those who were strong and those who were weak, some who spoke much and those who spoke little. Chief Joseph spoke seldom, but very seriously and eloquently when he did. Joseph's brother, Ollikut, however, talked incessantly and was a great joker, clowning around with everyone.

The next day Man Killer approached Geronimo about leaving.

The Apache said, "You cannot leave."

Man Killer said, "Why can I not leave?"

Geronimo said, "I should kill you. Will you not scout against us for the blue-coats?"

Man Killer replied, "It is my job."

Geronimo said, "It is my job to stop you."

The scout said, "I cannot stay."

Geronimo said, "If you leave, you must die."

Man Killer said, "When I can, I will go."

The Apache responded, "Then you will soon walk with the spirit trail with those who have defied Geronimo."

Man Killer said, "I was not given my name, because I pick many flowers."

He quickly flashed in his mind to Jennifer and wished he was in the Wet Mountain Valley in Colorado, holding her in his arms.

"Maybe I will kill you now," Geronimo said.

Man Killer said, "No, you will not."

"Why will I not?"

"Because that is not Geronimo's way," the Nez Perce said. "You will wait to see if I leave, then try to kill me."

Geronimo grinned. "Not try."

Man Killer smiled softly. "We will see what comes on the wind."

Geronimo said, "And so it shall be, young brother. My heart will be heavy when I steal your spirit. The wind is now blowing. What comes with it?"

"Geronimo!" An Apache ran up yelling, "Juh and others come with a white-eyes, a captive."

Geronimo watched as the small party rounded the trail along the steep cliff side and walked through the trees into the rancheria. In the background, trees dotted the other steep mesas of the Sierra Madres. Man Killer grinned as he saw a large, well-built, and ruggedly handsome man on a large black-and-white paint with eagle feathers braided into the mane and tail, red coup stripes around each foreleg, and red handprints on each rump. Clad in a Lakotah-made buckskin shirt, yellow-striped blue cavalry pants, rough-out boots, and large-roweled Mexican spurs, Chris Colt wore a leather scout hat with a single eagle feather sticking back on the right side from the beaded headband. Around his waist he wore a double rig holster with twin mother-of-pearl-handled Colt Peacemaker .45 revolvers, with an eagle biting and gripping a serpent carved into each butt. Fancy scrollwork was engraved on the metal parts of the shiny guns. A large bone-handled bowie knife rested in a fringed and beaded sheath behind the left holster. Geronimo noticed that the left little finger of the famous scout had been recently amputated. The stump was still pink where the scar tissue was building up.

What also excited Man Killer was the sight of Hawk, his horse, being led by one of the Apaches. Chris Colt, atop War Bonnet, was also led by a rawhide braided rope around his neck. He was grinning and nodding at Apaches right and left as he was brought up to Geronimo.

Smiling broadly, Colt winked at one ugly woman and said, "Morning, ma'am."

Looking at her husband, who also could not understand English, he said, "Howdy, sir. If we get into a fight, I'm going to let you live. That will fix you."

They pulled up in front of Naiche and the legendary shaman.

Geronimo simply said, "Colt."

Chris, grinning broadly, nodded at the Apache shaman and said, "Naiche, howdy. Geronimo, it's been a long time, you old throat-slitter. I came here in peace to parley. Your boys here don't understand it. I put my guns in my saddlebags and put the sneak on them at their cooking fire. I walked up and grabbed a piece of rabbit and started eating it. Finally, after seeing me, these brave warriors held guns on me, tied my wrists, and brought me here. Mighty brave warriors." Colt gave a little chuckle.

Geronimo looked at Juh, who looked down at his hands.

The Apache leader said, "Untie him. Give him his weapons you took from saddle-bags."

Colt held his hands back while another warrior cut through the bonds with a razor-sharp knife. He removed the noose and swung his left leg over the neck of the big paint, War Bonnet, and slid out of the saddle, landing in front of Geronimo, whom Colt towered over. He stuck his hand out, and the two clasped forearms. Of course Colt towered over most people anyway, having been able to look slightly downward into the eyes of six-footers his whole adult life.

Finally, Colt looked at Man Killer and said, "So, you got sick of white people and decided to join up with Geronimo, huh?"

Man Killer said, "Yes, Geronimo has been telling me to leave, and I have been begging him to let me stay."

"Colt," Geronimo said, "you have come far. Tonight you will sleep in the wickiup of your Pierced-Nose brother, and we will talk when the sun starts his walk across the sky again."

Chris Colt nodded and tossed Geronimo a small oilskin sack, explaining, "Coffee and sugar, for your fire tonight."

Geronimo turned and walked away.

Chris and Man Killer ate antelope stew and talked and smoked long into the night.

The next morning Geronimo came to the wickiup and said simply. "Let us three walk together and talk."

They walked away from the rancheria and sat on rocks on top of a thousand-foot-steep cliff overlooking the Sierra Madre range running deeper south into Mexico. Colt pulled out three cigars and lit one for each. They blew smoke to the four compass points, and Geronimo said a silent prayer, then they each enjoyed the cigars and talked.

Geronimo said, "You have come for your young brother?"

"I have."

"I cannot let him leave."

Colt laughed and said, "You are Geronimo. Most folks would say you can do anything you want."

Geronimo puffed his chest out a little and looked out over the mountains, saying, "Tell me, Colt, you were respected by Cochise when we first met. Do you think the white-eyes will treat my people right if I surrender?"

Colt said, "Probably not."

Geronimo said, "You are more like Apache than white."

Colt said, "There are honorable white men, Geronimo."

"Some," Geronimo said. "I cannot let your

friend leave. He leads the Long Knives against us. We are enemies."

Colt said, "You and I are enemies, but we respect each other. Geronimo, what if I give you my word that he will not scout against you?"

"Then he can leave."

Man Killer said, "I cannot give my word. I was hired to do a job."

Colt said, "But I am a chief of scouts, and you work only when I say so. You are fired."

Man Killer grinned.

Colt said, "It has been done."

Geronimo said, "You may go, but first I must have your word that you will not make war against me or my people, Colt."

"Unless my family is attacked by your people," Colt responded.

Geronimo said, "That will not happen. This is good tobacco."

They left the cliff side and returned to the rancheria. On the way Geronimo said, "You know the location of my rancheria."

Man Killer said, "So we do, but Colt's word has been given. We do not twist words when speaking from the heart." Saying this, he touched his breast.

Geronimo said, "Another Colt with red skin, this one is. He killed three of my warriors. He wounded the best, treated the man's wounds, and carried him on his shoulders, looking for water."

Colt grinned and said, "I would have slit your warrior's throat and left him there."

Geronimo gave out a howl and said, "So would Geronimo."

They took a few more steps and Geronimo added, "Perhaps Man Killer has stronger shoulders than us, old warrior."

Colt smiled, looking off at the horizon, and thinking of the real meaning of the wise leader's words.

"Perhaps," he replied.

At the rancheria Man Killer was given his weapons, and he went straightaway to Hawk and petted him all over.

Geronimo watched this while sharing another cigar with Colt and said, "He is a strange one, this warrior."

Colt said, "No, my enemy, his ways are just different from yours. He is of a different nation and has also lived among the whites a long time now." Colt then handed Geronimo a leather parfleche and said, "A gift for my enemy."

Geronimo said, "I must give you a gift, too."

Colt looked at Man Killer and back at the Apache and winked, saying, "You already have."

Man Killer mounted up and walked his

horse over to Colt. He started to say something to Geronimo, but was interrupted by the sight of Lozen, her jaw firmly thrust forward, striding up to them.

She said, "He cannot leave."

Geronimo said, "Why?"

She replied, "I challenge him to a fight to the death."

Man Killer raised his eyebrows and whispered to Colt, "Lozen, she is mad because I won't be her stallion."

Colt said, "She probably has her pick of stallions. She is mad because you won't be her mate."

The gauntlet had been thrown down, and Geronimo would not let them leave without accepting the challenge. Both scouts knew this.

Man Killer and Colt dismounted and said, "Lozen, you do not want to do this thing."

Lozen spoke between clenched teeth, her lips curled back, "Yes, I do."

She drew her knife and started circling him in a crouched position.

Man Killer crossed his arms over his chest, standing tall, and said, "I do not make war on women."

Colt said, "Friend, you better, or she's going to run you through with that pig-sticker."

Man Killer stood there firmly, arms crossed.

She said, "Fight or die!"

Lozen started to lunge, but Colt stepped forward, hand up, saying, "Wait, hold up. Geronimo, he will not fight her, but I will. Is that okay?"

Geronimo looked down at Lozen, and she was so mad now, she just wanted to stab anybody, so she nodded her head affirmatively.

Colt pulled Man Killer out of the way and whispered, "Stay with the horses."

Man Killer said, "No, this is my fight."

Gritting his teeth, Colt said, "But you aren't fighting."

Man Killer kept quiet when he saw the look on Chris's face, knowing that Colt meant he was not to be argued with.

Colt said, "I will fight you, Lozen."

She came forward and slashed with the knife. As her hand moved across his body with the blade, he pulled his midsection back and the blade passed by it.

Colt looked down quickly and pointed at her right foot, saying, "Your foot's bleeding."

She looked down and Chris launched a right uppercut from the hip that literally made her body arch backward through the air. Colt stepped forward and pulled the knife from her still fingers. She did not move.

Geronimo said, "Kill her. It is your right."

56

Colt tossed the knife to the Apache and said, "Nope, I was trying to prevent a killing. I don't make war on women either."

"Something to think about, old enemy," Colt added. "No matter how many whites and Mexicans you kill, it won't bring your wife and daughters back. And doing what the Mexicans did to them doesn't make you any better than them, does it?"

Geronimo said, "Maybe this is true. I will think on it."

He raised his hand and waved.

Man Killer said, "Wait, Colt."

He dropped from the saddle and picked up Lozen's prone body and carried her to the wickiup he had been in. He carried her in and poured water on her face. She sat up suddenly and looked around as if in a stupor, then started shaking her head. He poured more water on her face, and she snarled, starting to strike at him. He grabbed both wrists and pinned her back against the ground. Man Killer looked into her eyes and smiled.

He said, "Lozen, I leave now, but I want to tell you, if I did not promise my heart to another, I would be proud for you to bear my children and warm my lodge."

A tear appeared in the corner of one of her eyes, and she gave him a strange look.

He bent over and kissed her lightly on the

lips, and she kissed him back with all her being. Pulling back, he spoke softly, "Your smile and your face will always be in my mind. I have spoken."

He stood and walked out of the wickiup, jumped over Hawk's rump, and rode off with Colt without looking back.

Geronimo opened the parfleche given him by Colt and smiled. He reached in and pulled out a handful of cigars, an oil sack of coffee, and an oil sack of flour. He lit one of the cigars.

Coming down out of the mountains, Man Killer finally spoke, "Why did you come?"

Colt said, "Got a telegram from a friend at Camp Bowie. He said you were an outsider with Al Sieber's scouts and were sent out alone after one of Geronimo's war party. War Bonnet and I rode freights down, and I ran into Hawk after I crossed the border. He had found a nice meadow at a *tinaja* and was recovering pretty well, I'd say."

Man Killer said, "He found a water hole and grass and stayed there?"

Colt said, "I know you want me to say he bought himself a ticket and took a train back up to Colorado to fetch me, but he is a horse, you know."

Man Killer laughed at himself and his expectations. Then he said, "You backtracked him to me?"

"Yep."

They rode on a little and Man Killer said, "Would you really have slit the throat of the warrior?"

Colt took a swig of water from his canteen and handed it to his friend, saying, "That's for you to decide."

Chapter 2

>>>>>>>>>>>>>>>>>>>>>

Strangers

The two men held close to the Bavispe River and headed north toward Arizona. They talked of heading northwest to Tucson, but decided against it and crossed over the Chiricahua Mountains inside Arizona, then crossed over into New Mexico, heading north toward Lordsburg. They went up to Santa Fe and boarded a freight from there. In Pueblo, Colorado, they decided to give their horses more rest and took another train to Texas Creek along the Arkansas River about sixty-five miles west of Pueblo. There they unloaded and took the Texas Creek Road south toward Westcliffe and came to Coyote Run, the ranch of Chris Colt, about ten miles north of Westcliffe and only about seven or eight miles south of Texas Creek.

Man Killer was happy to be home, to get a hug from Chris Colt's beautiful wife, Shirley, and eat some of her apple pie. The former Shirley Ebert, who owned a thriving restau-

rant business in Bismarck, she and Chris
Colt had fallen in love and had gotten married a few years earlier. They had the type of
relationship Man Killer wanted to have with
Jennifer Banta. The two seemed to keep falling more deeply in love with each passing
day. They had two wonderful children now, a
little boy, Joseph, named after the Nez Perce
chief; and a baby girl, Brenna, a Gaelic word
for Raven, because of her dark hair and
lashes at birth.

Joshua Colt, Chris's half brother, rode in
from herding some cattle out of the mountains on Man Killer's second day back and
found the brave asleep in the bunkhouse,
still recovering from his ordeal. It was about
midmorning and Joshua walked into the
bunkhouse to welcome his young friend
back. Joshua had the same father as Chris
and a mother who had been a Negro maid in
Ohio, who had a love affair with Colt's father.
Chris had given part of the Coyote Run
Ranch to Joshua, and he was in charge of
the ranch operations, cattle, horses, and everything but Man Killer's own small herd of
Appaloosa horses, which he was breeding
and breaking when not out scouting. The
Colts had also given Man Killer a ten-percent
interest in the giant ranch, making him quite
wealthy, on paper anyway.

Two years older than Chris, Josh had a

light brown complexion and curly black hair, but other than that, looked almost like a twin to Chris Colt. Having spent years in the saddle and learning the handling of both men and livestock, he was the consummate cowboy. Wearing a pair of batwing, worn, shiny leather chaps, large Mexican-roweled spurs with tiny bells on the sides, jeans, a faded red bib western shirt, and a red scarf, Joshua had a twinkle in his eyes, like Chris sometimes. He had the look of a man other men just naturally followed. He shook dust off his big, black Stetson hat by brushing it on his right thigh and walked to the stove in the corner of the bunkhouse.

Burning his fingers on the handle of a blackened coffeepot, Joshua shook his hand, yelping, "Guldurn it! That blasted pot! Well, you decided to quit vacationing down in Mexico, so you could come home and sleep all day, huh? I tell you. These cigar store Indians. Don't know how to fight or ride. Just drink firewater and howl all night, then sleep all the next day."

Man Killer chuckled and pulled the covers up over his head. From under the blanket, he said, "Got any whiskey?"

Joshua's words were muffled through the blankets. "No, but here's some water for you."

Man Killer felt the bucket of cold water as it

splashed on him and immediately soaked through the blankets. The cold made him shrivel into a ball and hold his breath. He jumped out of bed in time to see Joshua laughing heartily and ducking out the door. Clad only in his breechcloth, Man Killer, laughing, chased out the door after him, carrying the wet blanket to throw at him.

"Joshua!" he yelled and stopped dead in his tracks. Before him, Joshua had stopped and stood by his brother and sister-in-law, who were in the ranch yard, talking to a gray-haired lady and a well-dressed man in a surrey, and they were accompanied by the beautiful Jennifer Banta.

The woman, upon seeing Man Killer, screamed and yelled, "Ooh, I say, a red Indian!"

And she fainted straightaway, falling into the grasp of her husband, who eased her to the ground. Shirley ran to her and started fanning her, as did Jennifer. Chris, smiling, walked over and grabbed a crate off the ground and placed it under the woman's legs. As the blood flowed to her head, she came to and got up unsteadily with assistance from her husband and the two women.

Man Killer didn't realize it, but Jennifer was breathing a little heavily, looking at his handsome face and muscular torso. They smiled at each other for seconds, then he snapped out of it.

He walked over and took the shocked lady's hand and pulled her lace glove back and gently kissed the back of her hand like any eastern gentleman, saying, "Pardon me, ma'am, for giving you a fright, but you have nothing to fear from me except for worshiping your beauty and grace and maybe being underfoot. My name is Man Killer."

"My word," she said, quite overwhelmed.

Jennifer hadn't taken her eyes off him.

She said, "Man Killer, let me introduce my aunt and uncle from Australia. This is Uncle Horace and Aunt Beatrice Windham. Uncle Horace, Aunt Beatrice, this is Man Killer of the Nez Perce, just recently held captive by Geronimo."

Man Killer stepped forward, shaking hands with Horace Windham and not liking something he saw in the obviously wealthy man's eyes.

Horace said simply, "G'day mate, pleased ta make yer acquaintance."

Man Killer noticed the way the man kept looking over at his niece and didn't like that either. Maybe he was just being silly, he thought, but he just wanted to get a reaction.

Man Killer said softly. "Excuse me," and stepped forward, sweeping Jennifer into his arms, whispering, "I missed you," and gave her a long passionate kiss.

Aunt Beatrice fainted again, and Chris and Joshua could hardly subdue their laughter.

After she recovered, Jennifer gently said, "You know, Aunt Beatrice, the elevation around here is well over seven thousand feet above sea level, and I bet you are having a frightful time becoming acclimatized. That's not unusual."

Horace looked at Man Killer, said, "So, mate, yer a bloody injin, huh? Don't act much like the abos we got at home, although I bet yer both cut from the same bolt of cloth."

Man Killer said, "No, we are not like the aborigine people of Australia, although I think our peoples are treated much the same."

Horace's jaw tensed, as he clenched his teeth together tightly. The Aussie said, "Well, yer educated, are ya mate? Ya know of the aborigines. Many white people here I've met don't know a thing about Australia, let alone the abos.

"Well, I have me a ranch, a spread, folks here call it. It's about as big as this whole state. If a man rides the boundaries, switching horses and riding day and night, mate, it would take him well over a month to cover the whole of my property. Got me a bunch of abos workin' there, I do. I treat 'em nice, too, mate, but they know their place."

"And what's that, sir?" Man Killer asked.

Horace Windham's face flushed, and he said, "Well, down-under, mate, an abo puts his lips on a white woman, and he'll soon lose his lips to a sharp blade. Probably lose a lot more, too."

Man Killer hid his anger, but said, "Good thing I don't live in Australia, sir, because I love your niece and am going to marry her, and I'm afraid a lot of white men with sharp blades would lose their lives, trying to remove my lips."

Horace said, "Well, you have to understand, me boy, these abos are all savages. They have no education like you do. They come from ignorant savages for ancestors, almost animals, for generations."

Man Killer said, "Tell me, sir. Are you descended from some of the prisoners who were first sent to Australia from Great Britain, like most white Australians?"

Jennifer walked forward and grabbed Man Killer's large biceps and smiled innocently at her aunt and uncle, both with red faces.

Horace showed how he could quickly regain control by smiling and saying between teeth clenched a little too tightly, "No, lad, you're mistaken. Many white Aussies were explorers, miners, farmers."

Man Killer said, "Oh sir, I'm aware of that. I know about people like Burke and Wills who explored from the top to the bottom of Australia, and the miners, and the ranchers, but I also know that Australia was originally a place where England sent prisoners and lawbreakers. Of course, the aborigines were there first, minding their own business."

"Pretty smart, aren't ya, mate?" Horace replied curtly.

Man Killer smiled and said, "Being primitive and being intelligent are two different things, Mr. Windham."

Windham just stared at the scout. Even Chris, Joshua, and Shirley looked at him in amazement, not realizing how much this young man had educated himself, besides the great deal he had learned in mission school. He was a voracious reader, always carrying books with him, even when scouting and sleeping by the campfire at night, or reading newspapers and magazines at every fort or town he and Chris ever entered.

Jennifer wasn't shocked by his knowledge at all. She just stared at him with love and wonder. The Australian couple shifted their feet uneasily, and Horace eyed Man Killer with what had to be hatred.

Shirley deftly broke the uncomfortable silence by saying, "It is hot out here. Why don't we all go up on the porch and sit in the shade and have some iced tea?"

Again covering his rage, Horace smiled and said, "You have ice here, Mrs. Colt?"

Pointing at the majestic fourteen-thousand-foot peaks above them to the immediate west, Joshua said, "Yes, one of our hands goes up and gets it above timberline on Spread Eagle Peak twice a week."

Horace gave a weak and polite smile, but then a glance at Joshua Colt that escaped everyone there except Man Killer and Joshua. Both were sensitive to racism, and knew what the glance indicated.

Man Killer walked toward the bunkhouse and said, "I have to check on my horses."

Jennifer started to him, saying, "Oh, Man Killer, I want to help."

Her aunt said, "Jennifer, we're your guests, dear, don't leave us. Please come sit at tea with us all?"

Man Killer said, "I have to ride hard, Jennifer. Stay here."

Joshua went after the Indian, explaining, "Nice to meet you folks. If you'll excuse me, I have a ranch to run."

He caught up with Man Killer and escorted the angry young man to the barn. Nothing was said, while Man Killer saddled Hawk. Joshua had given his horse to one of the ranch hands and had opted for a large

chestnut-spotted leopard Appaloosa he got
from Man Killer's herd. It was a mover and
ideal for chasing cattle in and out of the
many rocky, tree-filled canyons up above the
ranch in the Sangre de Cristo mountain
range. Planning only on coming to the ranch
briefly, he had simply turned his horse, Kitty
Cat, into a stall and removed the bridle.

He now replaced the bridle and then
looked over at the tight-lipped Man Killer,
patting the young man on the shoulder.

The two mounted up and rode toward the
big range.

Joshua said, "Partner, you'll never escape
it. I have had to deal with it from white men
my whole life."

Man Killer said, "Why are they like that?"

Joshua asked, "Why don't the Sioux and
the Crows get along, or the Nez Perce and the
Sioux?"

Man Killer replied, "Because they are enemies, but they do not call one another nigger
or red nigger. Even though they are enemies,
they still have respect for one another. They
do not look down at one another like one is
a dog and the other a man."

Joshua said, "Man Killer, I sure wish I had
the answer to that one. If I did, they'd elect
me president, brown skin and all."

They rode on a little farther through the
high green mountain grass and Joshua

chuckled to himself and added, "Maybe a lot of people with white skin are just born stupid."

Man Killer started laughing and Joshua joined in. They stopped while Joshua opened a gate at an irrigation ditch, laughing the entire time.

The two men continued on north two miles, then through two gates, before arriving at the pasture of Man Killer's Appaloosa herd and the Colts' quarter horse herd. They had several stallions, but they were kept in stalls in the barn and grained and fed daily, as well as being properly exercised each day. Numerous ranchers brought their best mares to the stallions at Coyote Run to be serviced and were willing to pay hefty fees.

The horses were cropping grass in the large pasture, and the two men observed several mares laying their ears back and chasing others away from different spots, then grazing there themselves. Both men laughed at this.

Man Killer said, "Why do horses always act this way?"

Joshua cut a plug of tobacco and stuck it in his mouth and started chewing. He spit, looked up at the big range, and said, "Maybe they think they're people."

He kicked his horse into a trot and went on, followed by the smiling scout.

Man Killer found two new foals that had dropped, and Joshua found two as well. All four colts seemed healthy, but then they came to a spot on the ground under a tree overlooking the pasture, which looked strange. One of the mares was hanging around the area and acting oddly.

They found the partially devoured remains of another foal from Man Killer's herd. It had been a roan-and-white Appaloosa. The intestines had been eaten, and there were teeth marks on the neck, which was broken, with four claw marks running down the shoulders and forelegs.

Man Killer looked up at Joshua and said, "Lion."

Joshua pulled his Winchester out and checked his loads.

Man Killer held up his hand and said, "No, Joshua, remember you have a ranch to run. This was my foal. I will hunt down the cat."

Joshua nodded and winked, knowing the man really wanted to be alone, and this would be a good excuse. In fact, he didn't blame him at all.

Man Killer vaulted onto Hawk's back and rode off uphill into the trees, following the trail of the mountain lion, for it was easy to see. Like Chris Colt, he had learned to deal with anger, sorrow, or any negative emotions by riding up into the high lonesome and looking down at the clouds in the sky.

The lion watched from under a large fir tree about seven hundred feet up the mountain. As it saw the creature come higher on his back trail, it got up and started padding higher on a switchback route that might bring him across the scent of more food. He had lost the foal, but lions didn't feed very long on carcasses anyway. Finicky eaters, they would generally feed on a kill, normally a deer, for just a few days, until the meat started to become just slightly tainted, and they would go on to hunt another quarry, leaving their carcass for coyotes or bears, which would eat anything no matter how spoiled or rotten.

Man Killer stayed on the track and followed the big cat up through the trees, where it traveled generally in a westerly direction across the face of Spread Eagle Peak, continually moving higher. Man Killer was now several miles behind it, and it no longer thought about the creature coming toward its lair. Cougars did not have many natural enemies, so it did not have an escape instinct about being stalked. Coming down into a large bowl, not far from timberline, Man Killer could look up and see the edges of the above-timberline glacier-fed lakes called Lakes of the Clouds. Teeming with brightly colored cutthroat and rainbow trout, Lakes of the Clouds was one of Chris Colt's favorite places to get away from everyone and all things human. Man Killer looked around at the high peaks, glaciers, and giant avalanche chutes carved into the mountainside and understood why.

In the bowl below, he saw a large harem of elk crossing the high mountain valley, jumping blowdowns and weaving in and out of a series of beaver ponds. Man Killer stayed where he was and just watched for movement. He saw two beavers towing branches in their mouths from aspen trees across one of the ponds. After fifteen minutes, one of the beavers slapped its tail on the water's surface and dived. Ripples emanated from the slapping of its tail, and the rings were twenty feet away from where it went under before Man Killer heard the faint slapping sound. The second beaver followed suit and slapped its tail on the surface as well, and went under.

Seconds later, Man Killer saw the cougar crouching and moving through the clear area between two groups of hardwood trees. Basically following the same game trail the elk were on, the cougar crossed the clearing.

The anger about the Australians was gone right now as he was absorbed in the hunt. Man Killer knew this area and had a good guess where the cat would come out. He vaulted onto Hawk's back and headed down the hill. By the time the cat passed along the face of Horn Peak, Man Killer had gotten around it and was waiting in ambush. The lion, as was habit with the creatures, would cross over a saddle between two hilltops on one of the mountain's ridges. Many cowboys and ranchers would sometimes just happen on a lion, but generally never saw one. Those who actively hunted them almost always put a pack of hounds on a hot trail and let the dogs work it out until the pursued cat treed. With the tracking skills of the American Indian and the knowledge gained under the tutelage of Chris Colt, Man Killer knew how to hunt the lions by understanding their behavior. One of the things he had learned from Chris was that mountain lions, for some reason, would go out of their way just to cross saddles between hilltops. It was simply a type of terrain feature that attracted them.

The scout hid Hawk back away from the saddle and south of his location a quarter of a mile and waited with his Winchester carbine. He had a .44 caliber round in the chamber and seventeen others in the spring-loaded magazine built into the lever-action walnut stock rifle. Like Chris Colt and many Indians, Man Killer had decorated his carbine with brass furniture tacks in the stock and an eagle feather hanging from the swivel for the leather sling on the bottom of the barrel. This was not only there for decoration but also to let Man Killer know which way the wind was blowing.

He sighted down the iron sights on the top of the rifle and picked out several likely spots where he thought the lion might pass. He worried about the big cat moving between some rocks at the far side of the saddle, so he was careful to sight in between those rocks. Man Killer practiced raising the barrel over and over and sighting at these targets. He did this until his eyes started to water, so he relaxed and let them rest.

Fifteen more minutes brought Man Killer what he had been waiting for. The cougar started across the saddle, but stopped right at the beginning, most of his body shielded by a rock. He stopped and tested the wind, which had just shifted. Man Killer was upset. Maybe the big cat smelled him, but he didn't think it was blowing directly from him to the cat right now.

Something was wrong though. The cat backed away from the saddle and disappeared into the trees. Man Killer strained his eyes and tried to see where it went, but to no avail. He lay there, watching the saddle carefully for the reappearance of the big cat. Straining his eyes, he kept looking until they began to water once more. He blinked but would not dare rub them.

The scout waited, watched, listened. He wanted to rub his tearing eyes, but would not consider moving, for that was not the way of a warrior. Patience was what he had been taught and had practiced since his earliest memories. A sand flea crawled across his left cheek, but was ignored. Man Killer realized that the wind was blowing from him to the far side of the saddle, but by looking at some tufts of grass and some leaves, he could tell that a cross breeze had then blown his scent back across the saddle into the nostrils of the cougar.

Would the cougar circle downwind to keep his scent in his nostrils? That was the way of most animals with good olfactory sensitivity. Man Killer assumed that the cat, now alerted again to man scent, would leave the area as quickly as possible, but he would wait just to make sure. He would watch and listen.

Mountain lions were very wary animals. They feared humans and, just in the short period of time Man Killer had lived among the whites, he had seen and heard of several instances when a single common ranch dog had treed a cougar by itself. Creatures of the night, they did most of their hunting and moving around after dark. They were very afraid of humans and hardly ever attacked men or women, but did sometimes attack children. For the most part, cougars hunted deer, which comprised about ninety percent of their diet. They loved the taste of skunks and porcupines when they could get them.

They were deathly afraid of humans and would normally run at the smell or sight of one, but as it was with many animals, this big tom cougar Man Killer had stalked had not read the books on mountain lion behavior. Nobody told it to fear man and not attack them, because it was now slowly creeping up behind the prone Man Killer, who intently watched the saddle for the possible return of this cat.

Man Killer felt a chill running down his spine. He was conditioned not to move when lying in wait for an animal, but he just had to turn and look behind him. Slowly, ever so slowly, he turned his head around a little at a time.

When he got half around, he heard a low growl. Instantly, Man Killer knew that this mountain lion had not heard stories around the campfire about how shy it was supposed to be. He spun and swung the Winchester carbine around, only to look up at a mighty silvertip grizzly bear, no more than ten feet away. It stood on its hind legs, its nostrils flaring, testing the wind.

Bears have poor eyesight and not much

better hearing, but their noses are incredibly sensitive. Although it was upwind of the Indian, the bear was still curious about this creature lying in his path. The cougar coming down the mountainside had made a noise and frightened the bear from its bed. Suddenly, it was upon this creature lying among the trees.

Man Killer's sudden turn made the bear give out a mighty roar, and it popped its teeth from side to side. Grizzly bears could outrun a racehorse on level ground, so all it had to do was drop down on all fours and pounce forward.

Man Killer's .44 took it through the throat however, and stood it back up in pain and anger. The Indian then worked the lever of the carbine as quickly as he could, while holding his finger out where it automatically hit the trigger each time the lever came back. Blood spurted from numerous wounds as the mighty beast was torn with hole after hole from the quickly shot bullets. It threw its head up a full eight feet in the air and fell forward, so close that Man Killer could not get out of the way. The bear's body just missed crashing down on the Nez Perce, but the fall was so close it rolled over on the scout's legs. Weighing well over half a ton, the lifeless body pinned the Indian's legs against the ground.

Man Killer lay on his back and started laughing, partly to ease the tension and partly because, looking up, he saw the big tom mountain lion in a fir tree just a short ways down the hill behind him. Ears back, the cougar looked down at the Indian from his perch and hissed. Man Killer raised the carbine, placed the bottom of the front bead across an imaginary line running from one side of the rear V sight to the other, centering the bead on a spot just behind the left front shoulder of the lion, and he squeezed the shot off. The bullet went through the center of the cat's heart, and it died instantly, the big body tumbling from the tree and breaking branches on the way down. It was so close, several of the branches came within five feet of Man Killer, still pinned under the mighty bear.

The scout's legs were not really hurt, but he could not pull them out from under the bear's dead weight. He used the stock and butt of his rifle for support and tried to pull himself free, then even pry himself free, but to no avail.

Man Killer admired the two large trophy-sized animals he had just killed and gave a prayer of thanks to God. Then he started laughing at his ridiculous predicament. He sat back and looked up through the trees and the cloudless blue sky and cupping his hands in front of his mouth, he gave off the crying whistle of a red-tailed hawk.

Within seconds, Hawk arrived, prancing and snorting as he smelled blood and death on the ground. Nevertheless, the big Appaloosa walked forward to nudge his master with his nose. Grabbing the reins trailing on the ground, Man Killer maneuvered the horse where he wanted him, and using his carbine, carefully tried to undo the slip knot holding his coiled-up leather riata just below the right side of the saddlehorn. Today he used a roughed-out leather saddle, instead of the hornless army McLellan rig he usually used on military campaigns.

Man Killer finally got the braided leather rope loose and, on the third try, tossed a little loop up over the horn and tightened it. He took a turn around the bear's neck and tied a slip knot, then sent Hawk downhill. The horse pulled hard, and the bear was pulled off the scout's legs.

Saying, "Good boy," Man Killer immediately jumped up and started stomping his feet, trying to recapture the circulation in his legs.

A large timber wolf appeared out of the woods, and Man Killer's hand dropped to his Colt Peacemaker, but stopped at the voice from behind.

The man said, "Don't do that, pilgrim.

Don't want ta shoot ya afore we become friends."

Man Killer turned to see a giant of a mountain man, with snow-white hair and beard, come down out of the trees. He was pulling a skinning knife from his buckskins and didn't even look at the scout. He simply knelt down and started skinning out the bear.

"C'mon, boy, daylight's a-wastin," the man said; "I'll take care a this here griz, and you gut the cat. Thet's some durned good eatin."

Man Killer walked over to the mountain lion and dragged it by the tail so the hindquarters were facing downhill. He kept looking at the big man with much curiosity, but kept quiet for now. Before he was done dressing out the lion, the bear was dressed out, the hide skinned out, and head cut off, attached to the hide. Sweat dripped off the man's face, as he did the finishing touches on the bear.

Finally, looking over at the wolf lying by a log, the Indian said, "Is he your pet?"

The mountain man said, "Naw, he's a wolf. Nobody's pet. Jest an amigo."

Man Killer said, "You going to give him some of this meat?"

The man said, "Nope, he gits his own vittles, and I git mine. He'll probably eat what we leave, but that's up to him, not me."

The man finished his work and immediately started sharpening his knife with a whetstone, while he walked away into the trees. The wolf stayed, closing its eyes and napping. Man Killer grinned as he saw the man take a long swig of water from his canteen and hold the liquid in his mouth. He would spit a little stream of water on the whetstone and start passing the big skinning knife across it, the blade looking like it was slicing off pieces of stone. He would spit a little more on the stone and keep sharpening.

Five minutes later, the man reemerged from the trees, leading a large bay mule, which was leading still another large mule. Both had pack saddles and mining supplies lashed on their backs with diamond hitches. The first was led by a lead line, and the lead line of the second was tied to the tail of the first.

The two men loaded the meat onto the pack animals, and the wolf started feeding on the carcass of the lion. Man Killer tied the bear hide and lion hide on his own saddle.

The man said, "Where ya wanna take the meat?"

Man Killer said, "You can have the bear meat, and I want to take the lion meat back to the Coyote Run Ranch, where I live. I want to keep the skins of both animals."

"A course ya do," the old man said, "C'mon. Ye'll have to stay at mah cabin fer the night. I ain't walkin' all the way to Colt's place and goin' home after dark. We'll have us a feast tanight and ya kin head back come mornin.'"

The scout said, "You know of Colt?"

The old man said, "Who don't?"

The Nez Perce went on, "My name is Man Killer."

The old man said, "Yep, I know."

Man Killer shook his head and looked at the big shaggy mane and shoulders as broad as a draft horse, as they walked up the mountainside.

Finally, Man Killer said, "What is your name?"

The old man didn't stop or look around. He just said, "Beaver."

"Beaver?"

The old man said, "Yep, now I want yer word ye'll never tell nobody about mah place when ya see it."

Man Killer said, "You have my word."

The man said nothing, just kept climbing higher at an exhausting pace.

Man Killer said, "Why are you called Beaver, old man?"

Beaver said, "Why're ya called Man Killer, young un?"

They kept heading south, up and down hills at a killing pace, before they got onto a well-traveled switchback trail on Crestone

Needles, the most rugged, jagged, harshest peak in the entire range of the Sangre de Cristo Mountains. Just before dark they went up over a lip on the trail and down into a rocky bowl, well above timberline. Man Killer was in excellent physical condition, but he could not remember the last time he had so much trouble breathing and moving his legs. This old white-haired man in front of him seemed to be hardly breathing, however, so the young scout would not even consider letting down.

Snow was everywhere around the cabin on the edge of a small glacier-fed lake. This was some of the most rugged, unforgiving country the young man had ever seen. The cabin was small and Man Killer could tell, very well made. A small trail of smoke drifted from the chimney. The old man, he figured, must have built a large fire before leaving so the one-room log building would remain fairly warm. Although it was springtime down below, the snow everywhere about them was deep, very deep. The wind was like the depths of a tornado, and Man Killer had to blink his eyes to see. He wondered how anybody could live in this place. Although they now were going downhill, before long the deep snow pulled at his thigh muscles and hip joints. Man Killer could not remember being so weary. Partway down the ridgeline, the man suddenly stopped and walked back to the side of the lead mule. He pulled a Sharps buffalo gun out of an Indian beaded and fringed leather scabbard on the side of the mule. Finally, Man Killer spotted a small herd of bighorn sheep on the other side of the big snow-filled bowl. They had spotted the men and mules and were moving quickly up the opposite slope. Beaver pulled up a sight on the back of the rifle and slowly set the elevation, then finally raised the rifle. He aimed for only seconds and pulled the trigger. The big gun boomed and several seconds later, Man Killer saw the big ram drop in midstride and roll back down the ridge, legs kicking still in death.

The scout said, "I have not seen such shooting, except by the mighty Colt himself."

The old man never looked back, just replaced the rifle in the scabbard, saying, "I can't afford to waste money on powder and ball. Cain't afford ta miss."

Man Killer grinned and shook his head from side to side. He huddled his shoulders against the cold and walked on down the mountain. They walked right past the cabin and kept on to the other side of the thirteen-thousand-foot-high valley and up the other ridge toward the body of the bighorn ram. The mountain man knelt down and skinned it out, waving away assistance from Man

Killer. Within minutes he was done and handed the cape and head of the ram to Man Killer. The scout admired the ram's head with the ends of the thick horns curling up higher than the ram's eye level.

Beaver said, "There's sumthin' what'll look nice above Colt's fireplace mantel. Taken it back with ya."

Man Killer said, "But don't you want it?"

The old man chuckled and said, "Why'n hell would I? I cain't eat horns."

It was well after dark when they finally made it inside the cabin, and snow was dropping out of the sky and swirling all around them. The wind was icy and cutting.

Inside the cabin it was as warm and draft-free as could be. The logs of the cabin had been extremely well fitted, and the few spots that had holes between the logs had been well chinked. Furs and hides were everywhere, along with a variety of traps and mining gear.

Man Killer tried to judge Beaver's age, but was not able to.

Accepting a cup of hot coffee, he asked, "Where did you learn to shoot so well?"

Beaver said, "My old sidekick. Died better'n a dozen year ago."

Man Killer said, "What was his name?"

"Kit Carson." Beaver said it with no feelings, just a matter-of-fact attitude, and kept checking the steaks he had grilling in the big stone fireplace. There was a scratching at the door, and the old man walked over and opened it. The big timber wolf walked to the fireplace and sniffed what was cooking, then brushed past Man Killer, and lay down in the corner, his big gray tail curled around his nose.

Man Killer had no fear of the timber wolf, knowing that wolves never attacked human beings. There were numerous old wives' tales, he knew, among the white men, about the big meat eaters attacking humans, but the shy animals abounded near his home in Idaho area, and all the Nez Perce knew that they would not have to ever fear wolf attack. That is, unless one had what the white man called hydrophobia, fear of water, though some whites called it rabies.

This old man was strange, very strange. Man Killer tried to figure him out, read his sign, but it was a secret trail from a hidden past. The scout had learned, among the white men, that many who came to the West had mysterious backgrounds. While traveling with Chris Colt scouting, he had met army corporals who had been officers, even generals, in the Civil War. He had met men who punched cattle but could quote Shakespeare. In fact, while chasing Victorio, Man Killer had gone to Tombstone, and the scout was introduced to Wyatt Earp and his brothers and Doc Holliday. Doc Holliday had turned to gambling and was a noted gunfighter, especially after the already famous gunfight at the O.K. Corral, in which he took sides with the Earps against the McLaurys and Clantons. But prior to coming out West for what was apparently tuberculosis, he had been a dentist.

Man Killer grinned to himself when he thought back to the meeting between the famous gunfighters. He had noticed men in the saloon who were watching to see if there would be action between the Earps and Holliday, and the famous gunfighter Chris Colt and his Indian sidekick. In fact, Man Killer had even been mentioned by several as almost as fast as Colt and very deadly. The watchers wanted some exciting event to happen, but it wouldn't, as all the legendary men present genuinely liked each other.

The scout had found that men like himself, Colt, the Earps, and Holliday could be really hellions with guns, but really didn't want to get into gun battles. Sometimes the adrenaline running through a person's body during such an event could become addictive, like a drug, but most of these men had an appreciation and respect for guns and the death they could deal. No matter how good or fast a man was, sensible men like these knew there was always that one time a gun sight could catch on the end of the holster, a round could misfire, or the other man could just be faster or more accurate.

He thought again of the mystery of this man in front of him and wondered what was in the man's past. Was there a lost love somewhere, years back? Was he wanted for murder?

Man Killer asked, "You were a friend of the mighty scout Kit Carson?"

"Yep," Beaver replied, "we was pals, good pals. Come through this area scoutin' fer old John C. Fremont. That's who they named Fremont County fer where Canon City is. Boy, thet ole Frontier Fremont was full a hisself. Kit was the one who done it all. Fremont was jest smart enough ta hire him and me."

The scout said, "How long did you know Kit?"

"Years, boy, years," Beaver said, placing their steaks on hand-carved wooden plates. "Fremont dint know jack nothin' but he was a hell of a promoter. He hires old Kit, and I kinda went along with the deal, on account I was kinda Kit's teacher so to speak."

"Teacher?" Man Killer asked, "You were a teacher?"

"Naw, I warn't no schoolmarm," Beaver replied, chuckling around a mouthful of mountain lion. "I learnt him how to live like this.

Taught him how to read sign and trap beav, hunt buffalers down on the flatland, fight Injuns . . . ah, no offense. Boy, I hated thet, too. Not huntin' buffs or fightin' Injuns, but bein' down there on the flatlands, most specially when civilization started to pour in. Yep, me and Kit had us some good times, and he was a man, I'm here to tell ya. Kit Carson was all man and an eager larner, too. I learnt him jest about everything I knowed about the wild, then he went an got hisself eddycated even more on his own. He used thet head a his fer more than a hat rack."

Man Killer loved the taste of the lion. It was the most sought-after meat of mountain men, red men, and true western men, and was even more popular than antelope.

Beaver poured some scalding hot coffee in two metal cups and handed one to Man Killer. Man Killer pulled out the makings and started rolling a cigarette, handing the makings to Beaver, who was wiping grease from the meat onto his chest.

Fixing a smoke, Beaver went on, " 'Member one time Kit an me was holed up in the Wind River Range." He paused and gave a queer look at the fire, and said, "Or was it the Grand Tetons? Anyways, we was holed up in some rocks an had bout a thousand Blackfoot attackin' us from the north."

Man Killer knew what was coming and had

heard this many times before, but he played along.

"Well, we was gonna cut and run to the south, but durned if about three hundred fifty Cheyenne fit us from that direction, so's we looked outta our perch and there was one way left and thet was the east, but jest then another force of about six hundred Dakota come at us a whoppin' and hollerin'. Man, old Kit and me shore was in a fix then."

Man Killer played along and said, "What happened?"

Beaver brightened up and said, "Hell, we got kilt, of course."

He slapped his knee and laughed as though it was the first time he had ever heard the joke, much less told it. Man Killer also laughed as if he had never heard the joke before.

Getting serious, Beaver said, "Say, boy, you still courtin' that purty little blond thing southwest a the big city?"

Man Killer laughed when he thought of Beaver referring to the berg of Westcliffe as the "big city." He said, "How do you know about that? Or me for that matter?"

Beaver laughed and said, "Ever go to a boxing match?"

Man Killer replied, "No."

"Wal, I got me a ringside seat, an I keep

abreast of what's goin on, kinda readin' sign, jest like Colt's taught ya ta do."

Man Killer thought that this man was really amazing, and his eyes wandered around the room, but locked on a brain-tanned cowhide with the Colt brand on it. His hand went to the handle of his right-hand Colt, and the old man laughed, pouring the scout more coffee. He said, "Speakin' a readin' sign, I was wonderin' how durned long it'd be fore ya seen thet."

Man Killer said, "Why do you have a hide with Colt's brand on it?"

Beaver said, "Joshua tole me ta take a steer fer meat whenever I'm a mind to. Colt dint seem ta mind thet either, so I do from time ta time."

Man Killer said, "Joshua? Chris? You mean you know them, and they know you're here?"

"Shore," Beaver said. "Run inta both of 'em several times. Good men. Both of 'em remind me of Kit Carson."

Man Killer was upset and said out loud what he had been thinking. "I wonder why neither one of them told me about you?"

Beaver laughed heartily and said, "Hell, boy, are you a man a yer word?"

Man Killer said, "Of course."

Beaver said, "Yeah, and so is them two. I tole each a them ta give me their word not ta tell about me ta nobody, so it seems they

both kept their word, jest like is which I
knowed thet they would."

Man Killer asked, "How long have you
owned the wolf?"

"Tole ya, I don't own the wolf. He's a
friend."

"How long have you lived up here?"

"Don't know, sonny. Ya shore ast a lot a
questions," Beaver answered. "Lessee old Kit
went unner in '68. How long ago was thet?
Decade an a half more or less. I was up here
long before he went unner. Ya know, I never
thought a thet. How come anyhow? What's it
matter?"

Man Killer thought for a minute and said,
"I guess it doesn't matter. Do you know your
age?"

Beaver chuckled and poured some more
coffee for both of them, saying, "Ya do ast the
queerest questions." He drank a little coffee
and added, "I do 'member somethin'. I was
born afore Carson, and he was born back in
'09."

Man Killer said, "Where were you born?"

Beaver glared at him and raised his eyebrows. He took another sip of coffee and put
a couple of logs on the fire. Then he gave
Man Killer a very serious stare. "Boy, if yer
gonna live among the white man," Beaver
said solemnly, "ya learn, out here, don't
never ast folks about their background. Let

'em tell ya if'n they want to. Some don't want to."

Man Killer felt his face burning from embarrassment. He did not apologize, for that was not the way of the red man. Like thank-yous, it was understood.

The next morning, with meat packed on one of Beaver's mules with the reassurance that the animal would find his way home if Man Killer just turned him loose, he got ready to mount Hawk and head back home. He shook hands with the old mountain man, and Beaver gave him a serious look. The Nez Perce instinctively paused, feeling the man was about to say something very important.

The old trapper said, "Boy, listen here. Them dudes what is visitin' down ta the Bantas hired themselves a gunslinger as a bodyguard. They ain't up ta no good."

Man Killer said, "How would you know they hired a gunslinger if you stay in the mountains?"

Beaver grinned, saying, " 'Member mah spy-glass I showed ya? Twas sittin' in the corner up against the fireplace."

"Yes."

"Boy, yer a expert tracker. I jest read sign like you do. Even from way up h'yar I kin see ever thing I need ta." Beaver went on, "Yisterday, when them dudes went back ta the Banta Ranch with thet beeyootiful golden-haired Banta gal what's gaga-eyed over you, I seen they had picked 'em up a gunslinger in Westcliffe, an he went with 'em ta the ranch. I knowed he was a slick by the way he wore his cross-draw holsters with twin Peacemakers, walnut-handled by the way, plus the fact thet he was ridin jest about one of the best put-together horses I seen in these parts. If'n a man who looks to be a puncher or ridin' the grub-line has hisself a horse like thet, he's either an outlaw or a gunslick. Anyone ridin' crosswise of the law needs him a set a legs thet kin outrun any posse, so outlaws an gunplayers always spend some serious barter on horseflesh."

He chuckled and said, "I s'pose I also figgered he was a durned shootist, too, 'cause I seen him practice-draw and dry-firin' out behind ole Chancy's barn. I also seen the way old Chancy was talkin' private like outside the house with Jennifer. The way he was shiftin' and holdin' his arms, he was a mite upset. I'm tellin' ya, boy. I don't like the cut a them dudes, an' you gotta take care a thet gal, mister. You gotta protect her, boy. Thar's danger on the wind fer her. I kin sense it."

Man Killer asked, "You know Jennifer and Chancy?"

Beaver spit out a big stream of tobacco juice and said, "Naw, not really. I jest know

bout some folks. I been a long time in this
area. Now, you gotta think a thet gal ya love.
Watch over her careful like."

The thing that had been bothering Man
Killer finally hit him like a twister hitting the
side of a barn. He knew he finally had this
old man figured out. Man Killer shook hands
again and mounted up, smiling down at Beaver. He said, "Beaver, many years ago, was
she a white woman or an Indian woman?"

Beaver looked off at the puffy clouds pushing up against the San Luis Valley side of the
peaks. His eyes seemed to mist. He waved as
he turned and stepped toward the door of
the cabin. Without looking back he said, "See
ya'. Gotta go fix up some meat fer jerkin'.
Thanks fer the bar meat. Come back some-
time, boy."

Man Killer felt bad about asking the
question and noticed that the old man's
shoulders seemed to be a little more
hunched than before as he walked into the
cabin. He turned and rode up toward the rim
of the snowy bowl. The grizzly hide and head
were rolled up and draped and tied over his
bedroll behind his saddle. The cat meat and
hide, along with the ram head and cape,
were packed on the mule he led.

This old man, he concluded, had lost a
love somehow, years and years before, probably blaming himself for her loss, then mov-

ing and staying away from people. He probably wanted to protect himself from ever being so hurt by anyone again.

When Man Killer rode up into the ranch yard, Joshua and Chris had just walked out the door, with cigars, after Sunday dinner.

"Missed a good sermon," Colt said, lighting his tobacco. "Were you in church, too?"

Man Killer smiled. "Yes, the one that you and I have enjoyed many times."

He turned and looked up at the towering white-capped peaks. Chris Colt gave him a knowing smile and wink.

Joshua said, "Thought you were going after a cat, not every critter hiding in the mountain range."

Man Killer said, "When I followed and shot the cat, the grizzly walked up and asked me to shoot him, too."

Chris said, "What about the ram?"

Man Killer said, "I did not shoot him."

Joshua took a puff and said, "Must have been Beaver. That one of his mules or ours?"

Man Killer said, "His," laughed, and walked in the door. He said hello to Shirley, and she told him lunch was ready for him, so he went out and unloaded the mule and horse, grained them, rubbed them down, and watered them. He put the cougar carcass and hides in the meat house, then took the mule out and gave him a slap on the rump, and the bay animal took off at a trot toward the big range.

The Indian washed his hands and went inside, eating lunch while talking with Shirley. He finished, cleaned his plates, and went outside with a cup of coffee, carrying a cigar from the humidor. The scout sat down with the two brothers, and the three talked while looking up at the beautiful range. The Sangre de Cristos were named by the Spanish explorers who first came into the area. Meaning blood of Christ, they were named for the red hue that so often appeared on their snow-capped peaks at sunset and sunrise both.

The chief of scouts looked over at Man Killer and wondered about the adventure the man had just experienced. Man Killer would tell him about it when the time was right. Colt smiled as he looked at his young protégé and thought about how far he had come since they had first met. Still a teenager, Man Killer had the height and build of a grown man, a man whom other men would step aside for. Chris thought back to their first meeting and his first experiences with the Nez Perce. Educated first by Catholic missionaries and a rough life, and growing up under the tutelage of the famous and wise Chief Joseph, the young Nez Perce was very intelligent and resourceful. Since the surrender of the Nez Perce, he had been Chris Colt's constant companion, and this was the final nail in the making of the framework of a real man of the West.

Colt looked up at the snow blowing off Spread Eagle Peak and the wind shifted, blowing a puff in front of his face. He thought back to the first cigar he shared with the wise Chief Joseph when they first met.

At the time, he and Shirley had not yet married. Hearing through the grapevine that Colt had been blinded by a grizzly bear attack and was helpless in Idaho, she had sold her successful restaurant and adjoining house in Bismarck, North Dakota Territory, left it all behind, and traveled west to find and stand by Colt. On the way she had been captured by a small band of Cheyenne. Finally hearing this, Colt had sent word to Crazy Horse, his blood brother, to find her. This was on his mind constantly when he was sent to the village of Joseph by General O.O. "One-Armed" Howard. He was to befriend the chief and convince him to move to the Fort Lapwai reservation. Colt first spent the night there, requesting counsel with the notable leader.

The next morning was a memorable one for Colt, as he got a full measure and insight into the man called Chief Joseph. He was a leader and an orator. It was no wonder that the perceptive Christian general wanted Colt to court the man. Other chiefs would certainly seek this man's counsel.

First, the wise, old Nez Perce leader surmised and told Chris Colt exactly why he was there. He explained that Colt had been ordered by General Howard to come and meet with him, win favor with him, and convince him to do as the general wanted.

After that, amazed by the chief's simple, yet profound wisdom, Colt sought his counsel on another matter. He wanted to know what to do about Shirley. It was time to speak about her and find out what Joseph thought he should do.

Colt said, "Chief Joseph, I have a woman who makes my heart beat hard and steals my sleep from me many nights."

Joseph grinned.

Colt continued, "She has been taken captive by a band of the Chyela or the Lakotah, but I do not know where to find her or what to do."

Joseph poured himself another cup of coffee, sweetened it, and started drinking. He kept sipping the coffee and enjoying his cigar, and it was as if he had not heard a word Colt had said. Chris knew to keep his mouth shut, as the intelligent leader was giving Colt's problem serious thought.

After ten minutes Joseph spoke, "You have worked with the cavalry. You felt you had to bring Ezekiel and our ponies to us. You have worry that the horse soldiers may start war with the Nez Perce. You think of all these things that weigh heavy on your heart, but your heart is also sad, because the woman you dream of each night is somewhere. She is captive, and your mind sees the many things you do not want for her. Should you just ride toward the lands of the Lakotah, or should you do your work for the cavalry first?"

Colt grinned and took a sip of coffee.

Chief Joseph said, "Where were you born?"

Colt said, "Back East, in a place called Ohio."

"I learned about it at mission school," the chief replied. "If my wife was taken from me by your people, and she was taken on the iron horse, and she was taken in the wagon—if your people took her and hid her somewhere in Ohio," Joseph said, "would I go to Ohio and find where she has been hidden?"

Colt said, "No. It would be impossible for you to do."

Chief Joseph said, "But does not Ohio

have trees and rocks and dirt and clouds like here?"

Colt said, "It doesn't look like this land, but it has all those things."

Joseph went on, "I grew up hunting and fighting and fishing as a Nez Perce. I have fought the bear and taken many scalps. I have counted coups. Am I not a good tracker, do you think Colt?"

Chris said, "Of course. You would have to be a good tracker. You wouldn't have become chief."

"Then," Joseph said, "could I not go to Ohio and look for sign and find my wife?"

Colt said, "No, it would still be impossible."

Joseph said, "Then who would I ask to go find her for me?"

Colt said, "You could ask me. I am white. I am from Ohio. It would be pretty easy for me to find a Nez Perce woman there."

Joseph poured another cup of coffee and spent another two minutes drinking it and enjoying the taste. Finally, he spoke, "Wasn't she taken by someone who was Sioux or Cheyenne?"

"Yes."

"Are not the Sioux brother to the Cheyenne?"

Colt said, "Yes."

"Are you not brother to Crazy Horse, who is Oglala Sioux?"

"Yes, I have sent word for him to find her."

Joseph said, "Then you have done the right thing. Crazy Horse will look because he is your brother. He will find her because he is Sioux, and the Sioux and Cheyenne are like the left hand and the right hand. You must now do your work and trust to your brother."

There it was: pure, simple, the answer to Colt's problem. It was brilliant because it was so simple, as is the way with most good answers. Again using very simple logic, the mighty chief showed Chris Colt that he basically could do nothing that many miles away and should trust to his blood brother, Crazy Horse, to see to her safety.

After that, trying hard to do the work he was hired to do, but finding his sympathies and common sense instead with Joseph and the plight of the Nez Perce people, Chris Colt joined them in their flight for freedom.

Chris had joined with the nontreaty Nez Perce and helped lead them on their famous seventeen-hundred-mile retreat across the wilds of Oregon, Idaho, and Montana. The journey had been perilous, and many women and children were lost, but he grew to love those noble people with each passing mile. His respect for the great Nez Perce leader grew as well. Chief Joseph had proved to be a brilliant military tactician, outwitting the U.S. military at every conflict. He had also won public sympathy and support, something unheard of at the time for the redman.

Colt again looked over at the young scout rocking and looking out at the same majestic sight that the three of them could never tire of, and he wondered how Man Killer would fare on his own throughout life. He smiled softly as he thought that Man Killer would indeed handle everything like a man.

Joshua looked at Man Killer and wondered about the killing of the cougar.

No sooner had he thought this than Man Killer said, "I followed the big cat south. I waited to ambush him at a saddle I thought he would cross. The winds decided to walk another trail, and he knew I was there. When I turned, the mighty bear thought I would be good to eat for lunch. My guns talked very fast, and the silvertip fell at my feet."

Chris and Joshua grinned at each other, and the young scout continued, "When Beaver and I reached the snowy valley where his cabin was hidden, he took a great shot across the valley and shot the ram. One bullet." Man Killer paused and added, "He is a strange man."

Colt replied, "I've seen a few like him,

though. Sometimes it's easier to live away from society than to learn how to get along with people."

"Sometimes, I can't blame people like that," Joshua added.

Man Killer said, "I think he had a great love, and his heart was broken by her in many pieces. I think that is why he lives with the eagles."

Grinning again and thinking of Jennifer Banta, Joshua and Chris glanced at each other.

"What is funny?" Man Killer asked.

Neither man answered, but soon both started laughing. Embarrassed, Man Killer stormed off the porch and headed to the meat house to butcher the lion and tend to the hides.

Chris took his cup and Joshua's, went into the house, refilled them, and returned. Still grinning, he said, "Must have gotten his temper from Chief Joseph, not me."

Joshua started chuckling and said, "Sure."

Joshua took a sip and said, "He's not angry anyway, little brother. He's got himself a disease."

Chris looked over, puzzled, and said, "What? A disease?"

Joshua said, "Jenniferitis."

Chris started laughing, and Shirley walked out the door, a scowl on her face. She said,

"He doesn't have anything other than a good heart, and you both should be ashamed of yourselves. I've been listening, and you two are being mean. Yes, he's very much in love with Jennifer, but it seems to me that one certain person on this porch even traded an entire herd of horses for me when a Cheyenne chief held me captive and demanded six ponies from any brave who wanted me. Now, you two get out there and make up to him right now."

Both men gave each other sheepish looks and headed toward the meat house. Their faces were red. Shirley stood on the porch, arms crossed, and watched them as the two tall heroes, men-among-men, shyly walked across the ranch yard and entered the tiny building attached to the side of the new barn.

Inside the meat house each man started to pick up sharp knives, when Man Killer said to both, "Have you washed your hands?"

They again gave each other sheepish looks and walked outside where they were met by another angry stare from Shirley. They walked over to the pump and washed their hands, drying them on one of the clean towels Shirley always kept hanging there. They went back to the meat house.

Chris whispered to Joshua, "I'd rather get between a she-grizzly with a toothache and her cubs, than to go through this."

Joshua said, "Me, too."

They again disappeared inside the building, and Shirley chuckled to herself, then turned and went inside at the crying of her baby girl, Brenna.

That evening, after supper, the four sat around the table, talking. Little Joseph sat on his father's lap.

Joshua said, "You know, Shirley, you mentioned that Chris traded a herd of horses for you, but I have never really heard the story."

Chris, Shirley, and Man Killer began telling Joshua the story. It was right before Chief Joseph and his followers were to surrender to Colonel "Bear Coat" Miles, just forty miles from the Canadian border near the Bear Paw Mountains. It was also when Chris first learned about the death of his blood brother, Crazy Horse. Shirley had been captured by the leader of a small band of Cheyenne, who was named Screaming Horse, and she had risen in the eyes of all in the village by nature of her beauty, cooking, work ethic, and spunk. During an attack on the village, a brave named Death Yell had saved her life and became enamored of her, like many other braves, and wanted her betrothal.

In the Nez Perce's location, Chris and Joseph had been smoking together again, and Chief Joseph became quiet for some time.

He finally spoke, "You have been a good and loyal friend, a brother to the Nez Perce, and our people will speak of you to their grandchildren. I will miss your tobacco, too," he said offering up another of his rare smiles.

Colt said, "What do you mean?"

Joseph smiled again and said, "You have sensed that your woman is near. It is in your eyes, and your heart has told your face to show how it feels."

"No, Joseph," Colt said, "I have looked sad because so many of your old people have left us to die along the trail and not slow you down. It is very sad what has happened to your people, but you are almost to Canada. You will not need me to speak with Sitting Bull. He is a very wise and reasonable man. I have to find her. She is near. I feel it."

Chief Joseph said, "You will take Man Killer with you. He wants to follow your trail, and it is a good thing."

Chris Colt took off, after some protestation, along with Man Killer and headed toward the nearby camp of Screaming Horse in the Bear Paw Mountains, and with him, he took a small herd of Appaloosa horses given him by Chief Joseph. Joseph had told Chris about Crazy Horse being stabbed with a bayonet by another Sioux, a guard, at Camp Robinson, Nebraska. Colt was upset to hear of his friend's death, but he was also happy that Crazy Horse had still been a free man when he was killed.

Just for a little revenge, Chris and Man Killer stole some cavalry horses from the men of Colonel Miles, who now surrounded the Nez Perce, and they added this to their small herd.

Just as Screaming Horse was about to accept several horses from Death Yell for Shirley's betrothal, Colt galloped into camp with the entire herd of horses and offered them for Shirley. This had been unheard of among the Cheyenne or any of their allies. No man had ever offered an entire herd of horses, especially good ones like these, for one woman. Screaming Horse gladly agreed, though Death Yell didn't seem quite so delighted about the arrangement. Colt, however, diffused the problem.

Chris took Shirley and headed toward the nearest railhead, wanting to ride to Denver and get her safely to her own environment.

In the meantime, however, Chief Joseph would soon be making his famous speech while surrendering his people almost in sight of the border. Colonel Bearcoat Miles had been a blocking force with General Howard's troops in distant pursuit.

Colonel Miles kept the camp surrounded, but talked with Joseph several times each day until the fourth of October. Six Nez Perce had been sent to try to marry up with Sitting Bull. The chiefs were again meeting in Joseph's tent and hearing the approaching cavalry. Looking Glass said hopefully the six were coming back with Sitting Bull. He stepped out of the door of the tepee and took a long-range cavalry bullet in the forehead from General Howard's approaching column. He died instantly. He was the very last casualty of the Nez Perce War. Joseph and White Bird were left, and Joseph sent word to Miles and Howard that he would meet with them the next day. He purposely did not say that White Bird would be there.

That night, White Bird, fourteen warriors, and seven women, worked their way through the soldiers' lines and made off to the north. They were in Canada before daybreak.

Only Chief Joseph remained to take care of his people. After eating, he dressed in good clothes and sent two men to fetch Howard, Miles, and their staff into the camp.

Chief Joseph said, "It is cold, and we have no blankets. The little children are freezing to death. My people, some of them, have run away to the hills and have no blankets, no food; no one knows where they are—perhaps freezing to death. I want time to look for my children and see how many of them I can find. Maybe I shall find them among the dead. Hear me, my chiefs. I am tired; my heart is sick and sad. From where the sun now stands, I will fight no more forever."

The 700 nontreaty Nez Perce now numbered 431. Joseph and the rest were given some blankets, and the Army helped look for the sick children. The Nez Perce were headed off for Fort Lincoln in North Dakota Territory, Colt's old post with Custer. They did not know that they would be marched through the main street of Shirley's former home, Bismarck, and there would be throngs of cheering citizens applauding them and handing them food and clothing while a band played "The Star-Spangled Banner."

Man Killer and Shirley both were misty-eyed when they finished telling Joshua the story. She jumped up and walked to the windowsill, bringing to the table one of her famous apple pies with crumb dough. She cut it and handed pieces to each. Chris poured Joseph a glass of milk, and the little boy stared wide-eyed at his large slice. The chief of scouts then poured each man a cup of coffee.

They talked long into the night and heard in detail all about Man Killer's hunt.

Chapter 3

>»»»»»»»»»»»»

Shootists

The next morning, Man Killer left at daybreak, headed for the Banta ranch, carrying with him some cougar meat and fresh vegetables Shirley packed for him. He kept Hawk at a trot most of the way, arriving in just over an hour.

When he rode into the ranch yard, he knew there would be trouble. He spotted the big, well-built chestnut horse that Beaver had mentioned. It was a thoroughbred and the type of mount any man would love to have bragging rights on. Man Killer unloaded the vegetables and cougar meat and turned toward the house, only to be stopped by a man standing in a gunfighter's crouch, ready for a quick draw. He had a pair of matched Colt ivory-handled Peacemakers in cross-draw holsters, and his face looked like that of an angry sidewinder.

The gunsharp said, "Freeze, red nigger. War thee hell do ya think yer goin', boy?"

Man Killer dropped the meat and vegetables just as Jennifer, followed by her family, poured out of the house. He looked at the gunfighter, with no emotion on his face, but made sure his right hand was near his gun.

Man Killer said, "Would you like it put on your tombstone that a boy killed you?"

Jennifer said, "You, you there! He is our guest! What did you do, challenge him?"

The shootist said, "Wal, Miss Banta, I was hired by yer uncle ta protect ya and them from all intruders ma'am. I draw my pay from yer uncle, but rat now I don't cotton to the uppity attitude a this heah Injun. He don't know his place."

Jennifer turned to her uncle and said angrily, "Uncle Horace, you tell that man he is fired and get off this ranch right now, or you and Aunt Beatrice may leave now as well."

The gauntlet was thrown down, and Horace did not want Jennifer angry with him. It would ruin his plans. He looked at the gunfighter and tossed him a sack of money, saying, "Well, you 'eard 'er, mate. Sorry, but this is their spread, and yer not needed anymore. G'day."

The gunfighter said, "I leave places when ah'm a mind ta, and I ain't a mind ta leavin'. Least not till I larn this blanket-nigger some manners."

113

Man Killer said, "You don't have to do this thing. You can just leave."

The gunfighter said, "Ya jest don't git it, do ya, boy? I don't like uppity blanket-niggers and ah'm gonna put ya in yer place."

Beatrice said, "Oh, my goodness, there's going to be violence."

Man Killer didn't look at her, but said, "I hope not, ma'am. There doesn't need to be any violence."

"Real sceered ain't ya, redskin?" the gunfighter drawled.

Man Killer calmly replied, "No, not really. I am a warrior, but a real warrior is first a man of peace. I do not want to fight you, but it sounds like you want to be stupid. You have good taste in horses. Where do you want your horse sent when you die?"

The shootist chuckled and said, "Thet ain't a gonna happen, Injun. Make yer play."

As if the words were spoken by Chris Colt himself, Man Killer said, "No, you mounted this horse. Ride it."

The man's eyes opened a little, and his hands flashed for his guns. Horace and Beatrice had never seen anything like the man's fast draw, but both gun barrels didn't even clear the leather of his holsters before they heard two gunshots fired almost as one, and the man took several steps backward and looked down at the giant blossom of crimson on his chest.

He looked up at Man Killer, who held his one gun in his right hand, smoke drifting out of the barrel.

The gunfighter had a look of horror on his quickly paling face. He said, "Ya kilt me, ya damned blanket-nigger. Ya kilt me."

Man Killer said, "You could have ridden away."

The gunfighter dropped to one knee, then two, and looked up at Man Killer and said in a whisper, "Take good care a mah horse?"

Man Killer said, "I will. I'll give her to the girl."

The man smiled weakly and said, "Obliged."

He fell face forward and slammed into the ground. His left foot twitched and a hissing sound came from his mouth, then there was silence.

Man Killer calmly replaced fresh bullets into the spent cylinders and spun the pistol backward into the holster, while the rest stared at the scene in silent amazement.

Inside, he was shaking, but it was not the Nez Perce way to show it.

As if nothing had happened, he turned, smiled, and said, "Jennifer, I have brought you lion meat and Shirley sent vegetables."

He handed the groceries to her and vaulted

into the saddle. Beatrice fainted again and nobody paid much attention.

Jennifer said, "Wait, Man Killer, why are you leaving?"

He said, "They hired that man to kill me."

Horace smiled and said, "No, no, ya got it all wrong, mate. We got lots a money. That's all. I just hired that man to be a bodyguard, while we're 'ere visiting, lad. I didn't know 'e was from bad seed, mate."

Chancy Banta stepped off the porch, holding a .44 in his right hand.

Man Killer said, "Why do you hold that?"

" 'Cause ef'n you missed that cayuse, I wasn't about ta," the white-haired, wrinkled, bow-legged rancher said. "Boy, yer a guest at mah ranch and yer family jest about. Anybody wants ta stir up trouble with ya at mah place has got hisself a fight."

Man Killer could not help but notice the icy glance that Chancy shot at Horace Windham.

Chancy then chuckled, wrapped his arm around Man Killer's shoulders, and said, "Hee hee, now thet was some shootin'. C'mon, son, we gotta git this body down ta the sheriff fer he starts gettin' ripe. You go hitch up mah buckboard, whilst ah set mah relatives up ta the table."

They took the corpse into town and gave a statement to the Custer County sheriff.

Sheriff Schoolfield stood up and shook

hands with both men, saying, "Sounds like a righteous shootin' to me. What about his horse?"

"He asked me to take good care of it, before he died. I told him I would give it to Jennifer. It is a large chestnut gelding with four white stockings," Man Killer said.

Chancy added, "The horse had a lazy B bar S on the left hip, and I'll add my brand to 'im."

"Good enough," the sheriff replied. "He had two hunnert in gold in his poke. Thet's raght much, I'd say. Guess it buries him and the rest goes inta the Custer County general fund. He dint have no old letters or anything. Heerd his name was Del Johnson or some sech, probably a name borrowed off a tombstone. He was ridin' the owlhoot trail for sure."

The two left the office, and the sheriff came out as they mounted the buckboard. He said, "Man Killer, you and Colt watch yer backtrail. Jest got word that Buffalo Bob Smith and Durango Hobbs rode into Rosita. Don't know why them two would be coming here, but they're rattlesnake mean and always on the prowl. You and Colt got sech big reps, that might be why they come here."

Man Killer said, "Thanks for the warning, Sheriff. We will be careful, but we always are anyway."

The two men waved and headed back south to the Banta ranch. Even walking the horses, the ride was less that half an hour.

Beatrice and Jennifer were working on a quilt on the front porch when the two men pulled into the ranch yard, and Horace was out behind the house. He was shooting a Henry repeater at a distant buck antelope. Man Killer was impressed. The pronghorn took off at the first shot, a near miss, but the man hit it on the run with the second shot, and it was about a one-hundred-and-fifty-yard shot. The antelope fell sideways, lung shot, and did not move.

Chancy said, "Durn good shootin' fer an Aussie rancher, Horace."

"Well, Chancy, I done me a might a shootin' in my day, y'know."

"Naw, I don't know," Chancy said, "Ah jest know ya married the sister of mah sainted wife, and y'all got a big spread, but thet's about all I ever knowed about ye."

Man Killer could sense something boiling under the surface between these two brothers-in-law, but he was not sure what it was. He did know that he had tremendous respect for Chancy Banta. He was a true western man. If he gave his word, he looked you in the eye and would die keeping that word. This was one thing Man Killer had learned about some men that he likened to his own people. There were liars and cowards among the Nez Perce, but they seemed to be few and far between. Chancy also had a good work ethic and deep moral values. He was a tough man, not one to be trifled with, and he loved his daughter very much, which was something he definitely had in common with Man Killer.

Man Killer visited until late afternoon, then decided to head back to the Coyote Run. He enjoyed the afternoon with Jennifer, sitting on the bank of their small ranch pond and fishing. He was a warrior, but a true warrior was first a man of peace, and he was bothered by killing the gunman who braced him in the morning. It seemed like so many hours before, but on the other hand, it was also fresh in his mind. Killing another man was never an easy thing.

After Man Killer had mentioned that to Colt at one time, the chief of scouts simply smiled and said, "Good. If it ever does become easy for you, it will be time for us to ride different trails."

He had to first ride into Westcliffe, then take the Texas Creek Road north to the ranch. Right before he rode out of the ranch yard, Man Killer was joined by Chancy Banta, who trotted out of the barn on a solid-looking line-back red dun. He rode up next to him and gave him a wink and a smile.

Chancy said, "Gonna ride with ya as fer as Westcliffe, son, git me a cold beer, an' see what's been happenin' roun h'yar."

In the West, the local saloon was like the local news office. It was the gathering place for men from miles around, and all the latest information was passed out about range conditions, Indian attacks, crop projections, gunfights, court battles, and myriad other things of interest to these rugged frontier men.

The two rode toward the town, the edge of which was clearly visible from the ranch, without speaking. They both just took in the majesty that lay before them with the width and breadth of the high mountain valley. Westcliffe lay at close to eight thousand feet elevation. To their left, just a few miles away, the gently sloping green valley fringes turned into numerous stands of scrub oaks and suddenly went up, up, up into timber-covered, high mountain ridges—each one quickly becoming devoid of tree cover at somewhere above eleven or twelve thousand feet. For ten or eleven months out of the year, those bare mountaintops were covered with giant caps of shiny white ice and snow, giving each mountain the appearance of being a pointed green cake with whipped cream heaped all over the top.

Just outside Westcliffe, Chancy said, "Boy when you gonna ast my girl to git hitched?"

Man Killer smiled and said, "I hadn't thought of it." Then he cringed, as he knew what he said was a misstatement. It ate away at his insides, so he finally said, "I mean, I have thought of it, but I have not thought about when to ask her. I do not have much to offer."

Chancy chuckled, and said, "Hell, boy, all that gal wants you to offer is yerself. When I go unner and my older brother does, she'll inherit the family fortune. She ain't interested in money, and she ain't interested in Australia, although my relatives are doin' their damndest to make her interested."

Man Killer said, "What do you mean?"

Chancy said, "Well, they figger I ain't got too many winters left in me. Probably don't at thet, and it's a durn miracle mah brother, Larry, is still kickin'. When we're gone, though, Jennifer's gonna inherit an estate. Well, we inherited it, and it jest kept gettin' bigger over the years. Mah brother and I come out here from Maryland together, but our family had money from shipping in New England, making ammunition back East, fertilizer, and sech as thet. When we're gone, Jennifer's the only one left on our side a the family. Now, I got cousins over toward Salida way and up past Cotopaxi, but my little gal will be the only one left direct from mah family, and she'll be the richest gal in Colorado probably, and I always wanted her ta marry her a good feller who wanted her fer herself, not her money. I know how yer people raised ya, and the money don't make no difference to you."

"How do you know?" Man Killer asked, grinning broadly.

Chancy said, "Anybody else woulda ast me right off why I live the way I do, if I'm so durned rich. You know why I do."

Chancy turned slightly in the saddle and looked left to right from one end of the fourteen thousand footers to the other. These beauteous snow-capped peaks stretched to the north and the south as far as they could see.

He looked at Man Killer and said, "Ain't no money in the world kin buy thet, mister."

Man Killer said, "Are you sure you're not Nez Perce?"

Chancy nodded and said, "Take thet as a real compliment."

They rode into town, and Man Killer stopped briefly at the telegraph office to see if there were any telegrams for the Colts.

When he came out with several telegrams, Chancy rode over to him and stuck out his hand to shake, and the look he gave Man Killer sent a chill down the scout's spine.

Chancy said, "You make sure ya take good care a my girl, mister. Don't never change from the kind a man ya are now."

Man Killer didn't know what to say and was embarrassed. This was the first time he had seen the old man show so much emotion, and it made him feel very good to think that Chancy wanted him, an Indian in a white man's world, to marry his only daughter.

Man Killer didn't know how to respond, so he just waved and took off at a trot up the Texas Creek Road. Wagons were moving along the road north and south, and the scout had to ride off the road every few seconds to avoid running into anyone on the major artery into the boom town.

At the Colts house, Man Killer sat down and drank hot tea while Chris read the three telegrams for him and Joshua read the one sent him. Joshua's was about a bull a man was leasing to him, and it was being sent up to Canon City by rail from Santa Fe. All three of Chris's telegrams were about one thing.

They were from the army at Fort Union, New Mexico. Colt had heard that Fort Union had lost importance as the biggest supply depot west of the Missouri, as the Santa Fe Trail withered down to nothing and the railroads really started taking over the West. A small garrison still remained at the fort in northern New Mexico, and they did not have much to do. There were occasional forays out from the fort to assist U.S. marshals operating in the area and some patrols to ensure that Geronimo didn't head that far north and east, but who understood the unpredictable Apache. The telegrams dealt with such a thing.

During the previous year, Colt, Man Killer, and Colt's attorney Brandon Rudd, had been officially appointed deputy U.S. marshals and had been asked to just hang onto the badges in case they would be needed again in the future. Brevet Lieutenant Colonel George K. Brady was in command of the 23rd Infantry regiment and the garrison at Fort Union. Colt and Man Killer were to report to him and were to scout for a detachment of cavalry troopers who would be looking for the rapist, murderer, and robber known as the Apache Kid.

Colt had heard of the wily criminal and was impressed. The man, apparently a White Mountain Apache, had been living among the whites in Arizona. He killed a white man to avenge the murder of his father and was tried and convicted of murder. Several people intervened with letters to Washington on his behalf, however, and he was pardoned by the President of the United States.

After that, he fled into the mountains and

started a campaign of terror against the whites. Numerous posses and several cavalry patrols pursued him, but could not even come close to finding the wily renegade. Several military intelligence reports now placed him in northern New Mexico and southern Colorado, and they concluded he was responsible for a number of unsolved rapes, robberies, and murders in the area.

One telegram said that both men were still deputized and could fulfill their duties as federal marshals on the campaign or as scouts for the U.S. Army. Further, it stated that possibly the Apache Kid would die a "quiet death in the solitude of the Rocky Mountains," but in either case, they felt that Chris Colt would have the best opportunity to locate him of anybody living.

Colt said, "Man Killer, can you leave with me before first light."

Man Killer said, "That is what I do. I will leave whenever you want me to."

He couldn't help but notice the tear forming in the corner of Shirley's eye, but she quickly turned away. He thought about Jennifer and wondered if she ever cried when she learned he was gone on a mission. It bothered him, thinking about her aunt and uncle trying to get her to go with them to Australia. He also wondered about Chancy's brother, Larry. Man Killer had not heard of him before and wondered where he lived.

He had acquired a new habit that few white men even did, but Man Killer was proud of himself for it. He walked over to Shirley and gave her a hug and kiss on her cheek, saying, "You will be asleep when we leave in the morning. When we come home, maybe you will have an apple pie cooling on the window-sill. I will steal it."

She said, "You won't have to. I'll make you one. That's a promise."

Man Killer put his hand on the door latch and said, "I will sleep. Joshua, that roan Appaloosa mare has."

Joshua interrupted, "I know; I know. I checked her yesterday, and she's bagging up. I'll keep an eye out for her foal. You want me to breed her back to one of the quarter horse studs or the Palouses?"

Man Killer said, "The leopard Appaloosa stallion."

Joshua said, "That's no problem. You two go do your work. I'll watch out for your mare and foal."

Man Killer said, "Good night."

Everyone responded.

Joshua got up and said, "I'm going out to the barn and check on Hawk's and War Bonnet's shoes. Good luck, Chris."

Colt said, "Take good care of this mommy

here for me while I'm gone, will you, big brother?"

"Of course," Joshua said, "I watch over everyone and everything on this ranch. That is what I do, as Man Killer puts it."

He also gave Shirley a kiss on the cheek and walked out.

It was dark shortly before dawn when Chris Colt and Man Killer rode out the end of the northwest gate of the Coyote Run Ranch. They had only to ride downhill on the Cotopaxi Trail for five miles, and they would be at the Arkansas River and the tracks running down to Canon City. A freight train came by around daylight, which they were able to board in a boxcar and ride on to through Canon City to Pueblo. From there, they transferred to another freight train that ran south to New Mexico. North of Las Vegas, they unloaded near Fort Union, and made the short ride into the fort on the remnants of the now dwindling Santa Fe Trail. With the introduction of the railroads all over the West, many trails like the Santa Fe had dwindled down to a small trickle of traffic. Prior to that, the Santa Fe Trail, which came down through old Bent's Fort and went south along the Front Range into New Mexico Territory, was a mile wide with many deep wagon ruts in it. Fort Union had been the major quartermaster depot for the entire Southwest, and freighter wagons arrived and departed several times each day, 365 days per year. Besides that, numerous wagon trains used the trail to flood into the Wild West frontier.

At Fort Union, Chris and Man Killer first saw to their horses at the livery, then reported to Brevet Lieutenant Colonel Brady. He was a military man for sure, and the post of Fort Union seemed to be a nonchallenging job for him.

He would leave his executive officer in charge and lead the patrol himself, as he explained to the scouts, "To get the hell away from this God-forsaken post and garrison duty. I need a horse between my legs, not a damned desk chair."

Brady told the scouts that they would take the railroad up above Raton Pass to Trinidad and use that southern Colorado town and known outlaw hangout as the jumping-off place to begin the operation. Colt figured that's what they would do and really wanted to just meet the detachment there, but he was used to doing things the military way, which could, at times, be extremely efficient, and at other times, extremely stupid. He and the Nez Perce wanted to see the fort anyway, having spent some time there a few years earlier. They were surprised at how deserted and quiet the formerly bustling military installation had become.

Man Killer and Colt, after looking around, went to the sutler's store for a game of bowling and then some billiards. All the soldiers hung out at the sutler's store when they were not on duty, as it was the only place to go for miles around. It had had a bowling alley in it for years, and that and the billiards were favorites with most patrons.

As they walked in the door and blinked their eyes against the dark, Man Killer thought about his first time in this place. It was a day he would never forget. He waited a few seconds, then was able to see a little better, and the place made him feel sad in one sense, elated in another.

When Chris Colt and Man Killer were first summoned to Fort Union, the young scout was much younger. That was when they were contracted to guide the buffalo soldiers of the Ninth and Tenth Cavalry in operations against the renegade Mimbres Apache chief, Victorio, and his followers, who had been terrorizing the citizens of Arizona, Mew Mexico, and Mexico. While Colt met with Colonel Edward Hatch, commander of the Ninth Cavalry, Man Killer had looked around and had agreed to meet the chief of scouts in the place.

Man Killer was drinking his second sarsa-parilla when a gravelly voice behind him said, "Didn't know they let any a Chief Joseph's red niggers in this here drinkin' 'stablishment."

Man Killer knew he had just heard trouble, and he turned around slowly, wishing Colt was here to help him out with trouble in a white man's world. He looked at the giant barrel chest of a big behemoth of a man with a gray-streaked bright red long beard and long salt-and-pepper unkempt hair. Beer suds were sitting on his beard, and he had a giant grin on his scarred and wind-burned face. He pointed at the lad and laughed loudly, guffaws rumbling out of a chest that looked to Man Killer to be bigger around than Hawk's. A Sharps buffalo gun rested against the man's side, and he wore, across his rib cage, a large beaded sheath and bowie knife, not unlike Colt's.

He said, "Got ya, didn't I, youngster? Yep, yer a salty one, ain't ya. No wunner old Chris Colt taken ya in under his wing. Reckon you'll do to ride the mountain passes with. Here's to ya."

With that, the big man gulped down the rest of his mug of iced beer and slammed the big thick glass down on the bar and nodded for a refill.

"Barkeep," he roared, "give my young

friend here a refill of his sasparilly, will ya? Man Killer's yer name, ain't it?"

Man Killer nodded at the jolly big man. He accepted the sweet drink and started downing it. Finally, he spoke, "You know my name."

"Shore have. I'm a man a the mountains, son, but up there we hear the news, too, time to time," he said, "You and Colt been the talk a the West past coupla year. Heard bout his rescuin' his woman from the Sioux, grinnin' down Crazy Hoss, an' becomin' friends with him, and rumor has it that he was with Chief Joseph on his famous retreat crosst the mountains. That ole Colt's shinin', boy. He'd be one fer ya ta stick with if'n things was different."

"What do you mean, different?"

"No matter. Drink up," he said, "I'll buy ya 'nuther."

"Why?" Man Killer said out of honest curiosity.

The man said, "Yer famous, and yer still a lad. I like the cut of ya. I'm an old white nigger come down outta the mountains, smelling a woodsmoke, beaver guts, and bar grease. I don't never git to see other folk hardly, much less someone famous."

Man Killer was suspicious. "You know my name. I don't know yours."

The man grinned and stuck out a giant

ham-sized palm that engulfed the Nez Perce's
hand as they shook.

Man Killer wiped his hand on his leg right
now, as he thought back to that day. He
slowly looked down at his hand, turned it
over, and remembered how the giant's had so
completely enveloped his own.

He said, "Name's Thadeous Webster Sawyer, but folks call me Barrel on account a one
time I picked up a big barrel a nails with my
arms wrapped roun' it and carried it crosst a
room. Won me a couple a double eagles, too,
I did."

Man Killer said, "Sawyer. You said your
family name is Sawyer. Chris Colt killed the
Sawyer brothers."

"My cousins," the brute said, "Will an me
was jest 'bout brothers growin' up."

Man Killer felt his heart pounding in his
ears and neck. Earlier, Chris Colt had shot
and killed another giant of a man, Will Sawyer, who had kidnapped, held hostage, and
repeatedly raped Shirley before she and
Chris were married. Neither one of them had
told Man Killer that Sawyer had raped her,
but it didn't need to be explained when the
two spoke with him about it. It was something left unsaid but understood.

"So you are here to kill Colt?" he asked.

"He's a hell of a man," Barrel said, "but it's a blood thing. Yer Injun. You understand."

Man Killer said, "How long have you been after him?"

"Coupla year. Went to his ranch up in the Wet Mountain Valley, but he wasn't there. I ast aroun' and found out he was headed down here."

Man Killer was very concerned now about Shirley and said, "What happened at his ranch?"

Barrel said, "Aw, some uppity nigger run me off with a scattergun. Claimt he was Colt's brother. Imagine that? I figgered he was some stable nigger what was teched in the head, so I paid him no never mind."

It had been quite a shock when Chris Colt learned that his father had had an affair with a Negro slave and bore a son by her, two years older than himself. When Colt learned about Joshua, he had to deal with his prejudice first, but then accepted Joshua fully and totally.

Man Killer said to Barrel Sawyer, "You left the ranch, didn't you?"

Barrel's watermelon-sized head got beet red, and he said, "Careful, young un. I jest bought ya a drink. Learn respect."

Man Killer replied, "I didn't ask for a drink. You have wasted such time. Outshooting Chris Colt would be like trying to lasso a windstorm."

"Hell"—Barrel laughed—"I don't even own me a short gun. I'm a gonna kill him with my blade."

With that, he pulled his bowie out in one easy move and admired it like a family pet. He replaced it in the sheath.

Man Killer said, "Will Sawyer tried that already, and he is sleeping now at the bottom of a burning mud bowl in the Yellowstone."

The big man roared with laughter again. "Nobody seen it but Crazy Horse supposedly, an' he's conveniently livin' in the happy huntin' grounds. Naw, I knew Will, and the only way Colt coulda kilt him was ta backshoot him."

Man Killer's gun came out in a flash and was cocked with the barrel literally stuck up the right nostril of Barrel Sawyer. He surprised himself with his anger and hand speed, but this man had just accused Chris Colt of a cowardly act. Colt was Man Killer's hero, and he would not stand for that kind of talk. He was seething inside.

"You have called my brother a coward," Man Killer said, "Before killing him, you will first have to kill me."

Man Killer remembered the lump in his throat after challenging the mountain man to a fight to the death. He was afraid, but he was more afraid of being a coward and not standing up for Chris Colt.

One thing led to another and before long Man Killer was in a fight to the death with the giant of a man. Soon knives were brought into play, and both men ended up very bloody, up to that point receiving superficial wounds, until the end.

Barrel was now holding the bowie underhanded, straight out with the blade up, hoping to thrust it into Man Killer's stomach and rip his intestines out. Man Killer's own knife suddenly appeared in his hand from the sheath hidden inside the back of his war shirt, and he rolled to the side while thrusting the blade into Barrel's chest. The momentum from the big man's rush helped bury the blade almost all the way to the hilt into the left side of his chest.

Man Killer rolled three times and grabbed a bowling pin. It had been set on the bar for patrons to inspect close up. Sawyer, face white with shock, came forward, hands outstretched, but the young Colt protégé never stopped. As he grabbed the heavy wooden pin, he spun around and swung it backward, striking the end of the handle of his knife, driving it all the way into Barrel's chest. The big man let out a death scream and fell face first, his body convulsing in death for a full half minute before it stopped forever.

All Sawyer could see was darkness and the image of himself with a trident and horns. Mentally he said to the image, "I was killed by a red nigger kid."

The image laughed, and Barrel Sawyer heard a voice in the darkness say, "Damn, that kid killed that big monster."

He screamed inside his brain, but his blank eyes just stared at the bright red pool of blood all around. He felt hands touch his body and roll him over, but he could not see or hear or move anymore. He panicked, then everything in his brain stopped.

Man Killer stood, and one of Colonel Hatch's orderlies started forward to help him but was stopped by Colt's touch. The Nez Perce stood, straightening his shoulders and sticking out his chest. He walked to Sawyer's body and stepped on the giant's chest and grabbed the handle of his knife. He yanked hard and pulled the blade free with a sucking sound. He then wiped it on the dead man's wool undershirt. Man Killer replaced it in his sheath and took a big swallow of sarsaparilla. He walked over to Colt, the room spinning. Chris was grinning.

Man Killer reached down and rubbed his severely bruised rib. It hurt more than any of his other wounds, and breathing came hard.

He now touched it subconsciously, and Colt gave him a sidelong glance and knowing grin. Man Killer was positive his mentor knew what he was thinking about. It was Chris's job to read sign and know things like that. The evidence that he did know was soon laid out.

Chris Colt snapped Man Killer back to the present when he said, "You know killing a man is something that you never forget."

Man Killer gave Chris a knowing smile.

The scout went on, "In civilized society we need men who can do that when they have to and don't forget to feel bad when they recall it. Those that do forget are no good to society, but become the coyotes and buzzards around us. Come on. I'll bet you a beer that I can beat you in a game of billiards."

Man Killer, larger, stronger, older now, gave the room another sweeping glance, thinking of that day, and grinned, saying, "You're on, Great Scout."

Colt smiled, thinking that Man Killer had not used those terms so often anymore, as he did when he was younger. Man Killer had become so educated and self-taught since they first met, it was amazing. At times, he spoke in the poetic manner of the American Indian, especially one who was raised in the band of the famous orator, Chief Joseph. At other times, he spoke like a young white man, fast approaching his twentieth year, with many years of proper schooling behind him. Although the Nez Perce were farther west than many Indian nations, they were one of the most educated in white man's ways and language. Christian missionaries had lived among them after the Lewis and Clark expedition, which had occurred many years before Man Killer's birth.

Colt worried about his not speaking poetically as often, because he never wanted the young man to forget or get too far from his Indian ways. That was one of the things that made Man Killer special. Like Chris Colt, he could walk in both worlds, red and white, although he could do it even better than Colt.

They played billiards and Man Killer won.

The next morning the twenty-man patrol, led by a brevet lieutenant colonel no less, departed from Fort Union, headed toward the railhead a few miles to the east. They would head north for Trinidad, one hundred and thirty some miles, arriving later in the afternoon.

That trip was taking the two, Colt thought, part of a morning and afternoon, when, just a few years earlier, pioneers in wagons could only make the trip in over a week, sometimes several. A man on horseback would generally take two to four days to make the trip.

In Trinidad the detachment rode into town where they met a small patrol that had been staying fairly close to the town, gathering as much intelligence as possible on the Apache Kid. There had been several robberies and rapes by an Indian, his hair cut short and parted in the middle, near the towns of Walsenburg, Trinidad, and the general area. It was obvious he was taking refuge in the Greenhorn Mountains.

The detachment made bivouac outside the town on a ridge climbing north away from the community and looking down over it. To the south, beyond the town, were several mountains that were actually flat-topped and tree-covered mesas.

While the troopers stacked their rifles, set out night sentries, and prepared their camp, Chris and Man Killer rode down into Trinidad to nose around and see what they could stir up about the Apache Kid.

They went into the busiest saloon in town and bellied up to the hand-engraved mahogany-topped bar. The bartender had a pot belly and broad shoulders. He wore garters on his sleeves to hold them up and a big, brown handlebar mustache.

Colt said, "Two beers."

The bartender smiled nervously and

stared at Colt, saying, "We don't serve Injuns here."

Man Killer said, "Good, we did not order any. We ate already tonight. We want two beers."

The bartender gave a sarcastic laugh and turned away. He felt a tap on his arm and turned back to Colt and Man Killer. They just smiled at him. He shrugged, turned back away from them, then felt both sleeves fall down over his wrists. The barkeep tried to push up on his garters, but was surprised to feel them missing. The surprised man looked at both arms, and the garters *were* missing. He looked around, spotted them lying on the floor, picked them up, and inspected them. Both garters were cut in half and were stretched out straight. He looked as if in shock, then at Colt and Man Killer. He said, "What did you do?"

Colt reached back between his shoulders and pulled out his giant bowie from the sheath hidden inside his shirt. He started cleaning his fingernails with the giant blade and grinned broadly at the mixologist. "Just standing here, minding our own business, waiting on our beers, partner," Colt said.

The startled bartender felt a cold chill run up and down his spine. He immediately went to the tap and poured two beers, sliding both down the mahogany bar to the two scouts.

Colt pulled out a couple of coins, and the bartender shook them off, saying, "On the house, sir."

Man Killer said, "Pour another one, please?"

The bartender gave a funny look, and Man Killer slid coin to the man, saying, "For you. It's on me."

The bartender really gave the young man a queer look now, but nodded, blew the foamy head off the cold brew, and gulped it down. He nodded in appreciation and forced a smile.

An upright piano stood in the corner, and a faro dealer left his deserted table and sat down, starting to play it, for two of the upstairs ladies seated in the corner. Both had been eyeballing the two scouts since they entered, but both men ignored them.

On the other side of the back of the room two tablesful of men hosted poker games. Four more cowpunchers and one teamster stood at the large bar, drinking.

Colt tossed a coin on the bar, and the barkeep walked down in front of the man. "Yes, sir?"

Chris said, "What have you heard about the Apache Kid?"

"Only what I've read in the papers, mister," the bartender said, warming up slightly. " 'Cept a coupla punchers was in here the
141

other day from a spread down to Raton. One of them said they seen the Apache Kid with a spyglass from a ridgeline up high, northwest of here. It was near Greenhorn, I recollect. The puncher hadn't been drinking yet and seemed like straight-shooter, but you never know."

Just then the batwing doors flew open, and a large man walked in, followed by a gang of eight others. Colt recognized four of them as gunslingers, and the way the rest wore their sidearms, it was obvious they were shootists as well. The swaggering leader was a gunslick from Tombstone who had been run out by the Earps at the business end of a scattergun. His name was Rattle-snake Jack Colby, and he wore a rattler hat band with mounted head, fangs open, on his black Stetson, which he was always carefully brushing off. He claimed twenty dead in gun fights, but there were only three Colt knew of, and one was a fifteen-year-old kid who fancied him a gunhand. He learned the hard way he wasn't.

Chris sipped his beer slowly and looked at Man Killer in the mirror. They both gave each other an oh-oh-here-comes-trouble-look and tried to ignore the gunhands as they bullied and pushed their way up to the bar. They laughed and chuckled and made loud, obscene comments to one another.

Colt whispered, "We ran two of those boys out of Oregon. Remember, they worked for Rufus Potter and tried to punch our tickets?"

Man Killer whispered. "But they seemed much, much bigger then."

Colt said quietly, "You were much, much smaller then. Everyone seemed big."

Man Killer smiled and stood up a little straighter then. He was a grown man now, but barely a teenager when that incident had occurred. Colt knew that some of the men had to know who they were. The two scouts were very hard to miss, especially with their big, colorful horses tied right outside at the hitching rail.

Colt lifted his glass and whispered, "Drink up."

Man Killer knew that Colt wanted them to get out of there, so he drank the rest of the cold brew and nodded, almost imperceptibly. They set their empty mugs down and turned toward the door, but only made two steps when they heard the distinct cocking of several guns behind them. Both scouts turned slowly and were staring at the drawn guns of the two men who had worked for Potter.

With mild amusement Colt said sarcastically, "It takes a big man to draw down on a man's back."

One of the slingers said, "Señor Colt.

Damn you, gringo. You made me and me amigo take water a long time ago, but I have learned a lot seence then, and we have waited for thees day."

Colt, again sarcastically, said, "So you can shoot us down while you have the drop on us? What a couple of hardcases."

Just then the door opened behind Colt and Man Killer, and everything in the bar just stopped. The gang of gunmen stared. Chris and Man Killer couldn't risk turning their heads, so they just listened as two men walked behind them and then slightly past them, bellying up to the bar as if nothing had happened.

If Chris Colt and Man Killer were a pair of noticeable characters, these two men were the ultimate. The first was very short and stocky. By his wardrobe, he looked, from behind, to be Comanche, but he wore a large sword in a scabbard angled crosswise across his back. The handle alone was close to a foot long and had very fancy gold inlay work in it.

The other was a tall man in blue denim jeans and a sun-faded green bib shirt. A faded red scarf was draped around his sun- and wind-burned face, and he was topped by a dusty black Stetson. He was probably a couple of inches taller than Colt, who was a notch or two over six foot, and the man was slender, but Colt could tell the man moved easy and the muscles under his shirt were like steel cables.

He had two things in common with Chris Colt: He wore large-roweled Mexican spurs with a loud jingle; he wore a pair of handsome Colt .45 Peacemakers with the hand-carved mother-of-pearl handles with an eagle perched on a serpent and ready to bite. He spoke to the short Comanche in sign language and asked if the man was thirsty. The warrior nodded, and the tall man reached across the bar for two shot glasses and a bottle and poured two shots of whiskey. He swallowed his quickly, placed both hands on the bar and gave a shiver, then turned around and leaned his elbows on the bar.

The Comanche turned around and slowly sipped his shot of whiskey. Colt and Man Killer looked again and were amazed. He was not Comanche. He wore beaded soft-soled Comanche moccasins, fringed leggings, and a faded red breechcloth, with a very long knife scabbard stuck through the belt. He also wore a bright red shirt with white polka dots and a few brightly colored ribbons sewn across the chest, shoulders, and back. He wore a beaded Comanche headband and a single red-tailed hawk tail feather with yellow plume at the base. His black hair was parted in the middle, but his face was not Indian.

His eyes were narrow slits, and he looked almost Chinese, but somewhat different. He looked around the room while sipping his whiskey, taking everything in.

The tall, slender man had a familiar look to Colt and a shock of dark brown hair peeking out from under his hat, but what amazed Colt and Man Killer both were his very light, sky blue eyes. Man Killer had to admit that the man's eyes were as amazing a color as Jennifer Banta's. He never thought he'd see any as light blue and piercing as hers. The man's face was brown from the elements, and he had a twinkle in his eyes that would make any available woman interested. He also was grinning.

The man said slowly, "Chris Colt, looks like you got yourself into one of those shooting scrapes."

Colt smiled and said, "Yep, stranger. These gents here are upset because we turned around when they pulled iron, and they couldn't plug us in the back."

Rattlesnake said, "Who are you, mister? Just shut up."

The tall man said, "Look out! Rattler!" His right-hand gun exploded with a blossom of flame, and the man's rattlesnake head on his hat band exploded, while the black Stetson flew off his head. The left-hand gun boomed, and the hat flew up in the air and across the room with a second hole through it. He did a border switch, flipping his right-hand gun to his left and catching the left-hand gun, which he flipped over top. He cocked and fired both guns simultaneously, and the hat was torn to shreds before hitting the wall.

Nobody had even seen the man draw, and he had just obliterated the leader's hat with four shots and some very slick gun handling.

The man now pointed both guns at the two men who had drawn on Colt and Man Killer. He smiled, and the men holstered their guns very carefully. He winked at Chris and Man Killer, and both scouts automatically liked this man. He had just pulled a stunt they might have tried themselves in a different situation.

The tall man now said, "Little more even now, folks. Suppose you two wanna draw on Chris Colt now?"

Both men were thinking it over.

To help them and their friends, the man added, "I didn't like the looks of the game, boys, so I dealt myself in, too. When I declare war, Tora here always gets involved. He'd rather fight than eat."

Rattlesnake, furious now, said, "You bought yerself a mess a trouble, boy. And that Chinese blanket-nigger looks like something to just step on. You and Colt and the other blanket-nigger might be good, but not good enough for all of us."

The slender man said, "My friend is not Chinese. He is Japanese, and he does not like to be called names."

The big bully laughed loudly past his anger and said, "Really, who gives a damn? Ain't that a shame, boys? The Chink don't like to be called names. If he wants, he can come over and complain to me, and I'll tear down his little yellow meat-wagon for him."

He guffawed loudly again and pointed and laughed even harder, as the little man walked forward, his eyes coming up only to the middle of Rattlesnake's chest.

The tall man said, "Tora can't speak. He lets his actions speak for him."

Rattlesnake said, "Whatsa matter, Chink, cat got your tongue?"

The other gunslingers joined in his continued laughter. Suddenly, the leading gunshooter drew his gun to shoot the man, but it didn't fire. He looked down and screamed as he saw blood spurting from his wrist, his right hand and pistol hitting the floor at his feet. Looking up, he saw a flash of steel as the blade swung across in a quick arc, and his head was severed from his body. It rolled off the back of the big body and hit the floor with a *thunk*.

The other gunfighters had never seen such

a thing and were amazed. Several looked to ambush the four men, but they were staring down six deadly forty-five muzzles from the stranger and the two scouts.

Chris Colt said, "One at a time, boys. Left hands, pull your iron and drop them in the water barrel in the corner."

The men very carefully walked to the barrel and dropped their weapons in, one man at a time. They also, at the stranger's direction, dropped their holsters in, too.

Colt pointed his left-hand gun at the two men who drew on him and Man Killer and said, "You take the head to the funeral parlor down the street. You take the hand, and you four take the rest of the body."

Most of the gunslingers were white-faced and in total shock. Blood dripped off the end of the long sword blade in the Japanese man's right hand, and the shorter sword, or long knife, was in his left hand. Nobody had seen him draw that. When he drew the big sword from his back and sliced Rattlesnake's hand off, the speed was blinding. His eyes shifted from one gunfighter to another, and a chill ran down each man's spine as Tora looked at him.

The tall man said, "I suggest that you boys mount up, one at a time, and ride out in different directions."

Finally, one of the shootists spoke up angrily. "See here, we have been hired for a job and are riding together."

Colt said, "Nope, you're all supposed to be gunfighters, but you just proved you're in the wrong line of work. All of you take different roads out of town and find new jobs."

The angry one said, "Mister, you butted in and started all this. I'll remember you, and we'll meet again. What's your handle?"

The tall, blue-eyed stranger smiled softly and said, "Colt. Justis Colt. Don't forget, anybody with that last name is someone you want to stay away from, because we are like glue. Understand."

Chris Colt laughed and said, "I'll be dipped in honey and set on fire. Justis Colt! Little Justis. My little cousin? Is that really you?"

Justis Colt smiled and said, "Chat later, cousin. Let's take out the garbage first."

Tora, Justis, Chris, and Man Killer escorted the four out of the saloon and watched each mount up, directing them in different ways at different intervals out of Trinidad. The marshal came up and introduced himself while this was going on and was totally amazed. He recognized several of the gunslicks and was glad he didn't have to tangle with them. A half hour later saw the last of the gunfighters, and the four men escorted the lawman into the saloon.

The marshall addressed everybody, saying,

"Boys, Trinidad's got a bad enough reputa-tion. Don't nobody spill a word about a man getting his head cut clean off in here tonight? I don't care what you say in some other town saloon, or what you say a month from now, but I don't want the dad-burned newspaper to start nosing around or wanting to take a photo of poor old Rattlesnake Jack Colby without his ugly head. We'll take him up to Boot Hill tonight and plant him quietlike with no muss or fuss."

He walked outside with the four and said to Chris, "Mister Colt, I know of you by your rep, and I've heard of your sidekick here, too. If you were involved in this, I know you didn't start it, so you'll hear nothing bad from me. Now, I want to know something. I've been hearing from time to time the past two years about Colt being with the Texas Rangers and cleaning house. I thought you were a cavalry chief of scouts, but wondered if you switched jobs. Was that you?"

Justis smiled and interrupted, "Yes sir, I've been working a bit with McNelty and his boys down there. That's where I met Tora, living with the Comanches."

Tora moved his hands quickly and said something to Justis. Justis just smiled at Tora and waved him off.

"What was that?" the marshall asked.

"Nothing," Justis replied.

Chris said, "Tora wanted him to tell you that they met when Justis fought it out and saved him from a band of Comancheros who tortured him and cut out his tongue."

Tora smiled at Colt and nodded his approval.

The marshal said, "I heard about that, but like I said, I thought it was your brother here, or is it cousin?"

Chris said, "Cousin."

The lawman went on. "Heard that you were shot to doll rags, but kept on coming till you took them all down."

Tora nodded his head enthusiastically.

Chapter 4

>>>>>>>>>>>>>>>>>

Justis Colt

The four left the sheriff and rode down the street. They spotted a small saloon that was part of a large hotel building and went in, figuring there would be less chance of trouble there. It was quiet and not crowded.

The four men sat at a table and drank coffee, talking long into the night. Justis talked about his big cousin, Chris, and what a hero he was after running off to join the Union Army as a teenaged boy and lying about his age to do so. He had become a big hero before that when he whipped the two town bullies in Cuyahoga Falls, Ohio, his hometown.

Justis was from near Pittsburgh, growing up on the Monangahela River, near its intersection with the Allegheny and the Ohio rivers.

He told Man Killer how his and Chris's families got together about once a year and enjoyed each other's company. His life was really affected when Chris and his pa came to Pittsburgh one time. Chris was about twelve and Justis was about five. There was a thirteen-year-old bully who went to Justis's school and took things away from the smaller boys all the time. Anything they ever had of value was not safe from the extortionist.

Justis had told Chris about how the bully had taken a jackknife away from Justis, and the younger Colt had gotten a shiner, trying to keep it. He also got a beating with a razor strap at home for bringing a black eye with him. Justis's pa, the brother of Chris's pa, was very tough on the boy and told him he could come home with a shiner, as long as the other fellow looked even worse. It mattered not that the other boy in this case was close to full-grown and Justis was only five.

The jackknife had been a birthday gift from his ma, who like Chris's ma, had died at a young age, and the knife meant an awful lot to the little boy.

They happened down the road in front of Justis's house the day after he told his big cousin about the bully. The bully was a head taller than Chris Colt, but the twelve-year-old braced him and demanded the knife back. The bully, with two friends to show off for, just laughed and shoved Chris back into the dust.

The young Colt came off the ground in a

154

lunge and waded into the larger, stronger boy with a fury. Colt, however, had not developed his fighting skills at that time. He had started developing his strength of character, though, and it served him well. Within minutes, Colt had a bloody lip, was bleeding profusely from both nostrils, and the bigger boy had only a welt on his left cheekbone. The big boy stood there, hands on hips in triumph, and laughed again at Chris.

Colt, swaying on his legs, said, "I told you to give my cousin his jackknife back."

The bully said, "Why? What are you going to do, beat me up?" He laughed again, as did his buddies.

Colt said, "No, but you have to fight me again." He drove headfirst into the bigger boy and started flailing with his fists. The boy tried to ward off the blows and yelled, "Stop it! I already whipped you!"

Colt kept swinging and took a vicious right to the rib cage that knocked the wind out of him. His eyes bulged, and he panicked, feeling as though he would never breathe again.

He quickly regained his breathing though, stepped back, and said, "No, you didn't whip me. I won't be whipped till I'm dead. You'll have to fight me and fight me and fight me again, until you give my cousin his jackknife back. If I have to take two black eyes and lose two teeth each time just to catch you with one lick, I will until he gets his knife."

The bully said, "You're plumb crazy."

Colt said, "That's right." He swung from the hip and caught the boy with a punch that rocked him and paralyzed Chris's shoulder. Colt waded into him again, and the bully added more bruises to Colt's battered body and face. His eyes were almost shut now, and blood was all over his shirt, but he kept coming.

The bully now had an eye swelling shut and three loose teeth. He tried to break away and said to his buddies, "Get him off of me! Get him off of me! He's crazy!"

The two other boys jumped in and pulled the two boys apart. Justis tried to pull Chris back, too, but got knocked down in the process. The bully walked away from the two Colts and reached in his left front pocket, producing Justis's prize knife. He tossed it at Colt's feet and walked away fast.

Chris yelled, "Touch my cousin again, and I'll come back! You'll have to fight me again!"

Justis helped his bigger hero stagger to the little home down the road. Chris looked so bad when they walked in the door that his father immediately wrapped him in a blanket and, with his brother driving the wagon, rushed Chris to the doctor. He had no threatening wounds, but he certainly looked as if he did when the elder Colt first saw him.

The story of what Chris Colt had done had not only impressed Justis, but Chris's pa and uncle, as well. It also impressed all the people the story kept getting passed on to over the months and years that followed.

Justis raised his cup of coffee in toast to Chris, saying, "To my hero, my big cousin, Chris Colt."

Colt's face was red, but he nodded, then quickly changed the subject. "You know most of those gunmen will meet somewhere and keep on toward their job, wherever it is?"

Justis and Man Killer nodded in agreement.

Man Killer said, "Weren't several from south of here?"

Colt said, "Yes, they were."

The Nez Perce scout went on, "They were headed north. Let us hope it is beyond Pueblo."

Colt got a grim look on his face and nodded. Canon City and Westcliffe were essentially west of Pueblo.

Chris asked, "What brings you two around here anyway, Justis?"

Justis said, "We're after two other gunslicks who were with the band of Comancheros that sliced off Tora's tongue."

Colt said, "Who are they?"

Justis said, "Buffalo Bob Smith and Durango Hobbs."

Man Killer said, "They were in Rosita when we left."

Justis smiled, stuck out his hand, and said, "Looks like we have to get riding."

Colt said, "Ask in Westcliffe, Silver Cliff, or Rosita how to get to the Coyote Run Ranch. You two can meet my wife and brother, rest up, and they'll give you some grub. Swap horses if you need to."

Chris was waiting for Justis to act surprised at the mention of his brother, but the younger Colt just nodded.

Justis said, "Heard about Joshua several times. Bet you were a little surprised to meet him."

Man Killer laughed and sarcastically said, "No, he was very happy and friendly with his brother when they first met."

The scout remembered Chris's initial reaction to his bastard half brother when the two took turns giving each other sore jaws.

Justis went on, "Heard that Joshua was a heck of a leader and had ramrodded some tough drives that other men would have lost everyone on."

Chris smiled, saying, "He sure has a way with cattle, men, and horses."

"He is much like the Nez Perce with horses," Man Killer said.

Tora spoke in sign language, and Man Killer nodded his head, answering, "Yes, the Comanche are excellent horsemen. I mean that Joshua knows how to handle horses and gentle them, not just ride them well."

Tora nodded in understanding.

The four men walked outside and found a chill breeze blowing.

Colt said, "I was giving Joshua a hand a few weeks ago, and we had one mustang that had just found his way through our fence somewhere and was with our herd of horses. None of the punchers could get close to him, but Joshua walked out into the herd, and they just milled around a little cropping grass. He walked up to the mustang and the critter ran off a few times, but the way Joshua acted kind of made him curious, because he would turn away from the mustang every once in a while and act like he wasn't paying any attention. Before you knew it, that horse had come up close enough that Joshua leaned forward and stuck out his nose, sniffing. The mustang walked up and did the same, touching noses with my brother. It was a sight."

Man Killer added, "The Nez Perce do the same thing. If you watch strange horses; first they smell each others' noses. That is how they start to make friends. If we do the same with a wild horse, he trusts us more."

Justis said, "Tora has taken a blood oath to find those two men, and I have taken an oath to help him, so we better get going."

Colt said, "I sure admire the way you handle that sword."

Tora bowed and Justis explained, "He was a Samurai warrior from the little country of Japan, but there was a problem with the niece of the Emperor. Tora always wanted to see America and decided that then was a good time to make the trip."

Tora smiled at this and so did Colt and Man Killer.

Justis went on, "He ended up saving my life when I was shot up and left for dead, and I got a chance to repay him later."

Colt said, "Interesting. Now, Justis, are you still a Texas Ranger?"

Justis said, "No, I quit when we decided to go after the band of comancheros that tortured him. They killed his wife, too."

Chris got a faraway look in his eyes, saying, "I can understand that."

He thought of his first wife, the beautiful Minninconjou Lakotah woman Chantapeta, who was raped and murdered by four renegade Crows. Colt had tracked them all down and disposed of each one.

The four men shook hands and waved as they walked off in pairs.

* * *

The next morning, Chris Colt and Man Killer were about two miles in front of the cavalry patrol looking for possible signs of the Apache Kid and any other dangers that might threaten the military unit. Justis Colt and Tora had spent what was left of the night traveling toward Rosita, a few miles east of Westcliffe. They had hunted down ten other men, so far, and finding Buffalo Bob Smith and Durango Hobbs would fulfill their blood oaths.

Chris Colt tried to put himself in the mind of the Apache Kid. The man raped, stole, and murdered, but he didn't seem to do it to accumulate wealth. Colt figured he did it to strike back and intimidate the white man's world. But why didn't he just join Geronimo, Colt wondered.

Many people thought that scouts simply went out and looked at tracks on the ground, but there was much more to it than that. Colt and Man Killer would try to visualize the Apache Kid riding through this country and figure out where he would go and what he would do.

They both tried to reason out what would be motivating the outlaw. Chris Colt concluded that the man had hatred and disdain for white men, but he also assumed that the Apache Kid was addicted to the exhilaration of the chase. That is why he did not go with

Geronimo or Nana, who were still on the warpath. He liked sneaking in among the enemy, wreaking terror and havoc, and sneaking away again unscathed, one man alone. Colt believed it had become an ego trip for the Apache Kid.

Many men would need a ranch house to operate from, but he was an Apache, born to the mountains and the wild. He would travel light, very light, and live off the land. The Apache Kid would not need a cabin, ranch house, or any kind of building. He would sleep under a tree one night, a ledge the next, the back of a pony the next, and maybe not sleep at all on the following night. One thing he probably would do, though, would be to spend the money he stole.

What would the Apache Kid spend the money on? That question seemed most important to Chris Colt. He would spend the money on liquor, for certain. He probably would not spend it on women, Colt reasoned, because he was a rapist. He used sex as a weapon against white women to terrorize and put fear in people's hearts. It was also a method for him to violate the security net that men thought they were providing for their wives and daughters. What better way for the man to strike out at the race he hated.

Chris also figured that the Apache Kid

would probably spend money on guns and ammunition. He was always well armed and had not spared bullets during frequent running gun battles. Many times, an outlaw being pursued was very careful about each shot, because ammunition was so scarce and expensive. In all the reports Colt had read about the Apache Kid, that did not seem to be the case.

Now Colt had to reason where the Apache Kid might spend money on both guns and liquor. Everytime Chris tried to buy liquor with Man Killer, it was proven to him how much the white world was willing to openly sell so-called firewater to red men. It would also be impossible for the Apache Kid to ride into a town like Trinidad and just order a drink in a saloon anyway. He certainly wasn't going to walk into a mercantile store and order several hundred rounds of ammunition. So where else would he find that?

Chris Colt came up with an answer to his two questions. North of Walsenburg and a little to the west, was a trader who had a shack on Apache Creek, at the base of Greenhorn Peak. That snow-capped mountain was the highest in the front range running up the border past Pueblo to Pike's Peak and Cheyenne Mountain. The mountains were covered with trees and were not tall enough to have a timberline, except for Greenhorn, which had been named for a Comanche chief, Cuerno Verde. He had been killed at the base of the mountain in 1819 by a Spanish captain named De Anza.

Chris Colt had heard two legends about the Greenhorn Peak area. One was about a miner who thought he struck it rich with a major gold strike. He had dug a wagon load of gold ore out of a hole on, or near, Greenhorn Peak. The miner rushed north with the gold to Pueblo and immediately went to an assayer, who inspected the rocks and said that the ore was worthless. Dejected, the miner took the wagon to the dump on the outskirts of the town and unloaded the worthless rocks. He left town and was never seen or heard from again.

A few months later, another man happened upon the ore in the dump and loaded some of it up, taking it to a totally different assayer. That assayer said it was extremely rich in gold. In fact, he declared it the richest ore he had ever seen. The problem was that the miner who first discovered it never told anyone where he had made his strike. That story was simply referred to as the Gold of Greenhorn Peak.

The second legend Colt had heard numerous times was called the Treasure of Apache Gulch. The gulch ran up about due east off Greenhorn Peak and was the site of many glory holes where mines were started, and a number of prospectors found evidence of Spaniards mining in the area. A couple of miners even found an old Spanish arras-tram, a device for crushing ore.

Supposedly some Spaniards had made a rich strike in Apache Gulch, then were killed by Indians. After that, a miner discovered the hidden gold ore and had it assayed at a value of $58,000 per ton. Supposedly, that miner was killed by Indians, and nobody knew where the ore came from.

Chris Colt, since moving to the Wet Mountain Valley, had heard many stories about secret treasure and hidden gold, silver, and diamonds in the multicanyoned mountains near his home, but he took each story with a grain of salt.

What he figured was the real treasure in Apache Gulch was the poke belonging to Boston Bill Brannigan. Boston Bill was a big man with a very heavy accent that most people could not identify. One man, who had traveled out west from Massachusetts, said that Bill Brannigan had a very distinct Boston accent, so he got the name Boston Bill. The funny thing was, though, Boston Bill denied the accent was Bostonian, and about a year after he was labeled and stuck with that moniker, a cowboy from Texas happened by and told numerous witnesses that he had

grown up less than five miles from Bill Brannigan at Austin, Texas.

Boston Bill ran a trade-goods shack in
Apache Gulch that was miles off the beaten
path. Because it was so far away from normal trade routes and possible customers, it
was known that he had to be dealing illegals
to those riding the owl-hoot trail. He claimed
to be in Apache Gulch for the convenience of
miners, but anyone with a half a brain did
not buy that.

A big man, broad of shoulder and stomach
too, with legs like oak tree stumps, Boston
Bill Brannigan had started out as a miner,
but soon found out how to make more
money by selling trade goods at inflated
prices to those with stolen booty, be it money
and other valuables taken in robberies or
stolen gold from claim jumpers.

If there was anybody in the area that the
Apache Kid would be doing business with, it
would be Boston Bill Brannigan. The man
was tough and hard and would not talk, so
Chris Colt would not try to force information
out of him. They would just keep watch.

Colonel Brady was smart enough to listen
to the battle-hardened and widely experienced chief of scouts. He readily agreed
when Chris Colt had him and his men bivouac on a distant ridge and wait for a smoke
signal from Chris Colt.

Colt and Man Killer dug in positions on the side of Apache Gulch and maintained vigil over Brannigan's store. The man looked like a bull terrier. Near dusk on the second day, he walked out the front of his store and started mopping the board plank wooden porch, unnoticed by anyone but the two scouts. It was late in the day and, with night coming in, the porch would take much longer to dry. Further, why would he even mop it when it was in the middle of a dirty, dusty gulch, they thought. Inside the store, yes, but not outside. Finally, why did he mop a dirty, dusty porch without sweeping it off first? The answer was simple: Mopping the porch had to be a signal that someone could detect from far off. Even if the Apache Kid, or whoever, missed seeing Boston Bill mopping, they could look at the porch from a distance and see that it had been mopped. It was a clever and subtle signal, but not clever enough.

There was no moon that night, so Colt and Man Killer took turns watching, using the binoculars that Colt carried in his saddlebag. About an hour before daylight, Man Killer heard the sounds of a horse making its way through some rocks on the side of the ridge far below. Several times rocks were jarred loose and rolled down the rocky hillside to the soft ground at the floor of the gulch. Man

Killer also knew that the horse was unshod because there was no metallic clicking of his horseshoes on the rocks.

He awakened Colt, and they saddled their mounts, leaving them ground-reined nearby. The small fire they had made was in a deep hole. Colt had dug a small trench, two feet in length, and covered the trench to form a tunnel that ran right up to the side of the fire hole. Wind would blow through the tunnel and keep the fire burning hot. The wood was very dry aspen and built underneath a thick tree, so the little amount of smoke was dissipated as it curled skyward through the branches.

The two men made breakfast, not knowing when they might eat again. They drank about a gallon of hot coffee each, then got rid of that much from their bladders.

Waiting patiently was something that seemed to Chris Colt to come easier to the red man than it did to the white man. Chris realized it was a matter of survival with the American Indian. Deer, for example, were creatures of habit. Many would go to the same water holes by the same routes day in and day out, but it took much patience to wait for one deer, then wait for a chance to get a clean shot at it. Chris had, because of his exposure to the red man's way of life, but it seemed more difficult for him than it did for his red friends.

An hour after sunup finally produced the results the two desired. An Apache on a long-legged buckskin horse walked down out of the rocks and went behind the trader's cabin. He tied the horse in the shade of some cottonwoods and walked back around to the front. Colt watched him through the binoculars and saw that he had his normal, short-cropped, greased-down hair parted down the middle and was wearing white man's clothing. Like many warriors, he favored a rifle, carrying a Winchester carbine in his right hand, and he had a .44 Russian tucked into the front of his waistband.

The Apache Kid looked from side to side and entered the cabin, and the two scouts mounted up, preparing to go down the mountain. Suddenly, Man Killer reined his horse and pointed. Colt looked down to see a wagon pulling up in front of the cabin. He looked through the binoculars and spotted a man and woman. She was not dressed for any kind of trip through Apache Gulch, including the lace-edged pink parasol she carried to block out the sun's rays. The man himself seemed to be dressed a bit stiffly for a miner.

Colt heeled War Bonnet down the mountainside, looking back over his shoulder and saying, "Come on!" Man Killer, on Hawk, was only two jumps behind the chief of scouts.

In the trader's cabin, Boston Bull Brannigan was horrified as he watched the Apache Kid tear at Lady Wimsley's clothing. She screamed in horror, but Colt and Man Killer were still too high up the steep mountain to hear the noise. Lord Wimsley also yelled into his gag and pulled at his bonds, but they were too tight, as he observed this killer preparing to assault his wife sexually. They had no sooner walked in the door and had been assaulted and subdued.

The Apache Kid ripped the woman's blouse, and her breasts fell out of her undergarments. He loved the look of terror on her face. Within two minutes she stood completely naked, tears pouring out of her terrified eyes, hands covering her private areas as best she could. Boston Bill just gave the killer sheepish looks as the Apache Kid kept looking at the white man for approval.

The outlaw undid his belt and started to drop his pants when something happened. Chris Colt swung his horse from one side of the steep mountainside to switch back in the other direction, and as he did so, the light happened to catch the shiny metal of one of his .45 Peacemakers. The quick flash caught the rapist's eye. The Apache Kid hooked up his belt and ran to the window and stared upward. He spotted the two scouts coming hell bent for leather down the side of the mountain. The coloring of both horses told him who the two men were. He was frightened, but not as much as he should have been. Many bad men became and stayed bad because they felt they were invincible.

The Apache Kid ran to the gun rack and yanked out a big Sharps .50 buffalo gun. He loaded up and double cocked it, running out the door of the trader's cabin. Colt and Man Killer were close enough now to make out the big gun and watched as he aimed in their direction. The killer, unfortunately, was not aiming at them. If he was, he might have missed at that distance. Instead, the Apache Kid aimed the big gun at some rocks well above the duo. The rocks were piled under a large overhang of precariously balanced boulders.

He fired, and some rocks started down the hillside, but the Apache Kid fired twice more, and the boulders started breaking loose.

In the meantime, Colt looked up, seeing the rocks moving, kicked his horse, and yelled, "Rock slide! Get out of here!"

War Bonnet sensed the urgency in his master's voice and the way he rode the saddle. So did Hawk. The paint bounded along the face of the steep ridgeline, kicking up pebbles and dirt behind him, as his four legs masterfully avoided stepping on any big rocks that would tumble him and his precious load, sending them down the mountain to be buried under rocks.

Hawk, however, was a pure Appaloosa. As sure-footed as War Bonnet was, in this situation Hawk was the true master. In just a few jumps the spotted mountain horse was inches behind War Bonnet and keeping up with him as he scrambled along.

Above, a giant landslide had now gained momentum and was falling down toward them at almost 120 feet per second. It sounded as if twenty freight trains were bearing down on them. They had only seconds to get out of harm's way, but the muscles in the rumps of War Bonnet and Hawk were the only things that could save them now, along with some blessing from God.

It seemed as if the whole mountainside was coming down now, and that the two men and two horses would be crushed under the rocks. War Bonnet saw a break in the game trail where a four-foot-high boulder had crashed down and stopped in the trail, and beyond it knocked a five-foot-length of trail down. This area was almost vertical. The horse instinctively knew that danger was upon them, but his instincts also warned him that he could not go forward.

Suddenly, a streak shot past him on the

uphill side. It was Hawk, and he vaulted the boulder in one smooth jump, his front legs landing on the trail, inches beyond the missing section of trail. His back hooves hit where the front ones had just landed, and he bounded down the trail. This show of bravado and athleticism was all that War Bonnet needed, and he followed his pasture mate over the boulder, his hind feet hitting right on the edge of the broken away trail. The trail gave way, and War Bonnet valiantly kicked and struggled with his hindlegs, finally catching on the solid foot-wide trail, and he shot along behind the spotted-rump horse.

Out on the prairie, on a mountain road, or any flat ground, War Bonnet, formerly the favorite horse of the great plains warrior Crazy Horse, could easily outdistance his partner, Hawk, in a long or short run, but in this rocky setting the Appaloosa was clearly at home.

When asked by Chancy Banta one time why he favored the Appaloosa, Man Killer replied, "In this country sometimes the rocks move. When they do, I want a horse that can move faster."

The roar of the mountainside was now deafening, and War Bonnet's nostrils flared as the first pebbles and dirt struck him on the rump, but two more powerful strides

took him and Colt out from under instant
death. The two men reined their horses up
thirty yards beyond the end of the slide area
and looked back, while the two beasts stood
hip-shot, their rib cages heaving in and out,
sweat glistening between their legs and on
their necks and chests.

Nothing but a giant cloud of dust now
came up at them from below, along with the
sound of the last of the boulders crashing
onto the rest and the splintered trees in the
gulch below. The dust cloud obscured the
cabin from view, but they knew the Apache
Kid must be on his way out of there. Colt just
hoped and prayed they might have stopped a
rape and double murder. The Apache Kid's
pattern had long since been established.

The two men decided they had to walk the
horses the rest of the way down. If they just
ran down the mountain, they were risking
serious injury to the legs of either horse, as it
was very hard on the front legs of horses to
go down a mountainside. Most often, going
down a steep-sided ridgeline, the two
mounts would slide almost on their rumps
with their front legs stretched out in front of
them.

Before starting back down, they dismounted and led the mounts partway, just to
give them more rest. The recent ordeal could
cause the two steeds to tighten up, and they

could die from twisted intestines. More than one dude, having grown up back East in towns, had inadvertently killed a horse out west by not protecting the animal's very delicate digestive system.

For this reason, too, both scouts knew that the horses had to cool off. If they just rode down quickly to the cabin without letting War Bonnet and Hawk cool off, the horses could die. As Man Killer started off down the trail, Colt hollered, "Wait!"

He left War Bonnet, reins hanging, walked forward, patted Hawk on the neck, and gave the horse a kiss on the nose, saying, "Thanks partner, you saved our bacon."

He walked back and picked up War Bonnet's reins, patting *his* neck and saying, "You did great, too, War Bonnet."

They started down, and Man Killer looked back, seeing a tendril of smoke rising into the sky. He said, "Our smoke is now speaking to the colonel."

Colt looked at the column of smoke coming from the ridge top and grinned. Anticipating what had just happened, in trying to go quickly after the Apache Kid, they had prepared a large pile of dry creosote brush, cedar limbs, and pinion limbs from dead trees. On top of this, they had heaped piles of green mesquite, creosote, and pine branches. At the base of the log-cabin pile of firewood, they had placed a large pile of dry tinder. Whey they started down, they did not want to alert the Apache Kid about their presence, so they couldn't just light the fire. They had to get close before the fire was lit so it could send a timely message to the distant cavalry patrol to come running.

As they rode by the big flat boulder where the fire was built, Chris Colt lit a cigar and got the ash going on the end. He then hopped onto the big rock and stuck the mouth end of the cigar into the pile of tinder, and the two took off down the mountainside. He knew that the constant mountain breezes would keep the ash in the cigar burning, until it finally burned into the tinder pile, where the breezes would get a flame going. This would give them many minutes to get down the mountain undetected.

Twenty minutes later, Chris and Man Killer burst into the store cabin. The Apache Kid, as expected, was gone, but they carefully checked to make sure. The woman was totally naked and was sprawled across the table on her back, her wrists and ankles tied with rawhide thongs to each table leg. A superficial knife slash stretched across her stomach. Her husband was ashen-faced and was bound to a support post in the middle of the room. Boston Bill was not to be found.

The woman looked horrified as the two

crashed into the room, Colt through the door, and Man Killer diving through the window. She screamed as she saw the Nez Perce stand up out of the somersault he did on the floor.

He quickly said, "You are safe now, ma'am."

Tears of relief flooded her eyes, and she whispered, "Thank you," as Man Killer looked around carefully, gun in one hand, but covering her nakedness with a buffalo robe lying on a nearby counter.

Seeing her tied up naked hit Chris Colt in the pit of his stomach. His mind went back, some years before, when he found Sarah Guthrie in similar circumstances, and his mind quickly flashed back to what happened.

It was Montana, near the Big Horn Mountains, and the year was 1876. Sarah Guthrie coughed on thick, black smoke and quickly opened her eyes. The smoke passed across her naked body and suddenly lifted with the angry wind. She couldn't help notice the bloody corpses of her son and husband on the front porch of the burning cabin, and she vomited again. Sarah closed her eyes again and bit her lip, trying to ignore the warrior on her, or the cheers of the rest of his war party. He was the third rapist, but Sarah decided she would survive this and not let them hear her cry out. She felt the warm, sticky blood running down the side of her head. They had staked out her arms and ankles near the well, so she couldn't even reach up to the nasty cut in her straw-colored hair.

Sarah Guthrie looked up at the wild face of Two Bears as he pulled his breechcloth off. He seemed the most aggressive of the Crow warriors and the most muscular. His look was psychotic and again, she considered the possibility that they would kill her like the rest of her family. One part of her wanted that, but Sarah was a pioneer woman, a woman of the West, and she really wanted to survive.

The mountains far off to the West had a purple tint to them with patches of green here and there. The prairie in between would seem to be just a mile or two to a visiting Easterner, but it was more than twenty miles to the high ground. The space between the cabin and the war party contained a lot of sand, rocks, sage brush, cacti, greasewood, mesquite, rattlers, bunch grass, and one lone rider, a white man.

The eight other Crows sat their ponies, laughing and cheering while Two Bears raped the well-built woman. Their graying leader, Thunder Talk, turned his head and spotted the rider approaching in the distance. The other braves looked that way, too, and a murmur started among them. Preoccupied, Two Bears didn't notice their noises or the approaching rider.

Even at a distance, they could tell he was a white man. Tall, he rode a large, muscular line-back buckskin gelding. Little puffs of dust flew out to the side every time the cantering horse's feet hit the ground. The man seemed to get much larger with each step. As he rode closer, the Crows saw the chiseled features of the man's face, and the copper hue of his skin from many hours under the sun. He wore jeans and a floppy leather scout's hat. His shirt was a porcupine, quill-decorated Minniconjou Lakotah war shirt, and he wore Sioux moccasins, as well.

Amazed by the sudden interference of this brazen white man, the braves stood transfixed and openmouthed in wonder, maybe awe. Finally, a few of their number snapped out of their temporary trance. Several warriors aimed Henry rifles at the white-eyes, but a signal from Thunder Talk made them put the guns down. The old war chief was amazed by this white man's bravado. He just kept coming, seemingly not even noticing them, but he had a great purpose in his bearing.

They didn't know that his mouth was totally parched and dry, and he felt as though it was stuffed with cotton balls every time he attempted to swallow. They didn't know that he could feel his heart pounding in his neck and ears, but he just didn't give a damn. If they killed him, he decided, he would just have to die. He was frightened all right, but he would not let them know it. He was a man with a mission. He had a job to do, and that was to kill Two Bears in hand-to-hand combat. He didn't want to do it to prove he could conquer fear. He didn't want to do it because he wanted to become known as a hero. He simply had to do it, because of a code he lived by, a code that was more important than fear, more important than common sense.

They all could see now that the man wore a pearl-handled Colt .44 in a low slung holster with a large Bowie knife in a beaded sheath on the other hip. The worn stock of a Henry .44 repeater stuck out of the boot under his right leg.

In the throes of passion, Two Bears, the current rapist, was totally unaware of the man's approach. He didn't even hear the grunts and gasps from the other warriors as the white man slid to a stop right in front of Thunder Talk and dismounted without looking at anyone but Two Bears. The white man briefly glanced at Runs Too Hard, the youngest of the group, as he handed the lad the reins of the sinewy buckskin horse. Shocked like the others at this brazen display, the teen-aged warrior accepted the reins and stared, then glared, at the white-eyes.

Finally, the white man looked up at Thunder Talk as he removed his gun belt and tossed it to the old man, after extracting his razor-sharp bowie knife.

Chris Colt stuck the knife in his belt behind his back, and stormed over to Two Bears, grabbing the pompadour hanging over the muscular brave's forehead. He yanked the brave up and back, as the white woman opened her eyes in more shock. Seeing the tall white man, a new sense of survival and relief swept over Sarah, and she fainted. She came to in seconds, however, and watched with renewed hope as the white man tore into the rapist.

Thinking of this in the cabin of Boston Bill Brannigan, Colt glanced over at the woman while he cut through the bonds around her husband's wrists. She had fainted, her lips and face white, a trickle of blood running down her chin. Chris flashed back to Sarah Guthrie.

Thunder Talk just grinned and watched as the gargantuan brave, Two Bears, went into a complete rage, attacking the white man with

181

a flying head butt and a very loud Crow war cry. The white man simply sidestepped and let the six-foot-five-inch brave fall on his face. Two Bears jumped up, lips curling back over his teeth. He reached for his knife, then suddenly noticed he was naked. His eyes went to the breechcloth and knife lying near the naked woman.

Colt walked forward, and his right foot suddenly lashed out, the instep smashing the brave's groin up against his body. This was followed by a quick left-right combination of punches to the jaw. His head snapping quickly with each blow, the Crow went up on his toes.

Colt knocked the Crow out cold, poured water on him, revived him, and continued the fight, even retrieving the brave's knife for him at one point. He then killed the big Crow warrior with his large bowie and walked over to Sarah to help her. The white man walked to the woman, awakened from her faint, and cut her loose, helping her to her feet. She wavered, but steeled herself and walked beside him to the chief. Sarah couldn't even swallow. The man then took off his quilled war shirt and placed it around the nude woman's shoulders. His shirt was so large that it covered all her exposed private areas adequately.

* * *

Colt, in the trader's cabin of Boston Bill Brannigan, walked to the British lady and cut her bonds as she awakened from her faint. Chris smiled softly at her.

The British woman looked at this tall, handsome man and the tall, handsome Indian and said a silent prayer of thanks. This man was certainly a hero and had saved her and her husband from certain death and further horror.

When Colt had removed his shirt to cover Sarah Guthrie in 1876, she and the Crow braves admired the rock-hard sinew and muscles that rippled all over Colt's upper torso, but what amazed everyone watching were the numerous scars on his body. Words didn't need to be spoken, for the scars on his body told an entire story like an Indian's winter count painted on a tanned and stretched-out hide.

On his pectoral muscles, right above the nipples, were the telltales scars of the sun-dance ceremony, where a shaman had pierced his breasts with the talons of an eagle and placed wooden pegs through the holes. He then, staring up at the sun through the hole in the sundance lodge's roof, danced in circles with leather thongs attached to the wooden pegs and the leather thongs going up over a pole in the lodge's ceiling, then back down to a number of heavy buffalo skulls on the floor. He danced and danced until he almost fell in a faint and had a vision. The white brave was then lifted up by the thongs and spun in circles in a feint while the flesh and pectoral muscles stretched out grotesquely.

Right above the ceremonial scar on his left breast was a bullet-hole scar with a larger exit hole in the back of his shoulder. There was another bullet-hole scar low down on the right side of his abdomen, and a small slash scar going horizontally across his washboard stomach, just above the naval.

Finally, four long claw-mark scars run down his very large right biceps. They had to have been made by either a bear or a mountain lion.

Since then, Colt had acquired even more scars and Man Killer was almost trying to catch up.

Facing the Crow war party, Colt reached out for his gun, and the chief, still overwhelmed, handed it to him. He buckled it on and slipped the knife into the sheath, after further wiping the blade on his leg. He started for his horse, but now was stopped by the other angry warriors. The old chief rode in front of him.

"I am Thunder Talk of the Crow nation," the man said in a loud, booming voice.

The white man said, "I am Christopher Columbus Colt, Chris Colt, and my work here is finished. I will take this woman and leave."

The chief stopped Chris by pointing his rifle at the brave man and cocking it. Chris felt the blood drain from his face, but tried to hide any fear.

Thunder Talk said, "You killed my best warrior. You will die here, Chris Colt."

Colt stared at him and said calmly, "Then, old warrior, you and I will sing our death songs here together and some of your braves will die with us. My fight was with him, but the woman and I will leave, or we will die here with you and your brothers. My knife is a lightning bolt, and my guns talk much thunder. I can go, or we can die, these are my words of death, but they are words of iron. The choice is yours, old man."

Thunder Talk grinned. "You are named good, One Eagle, for you are not meek like birds who fly in flocks. Why did you kill Two Bears?"

Chris looked away, then back into the war chief's eyes. He said, "My wife was Lakotah, of the Miniconjou tribe, your enemies, and so was my baby daughter. I scouted for the cavalry like many of your braves do. That man and three others came to my cabin while I was away. They took my wife and killed her. They killed my baby, too. I tracked

each man and killed them. Now I have killed
the last man. There is a wolf in my belly and
a pain in my heart. I will take this woman
and go, find food and rest. Look into her
eyes, old warrior. You have already killed her,
and you have taken all the medicine from
your enemy here."

Chris looked at the bloody, burned corpses
of her husband and son. The chief looked
over and simply nodded at Chris.

The gray-haired leader spoke, "You speak
of scouting for the Long Knives. You truly are
a strongheart, but why do you scout against
your own brothers?"

Chris Colt looked at the far off Shining
Mountains as the Indians called them, but
they were known to white men as the Big
Horn Mountains.

"It is a long story, Thunder Talk," Chris replied, "and better spoken of at a lodge fire
while passing a smoke."

Thunder Talk spoke again, "Two Bears
was not of our lodges and so must have been
his friends. If they were of my circle, you
would be screaming now, asking me to shoot
you."

"Old Thunder Talk," Chris replied, "I believe you that I would be dying now, but I
would not be screaming."

"It is so," the old chief said with a chuckle.

"You are indeed a warrior. Take the squaw and go."

Chris said, "She is a woman, not a squaw," making reference to the derisive term "squaw," which actually describes a female's genitalia.

Thunder Talk laughed and said, "Colt, you are like the mighty oak which does not bend even in the strongest wind. Yes, she is a woman. Now, take her and go, for I do not know how long I can make cool river water flow through the flesh of these young bucks, instead of the hot rocks and mud that runs through their veins when their ponies tails are tied." The latter remark made reference to tying one's horse's tail into a knot while on the warpath.

Chris Colt said, "You are not only a warrior of many years, but very wise. The Great Mystery must surely smile upon you for your wisdom."

The chief straightened his shoulders back a little and puffed his chest out, grunting pride and approval. Chris hoped that his last words would buy them a little more time before the old man would finally give in and let the young bucks go after the pair.

Colt had used some tricks and got her away safely. They had become lovers, and he always had a soft spot in his heart and memory for her, but he was very much in love with his wife, Shirley. Finding this woman in this cabin though, in this condition, brought all the memories flooding back, and also brought back the painful memories of finding his first wife, Chantapeta, "Fire Heart," and their daughter, Winona, "First Born," both raped and murdered by the Crows.

Like most people who had accomplished much in life, Chris Colt's worse scars were not on his skin but in his heart. He secretly vowed to find the Apache Kid and end his scourge in the West. The outlaw would not be going back to stand trial.

Colt did not know that Man Killer had secretly taken the same vow. If the Apache Kid had raped and killed the whites as those in Geronimo's band were doing, Man Killer could at least understand it. The raping was not for carnal pleasure, but to taunt and terrorize the enemy. The Apache Kid, however, was doing this out of a personal hatred and was not doing it to try to save or benefit his people. He also was stealing and spending the money of the people, whose ways he supposedly disdained. Not only that, the Apache Kid had been treated fairly by these people, for the most part. He had even received a presidential pardon from Washington at one point, but he spit on everything about the whites just because he wanted to become famous like Geronimo, Victorio, and Cochise. Those men, however, had been leaders and were not interested in becoming famous. They just wanted to save their people from the scourge of the "white menace." The Apache Kid was doing this for his own aggrandizement, and Man Killer was ashamed and embarrassed for the American Indians because of this. He would end this man's life. If a red man wanted to fight for his people against the white-eyes, instead of choosing the path Man Killer chose, the scout respected that. On the other hand, he knew that if a brave fought for selfish reasons, like the Apache Kid, it detracted from the principle and nobility of all red men and women.

Man Killer walked back into the cabin and sat down at a table with Colt where he talked with the man and woman. She was wrapped in the buffalo robe, and Chris was pouring them cups of coffee. Man Killer found a flask of whiskey and poured some into each cup. The man and woman acknowledged this and nodded thanks. She cried a little then wiped away the tears. Her husband kept giving her reassuring pats on the arm, but he looked totally devastated.

Chris and Man Killer also had coffee and made cigarettes while the four talked. Colt said, "The name is Colt, Chris Colt, and this is my sidekick, Man Killer of the Nez Perce nation. We are scouting for a patrol of U.S. cavalry, and they will be here shortly. You are safe, ma'am."

"Gentlemen, I am Lord Wimsley, and this is my wife, Lady Wimsley. We are from Kingston-on-Thames, London, England. I am a close nephew of Queen Victoria, Queen of the United Kingdom of Great Britain and Ireland. We wish to thank you so much. I suppose that I should never have brought my poor dear wife to this wilderness."

Man Killer spoke before Colt could say a word and shocked the Britishers with his command of the language and education. "Sir, if you are a relative of Victoria Alexandrina herself, why would she allow you to come to a place such as this with no escort?"

Chris Colt grinned slightly, knowing that Man Killer's appearance and conversation must be very confusing and disconcerting for these Britishers.

Lord Wimsley said, "I am afraid, dear sir, that I am a bit of rebel myself. I wanted to come to America and search for a gold mine, without the trappings of the aristocracy, of course. My dear wife here, as usual, was perfectly willing to leave our grand estate and servants to accompany me in my folly, God bless her. I just can't thank you enough for your intervention, gentlemen."

His words were choked off and tears welled up in his eyes. She grabbed his hand. "I say," she finally spoke, "you gentlemen seem so different and foreign from any that I have ever seen, but yet you are as chivalrous as those who walked the courts in Camelot. I cannot possibly express my gratitude."

Man Killer looked at Colt and said, "She speaks of England during the Crusades under Richard the Lion-Hearted. Is that not the name that an Indian would have, Great Scout?"

Colt grinned.

Chris said, "The Apache Kid?"

Man Killer replied, "He went west up the gulch."

"What about his horse?" Colt asked.

"Long strides, powerful muscles, well-built."

Colt asked, "What about Brannigan's horse?"

Man Killer said, "The Apache Kid rides alone."

Lord Wimsley said, "Excuse me, Mr. Colt. He is down there." The Britisher was looking at a trapdoor built into the floor near the fireplace. Man Killer stood gun-in-hand and walked to the back door. He said, "There was a door into a fruit cellar behind the cabin."

He stepped out the door. Colt walked to

the trapdoor and lifted it up, a Colt in his right hand. He could see only darkness.

"Okay, Brannigan, you snake, come up out of your hole!"

There was no response, but the scout did hear some faint noises. A minute later, the back door opened, and the very large Boston Bill Brannigan walked in the back door of the cabin with Man Killer's gun barrel stuck into his left nostril. His face was as red as a beet, and his jaws were clenched in anger.

Colt said, "Brannigan, you have been supplying a murderer and rapist and stood by while he almost raped this fine woman. You are hereby out of business. Pack up and check the weather out in south Texas. I hear their skunk population is down."

"See hear, you," Brannigan said, "if I didn't have a gun barrel up my nose . . . you can't make me leave."

Colt said, "I see that Mr. Brannigan needs some convincing. Holster it, Man Killer."

Brannigan heard the Indian's name and his heart jumped up in his throat. He said, "Are you Colt?"

Chris nodded.

Boston Bill felt a lump in his throat, but he still had never been bested in a fight. He said, "Makes me no never mind. I ain't a leavin'."

Colt said, "Please?"

He hit the big man, suddenly and unexpectedly with a looping right that came from the hip. The shock of the punch temporarily numbed his shoulder, and the big man backpedaled to the wall, which he crashed into and slid to the floor. He stood and shook his head, then came at Colt with a rush. He had stuck his right hand in his pocket and brought it out to take a wild swing at Chris Colt. The scout blocked the punch and felt sharp pain in his left arm, then smashed Brannigan in the ribs with two quick uppercuts. He stepped back and saw that the trader had slipped brass knuckles onto his right hand.

Colt put his hand up and said, "Wait. I want to show you something."

Boston Bill was already breathing heavily because of anxiety over the mystique of Chris Colt, so he welcomed the break. He also was not the most intelligent creature on God's green Earth.

Colt found a board lying across two barrels that had been covered with a pile of beaver and pelts, and he quickly removed the pelts. Lord and Lady Wimsley, Man Killer, and Brannigan all watched with total curiosity. Colt held the knife edge of his hand near the board. He signaled Boston Bull closer.

Colt explained, "I just met with my cousin and his sidekick, who was a Samurai warrior in the country of Japan. Tora can break boards with his hands and feet. He taught me a secret. Watch. Look at this board."

Colt picked the board off the two barrels and held it up. He suddenly and viciously jammed it into Brannigan's face, smashing the man's nose and knocking out all of his upper and lower teeth, pulping his lips. Chris dropped the board and waded into Boston Bill with both fists, punching him four times in quick succession. The last punch sent the big man flying off-balance backward through the four-pane glass window. Totally knocked out, he lay on his back on the porch, his heels still across the windowsill.

Colt turned to the others and said, "He had brass knuckles on, and they hurt. No Marques of Queensbery rules out here, Lord."

Lord Wimsley cleared his throat and said, "Obviously."

All looked at Lady Wimsley, tears streaking down her cheeks, as she said, "I shan't object, sir, if you should put a bullet through his brain."

"Helene!" the lord said. He walked to her and wrapped his arms around her, protectively.

Colt nodded at Man Killer, and the two slipped quietly out the door after Chris said,

"The cavalry will be here soon, if the Lady would like to get dressed."

Man Killer walked to the well, twenty paces out from the cabin, and drew a bucket of water. He carried it to the prostrate trader and dumped it on him. The big man came up blubbering and gasping for air, as if he were drowning in a river. He grabbed his mouth and moaned, feeling his bloody gums and no teeth. He said, "You knot out aw ov my teef."

Colt said, "You still have your life, for a while. Pack up and move out, or I'll really tear your meat house down next time."

Boston Bill stood up, weaving on his wobbly legs and said, "I heah da sun shines a dot in Tectus. I had nuff a you, Code. I'm goin'."

Colt said, "Hold it, Brannigan." He walked over to the big man, who winced in fear. Colt pulled Brannigan's brass knuckles off his ham-sized fist and put them on over his own knuckles. He punched the big man in the left arm, and Brannigan howled in pain and grabbed his arm. Colt removed the knuckles and tossed them to the well, where they fell down the hole.

Colt said, "Just wanted you to know how it feels, Brannigan."

Lord Wimsley suddenly appeared around the corner, leading a roan horse with a bridle and saddle on it. He handed the reins to Brannigan.

The lord said, "You are packed, as far as I'm concerned. You may leave with your life, sir. You almost caused the death of my wife."

Brannigan said, "He ted I tould pat up and go. I hab sebral dousand dowbbers wort of goods in dere."

Lady Wimsley stepped out on the porch in a green dress, looking very proper, her chin jutting defiantly. She held a can of kerosene in her left hand and tossed it through the open door. She lit a match and tossed it inside, shutting the door behind her. She lifted her dress and stepped off the porch while Brannigan stared in amazement.

He saw flames inside the cabin and screamed, "No! You can't do dat!"

Lady Wimsley walked out to Man Killer and drew his left-hand Peacemaker, pointed it at Brannigan, and cocked it. She said, "Good day, sir."

He mounted his horse and rode away at a canter without looking back. As he started to round the bend in the gulch, the cavalry patrol came into sight and all looked at him ride by. They rode up to the foursome and looked at the burning cabin. Colt explained to the colonel what had happened.

Colt then whistled for War Bonnet, and the big paint soon trotted around the corner and up to him. Colt grabbed the saddlehorn and swung up into the saddle.

Man Killer said, "What do you do?"

Colt looked over at Lady Wimsley and winked at Man Killer. He said, "I think, Colonel, that it will be very embarrassing for our government that a lady of English nobility was molested on our soil by an outlaw, and no one from our government was watching over her. Besides that, I believe it would be terrible for Lord and Lady Wimsley if the story gets out."

He looked at Man Killer and said, "I've told you about Sarah and Chantapeta. It is something I must do, Little Brother."

Man Killer knew that Colt was not just mentioning his wife, but first and foremost thought about the repeated rapings she fell victim to at the hands of the seven-foot giant, Will Sawyer, who Colt eventually killed in the Yellowstone.

Colt looked at the brevet lieutenant colonel and said, "Colonel, I think you ought to return to Fort Union and see these people safely off to the East and arrange for a military escort. I give you my word, you will not have to send another patrol out for the Apache Kid. Let's let him quietly disappear."

The officer thought for a minute and said, "Colt, if any other man in the world made such a claim, I would pay it no heed. You, sir, are no ordinary man, though. Good luck to you. Need any supplies?"

Colt said, "No thanks."

Man Killer said, "Do not worry. I will explain it to Shirley."

Colt smiled and accepted Man Killer's spare canteen.

Lady Wimsley came up to him and offered her hand, saying, "Mr. Colt, I shan't ever forget you, sir."

He tipped his hat and replied, "Nor I, you, madam."

Lord Wimsley shook hands next and said, "Sir, I shall always be in your debt."

Colt said, "No, you aren't, sir. Just get this fine lady back to her own environment and take care of her."

Wimsley's eyes welled up once more, and he said, "Like the most precious gem, sir, I must say."

Colt wheeled his horse and took off up the gulch. There was one thing first and foremost in his mind; the Apache Kid would rape no more women.

Man Killer watched his mentor until he was out of sight, wanting to go badly himself, but knowing that Colt had an even deeper reason to rid the frontier of the Apache Kid.

Chris found the tracks of the killer moving up the gulch at a fast trot, and the chief of scouts rode immediately up to the high ground. He knew that was where the Apache

Kid would go because that was the Indian way, and it was also Colt's way, because he had learned, years before, that, in the wilderness, the Indian way was the best way. He was lucky. Arriving on the high ridgeline to the north, an hour later, he found that the Apache Kid had chosen the same route. Colt rode with his Winchester across the swells of his saddle, and his eyes scoured the ground to his front in sweeping glances from side to side. He would look directly in front of his horse, and his eyes would travel out away from the trail and sweep left and right. Every few steps, he would turn in the saddle and look behind him.

Man Killer, in the meantime, was scouting ahead of the patrol as they worked back down the gulch on their way to the railway. The train would be flagged down, and Lord and Lady Wimsley placed aboard with a military escort. All agreed to keep the incident quiet for the sake of national interests and foreign relations.

Colt had a burning anger deep inside him. His wife, Chantapeta, had been the one person who had stopped his wanderlust, and she was raped and murdered. He had become a lover of Sarah Guthrie, and she had been raped. His poor little daughter never even had the opportunity to experience life, and she had been raped and murdered. His current wife, who was indeed his one great true love, had been repeatedly raped by a giant of a man, who was more like an animal.

Colt was careful and gentle with his wife. That was the only way he knew how to be with a woman. To him, the woman he loved was strong like steel but should be treated like the finest crystal. He did not know or understand what could make a man rape women or beat them. He just could not conceive of that type of thinking, but he knew very well it happened, and he hated any man who did it.

The one time in his life that he got a little taste of making things right was in the Yellowstone. It was also very meaningful, because it was one of the last times he had seen his good friend, Crazy Horse, alive.

Colt had been searching for Will Sawyer, the rapist who had kidnapped and assaulted Colt's then-fiancee, Shirley Ebert of Youngstown, Ohio, by way of Bismarck, North Dakota Territory. Sawyer had disappeared, but he was so large, Colt knew that he couldn't hide long. Chris would find him if it took decades. Chris Colt felt angry, killing angry.

He left Bismarck and began his search. It was days later when Colt stopped in Virginia City at the end of the Bozeman Trail, when he got word. He went into a saloon to wash away days of dust and get the latest news, as saloons on the frontier were like the newspapers back East, maybe better. Some miners conversing about a giant of a mountain man called Buffalo Reeves. Colt bought the miners a drink and invited them to sit at a table with him. They sat down and he said, "This Buffalo Reeves you're talking about. How big is he?"

One of the miners said, "Oh hell, at least seven, mebbe seven and a half foot and big, ya' know big, like a buffaler."

"Where does he trap?" Colt asked.

The other said, "Yellowstone country."

Chris was out the door before the miners could finish their drinks.

It was three days later, when the giant, buffalo-coated Will Sawyer, alias Buffalo Reeves, heard a noise and turned. He sat on a log, drinking a steaming hot cup of coffee after having just finished his morning trap line.

The setting was quite eerie, as he had made his cooking fire right next to a giant pool of bubbling hot mud and clay. In the background, steam poured from several geysers as well as off the pool of boiling mud. There was so much steam and smoke in the area in the early fall morning that it almost obscured the view.

Sawyer's long, scraggly beard and long

201

hair almost hid his face from view. His eyes strained to see what was making the noise he kept hearing, but he couldn't spot anything. What the hell, he thought, nobody or nothin' around can take me with gun or fist. Suddenly, he thought of Chris Colt and got a sick feeling in the pit of his stomach. He thought about Colt often because the man had beaten him with his fists. He hated Colt, and he always wondered if Colt would show up someday. He had become a full-time trapper, in fact, so he could shoot Colt from ambush if he ever did come and nobody would ever know.

"Sawyer." The voice was almost a whisper.

Colt's voice startled Will so badly he jumped, spilled his coffee, lost his balance, and fell backwards off his log. Getting up, he wiped coffee from his buffalo coat and looked at the man he hated so.

Geyser spouting steam behind him, Chris Colt sat perfectly still on his magnificent paint horse. Colt's half grin and his calmness scared Sawyer even more. Just the sight of the ruggedly handsome scout scared him. Dressed half-Indian/half-white on the paint with the eagle feathers in the mane and tail, three red stripes around each upper foreleg, and red handprints on each hip, Colt was the epitome of confidence and all that was savage and rough about the West.

Well, it was here. Will Sawyer could finally put his fear and humiliation behind him. Colt might have gotten lucky against him in a fight, but nobody could outgun him. Sawyer took off his buffalo coat and tossed it aside. He got in a gunfighter's crouch, and his lips curled back in a snarl. With deep booming voice he laughed nervously and said, "Ya' mighta got lucky and whipped me in that fight, Colt, but I'm gonna shoot so meny holes in ya', the miners kin use ya' fer a sluice box."

He laughed heartily at his own joke and went on, "I shore liked stickin' it to yer ole lady, Colt. She was nice. Oh, by the way, even if'n ya git lucky, my pardner, Red Williams, is aimin' a Sharps at yer back right now. He's in them rocks yonder."

They both heard a horse walking up toward Colt, and a figure on horseback suddenly started showing through the steam. He walked right up to Colt.

Will Sawyer just stared and said, "Crazy Horse!"

The tall Oglala warrior looked at Colt and tossed a Sharps buffalo gun toward Sawyer. He reached down next to his breechcloth and pulled out a bloody, red-haired scalp and held it up for Sawyer to see. Crazy Horse turned his horse and slowly walked back into the clouds of steam out of sight.

"Don't matter, Colt!" he yelled, "I don't need no help killin' ya! None, ya heah?"

Will Sawyer's hand streaked down for his right-hand gun, and Chris Colt's came up in one smooth motion. The gun bucked in his hand and Sawyer's gun flashed at the same time. His bullet, however, made the dirt out in front of Sawyer explode like a miniature cannon shell. Colt, like Crazy Horse had done before, flipped his leg over the neck of his horse and dropped down to the ground. He walked forward, ejecting the empty shell from his six-shooter, while giving Sawyer an evil grin. Will Sawyer tried desperately to raise his gun, but he kept staring down at the growing stain of red in the middle of his chest. He got his gun almost all the way up when he looked at Colt taking careful aim at him.

I think I can take him, he thought. I can take him.

Then Colt fired, and Will Sawyer felt a boulder smash into his chest, then another, and another. He was falling backward. He didn't want to do that. He threw his hands back to protect himself. They hit boiling water. It burned. He was underwater. It was burning like fire. Sawyer wondered if he was in Hell, then he didn't wonder anymore.

Colt said, "If you're going to shoot a man, shoot; don't talk."

Crazy Horse rode up next to Chris while Colt walked forward, reloading, and looked at the giant bubbling pool of boiling mud. Bubbles came up where Sawyer had fallen in. Colt walked over to Will's buffalo coat and picked it up. He handed it and Red's Sharps to Crazy Horse. "It will be a cold winter, my brother."

Crazy Horse looked at the bubbling pool of mud and said, "Not for the one you called Sawyer."

Both men looked at the boiling liquid and started laughing.

Colt said, "How long have you followed me?"

"Long enough," Crazy Horse answered.

Crazy Horse was stabbed by another Sioux, a guard with a bayonet, at Camp Robinson, Nebraska, less than a year later. By that time, Shirley and Chris were husband and wife with their first child on the way.

Chapter 5

>>>>>>>>>>>>>>>>>>>

The Apache Kid Blows
His Top

Colt kept on up the ridgeline for another hour. The tracks of the Apache Kid's horse showed he was getting tired, and the outlaw was heading into even rougher country. He finally came down off the ridge, crossed the next gulch south, and headed uphill, once again. Colt came to a spot where the ridgeline suddenly opened up and ahead, less than one hundred yards, lay a jumble of giant rocks. This was a perfect spot for an ambush, especially someone with a Sharps .50. Colt swung his horse off the trail immediately and went down the north side of the ridge into the trees. Just before dark, he was back on the trail on the ridgeline above and beyond the pile of boulders.

Colt was not about to stay on the trail after dark, as that would be certain death, so he swung down into a bowl of evergreens with many fallen trees. The growth was thick and the timber dark from up above.

Chris unsaddled War Bonnet and kept him close by, wrapping himself in his blanket under a large deadfall. Following an Apache who was a wanted desperate killer, Colt knew that spending the night where he was was an invitation to be attacked, but that made it easier than following the Apache Kid forever.

The Apache Kid had been stopping at every vantage point to watch his backtrail, and he had backtracked twice that day, tied pieces of leather tied over his horse's hooves when they crossed rocky ground, and several other tricks, but none of these things had deterred the man on his trail. The outlaw also knew who the man was, so he would be hard-pressed to lose the man. He recognized the man's horse and his looks. It was the famous scout and gunfighter Chris Colt.

The Apache Kid cursed his luck. If he had been living his life as he had in the old days, with his band, he would just ride his horse until it was exhausted, kill it, eat it, and keep on on foot for miles. He had, however, grown soft, growing accustomed to the ways of the white-eyes.

Colt slept on alert, something few men could do, always warriors. Although he allowed his senses and body to rest, they were still attentive to every sound, smell, even vibration in the ground. This type of sleep could give a warrior adequate rest; however, he would have to take a break after a period of time and go somewhere safe and totally relax. This could be evidenced by soldiers or braves, after a long campaign. Although they may have eaten well and gotten a full night's sleep each night, they would still end up with dark circles under their eyes.

It was well after midnight when Colt heard the noise. It was slight, something very minor. He didn't even know what it was, but he awakened. Colt didn't move, but his right hand wrapped around the carved mother-of-pearl grip of his right-hand .45. His eyes opened, and he looked all around to his front. First, he looked at War Bonnet, but the horse had put his head up, ears forward, for only a few seconds, then went to cropping grass. The moon was full. Earlier, Colt had mentally catalogued all the things in his field of vision.

He listened for every sound. He heard a bird in the trees behind him. A small animal off in the trees beyond his feet ran from one tree to another. Nothing made noise to his front. Suddenly, War Bonnet's head popped up again. The big horse sniffed and listened. Colt sat up slowly under the blowdown. He didn't know if he was visible or not, but he wanted to see better. From there, Colt saw a deer grazing across the small meadow away from War Bonnet. That was what the horse was staring at. A rattlesnake issued its warning in the same area as the deer and the small animal bounded off into the trees.

War Bonnet had instinctively catalogued the smells he heard and now felt safe. He dropped his head back down to graze. The snake was too far off to worry about. Colt, satisfied, lay back down, closed his eyes, and went immediately to sleep.

Something brought Colt up out of the blackness. It hit him as his eyes opened; he was at ten or eleven thousand feet elevation, and rattlesnakes never came up that high, never over eight thousand feet. As his hand streaked up with his Peacemaker, the new hissing sound struck his memory full force, just as he saw the sparks arcing through the air toward him. He fired at the black shadow running away, and he rolled as quickly as he could, but the dynamite landed very near him. Hitting the log above Colt, the three tied-together sticks were deflected slightly, but still the concussion was enormous. Instinctively, Colt covered his ears with his palms and kept his elbows in tight to protect his heart and lungs, a split second before the dynamite went off. He was catapulted through the air, his limp body crashing into the base of an aspen tree. The log deadfall that had been above him was completely splintered.

Chris Colt felt rain falling on his face and it was very cooling. He suddenly realized he had been feeling very hot. Lightning crashed overhead, illuminating the night sky, and the suddenness of it made Colt want to draw his pistol, but he could not move. He panicked, then quickly relaxed. The rain felt so good, he slipped back down into that deep pool of blackness, and he enjoyed the feel of the rain on his face until he could no longer feel it.

Chris opened his eyes to the bright sunlight. He looked up at the sky. The sun was very hot and was in the sky in the left field of his vision. He thought to break through the confusion. He was on a ridge of Greenhorn Mountain and was after the Apache Kid, when he stupidly put himself in a position to be attacked. Colt was angry at himself, very angry. He hadn't thought about the outlaw getting explosives from Boston Bill Brannigan. Chris Colt knew he had gotten cocky. He slept in a likely sleeping spot, knowing there was a good chance that the Apache Kid would seek him out, but feeling he would triumph with superior ability and firepower.

Now Colt realized he had been almost blown to bits by dynamite, and he ached as if he had been run over by an ore-loaded freight wagon. He was glad that he was in pain, though, as he slowly rolled over to survey the injuries all over his body. He believed he must have been temporarily paralyzed when he was previously out cold and came to several times.

Colt also had nagging hunger pains and thirst, but was thankful he had left his saddle and saddlebags near the big paint. Normally, he would have taken it into his night location, but the deadfall had been surrounded by other dead logs and branches, and it would have been hard for the big horse to traverse it so Colt could saddle up. Instead, he had placed the saddle, bridle, and bags over a log about three feet off the ground. If he had to take off in a hurry, he would be able to quickly saddle his horse and go.

Chris felt his beard stubble and knew by its length that he must have been unconscious for about two days, maybe even three. Every muscle and bone in his body ached, and his head ached about as bad as any other time it had. He didn't think he had a major concussion. He had had a major concussion, before and the aftereffects left him frustrated, because of trouble counting and short-term memory problems. He also had very big mood swings the first few days, and eventually, he went temporarily blind from the head injury.

Colt leaned against the aspen tree and made himself a cigarette, which he slowly puffed on while he worked up the energy to crawl to his saddlebags and canteens.

He thought back to the time and place when he had suffered the severe concussion. He had rescued Man Killer, who was then a younger boy named Ezekiel, from some rustlers and killers who had murdered the Nez Perce boy's younger brother. The rustlers were tied in their saddles while Colt and the young Man Killer, Ezekiel, were pushing the stolen herd of Chief Joseph's Appaloosa horses west back to their home in Wallowa Valley in Oregon.

Colt felt War Bonnet start flexing his muscles nervously under his master's legs. His ears twitched all around in every direction and the horse's nostrils were flaring in and out desperately. The herd was acting strange as well.

Colt said, "Do you smell the bear, Little One?"

"Yes, his smell is on the wind which runs into our faces," Ezekiel replied.

Colt reined his horse and those of the other three. The boy stopped next to him and looked at the scout's eyes, scanning like a Nez Perce warrior. Colt's eyes panned the ground immediately to their front, going left to right, then viewed a few meters farther out and scanned back to the left. He then viewed even farther out, his eyes going left to right again, checking every little piece of foliage and terrain, looking for a telltale patch of fur. The herd acted very nervous.

"Señor," the Mexican killer whispered, "What is it you look for? Ees it Indios?"

"Better hope not," Colt replied quietly, without looking, "Now keep quiet."

His nostrils flared slightly as he sniffed the air. He looked to Ezekiel like a mighty bear himself, testing the wind. The scout said, "He is between us and the ponies. See how they're moving forward fast now? They are beyond the smell and just want to get away. If he makes a charge, you take the horses and these critters, and I'll get between you and him and shoot him. No matter what, keep going."

Colt thought back to his first grizzly bear. He had been out with his father-in-law on a scout, looking for a bison herd. On the way back to the camp circle they made camp in a stand of cottonwoods next to a creek. The two men were sent up a tree for two hours by a very angry sow grizzly, who wandered along the creek bed with her two cubs. They could have shot her, but not with cubs.

Colt respected all the Indian nations because they lived with nature, not against it.
Every nation of warriors practiced self-
controlled conservation methods. In the
early days, some tribes would make piles of
stones and arrange them in a funnel, then
chase a herd of buffalo into the funnel and
run them over the cliff. That was wasteful,
but was about the only way they could har-
vest their meat then. After more sophisti-
cated bows and other weapons were
developed, they started taking individual animals. White men, on the other hand, were
starting to line up on trains and shoot bison
after bison from passing railroad cars. Such
a demand developed for buffalo hides, as
well, buffalo hunters would kill thousands of
buffalo, then waste the meat, taking only the
hides. Practices like this angered Chris, as
the Indians knew they had to protect all
herds of animals so there would always be a
supply for their tribes.

Chris felt the animal's presence, and it
scared the heck out of him. It was close, but
he couldn't pick up any sign of it. That
scared him, too.

Suddenly, with a tremendous roar and a
rush, a giant silvertip grizzly came from the
thicket on the uphill side of the trail. This
monster stood over eight feet tall on its

hindlegs and weighed well over a ton and a half.

A grizzly bear, on level ground, could outrun a race horse in a short distance, and this big bear was no exception. He closed the distance between the thicket and his hiding place in seconds, and Colt barely had time to spin and fire from the hip, his bullet taking the bruin in the front of the left shoulder with little or no effect.

The bear slammed against the rib cage of War Bonnet, his teeth popping and a roar emanating from deep in his chest that reverberated through the canyon like a mighty avalanche. Colt flew sideways, and the horse rolled once and bolted toward the herd and fleeing men in front of him. The bear stopped and stood on it hindlegs, nose testing the wind, while he swung his watermelon-sized head from side to side.

Ezekiel hesitated, and Colt yelled, "Go! Save the horses!"

The bear dropped to all fours and faced his small-sized intruder again, and Chris raised his pistol, aiming at the bear's face. The bruin charged, and Chris fired, the bullet glancing off the bear's skull, creating a crease along its head. It was as if it had been whacked with a fly swatter. The bear slammed into Colt, and only the pistol saved

Chris from the mighty teeth and jaws, as the bear bit down on the gun, mangling it.

He took a quick swipe at a sapling, and the tree splintered in half. Colt pulled his horn-handled bowie knife from the beaded sheath on his left hip and switched it to his right hand, facing the shaggy killer. The bear stared at Colt through his little pig eyes, while big heavy breaths poured out between spike-sized teeth.

Colt felt no fear. Yes, the bear weighed hundreds and hundreds of pounds more than Colt and stood almost two feet taller. He could pick up boulders with his mighty forelegs, or excavate an entire hillside, just to dig out a tasty marmot. The scout, however, was a true warrior, and he was now staring death in the face. He was conditioned not to feel fear until the combat was over. Much like many of the cavalry troopers he scouted for and American Indian warriors he fought against, he would feel great fear when the danger was past, but right now, his head was clear, his nerves steady. His adrenaline coursed through his body, and he was prepared to match his wits and strength against this superior foe. He knew the odds, but he felt that he could not be defeated.

With a roar like Satan unchained, the bear charged. Colt stood his ground, and the big furry body slammed into Chris with tremendous force, but Colt fell backward and let the big bear pass over him, striking upward full power and thrusting the big bowie into the buggy-sized chest just behind the left front leg.

With agility that seemed incredible for its size, the grizzly jumped in the air with a loud roar and twisted its body at the same time, biting at the knife that was buried to the hilt behind the joint. He rolled beyond Chris Colt, who lay unconscious on the ground, his head having slammed into a flat rock when the bear crashed into him.

Chantapeta, Chris Colt's late wife, wore a soft buckskin dress as she tiptoed into the tepee and awakened him with a large apple pie. Colt smiled and looked at the steam coming off the apple pie and thought about how good it would taste. Then he frowned while lying on his buffalo blanket. How could a Lakotah woman make an apple pie, in a pie pan, in the middle of a Minniconjou village? He couldn't figure it out, and it made his head hurt. He looked from the pie to her, and she had changed into the woman he loved, Shirley Ebert, who was now Colt's wife. Long, naturally curly, auburn hair hanging well below her shoulders, she had a smile that looked as though it had been stolen from a Greek goddess.

* * *

He had awakened after that but had to deal with frustration, pain, and even blindness. Right now, Colt was starting to feel alive, although he felt as if his entire body were one giant toothache. About the only part of his body that did not hurt, in fact, was the stump of his little finger, which had been amputated by another torturous villain from Colt's past.

After that, Chris stood on the log by his saddle, climbed onto his horse's back, and let the animal take him to where he had been watering, a small seep a few hundred yards into the woods. Canteens slung over his shoulders, he drank as much as he could and returned to the fire. He made another pot of coffee and drank some more while he smoked another couple of cigarettes.

Not worrying about anything now, Colt curled up around the fire and decided to let sleep, food, and water do their work on his sore body. He was angry, and the Apache Kid was going to pay. He would pay in spades, but Colt knew enough to first take care of himself and then go after the rapist/killer. Chris knew that every hour he could let his body heal would save him ten hours in the chase.

In the morning, after a good breakfast, shave, and more water, Chris Colt felt much better. He was still very sore, but he felt he could handle a day, or part of a day in the saddle. War Bonnet had not been affected by the explosion and had plenty of graze and water, so the big gelding was ready to travel and crunch some gravel under his black hooves.

Within two hours, Chris Colt was eyeing something that made him feel very good. The Apache Kid was not covering his backtrail or trying to kill his horse getting away. Apparently, seeing Colt's limp body flying through the air, he thought the chief of scouts was dead. That was what Chris Colt could only surmise. In fact, what actually had happened was that the Apache Kid had looked back, as he tried to escape the scout's deadly gunfire and had seen the big man fly through the air when the dynamite went off. He did not know how any man could live through that, even if it was the legendary gunfighter.

Chris Colt made camp that afternoon on the shoreline of Lake San Isabel, as the outlaw's trail took him in a northerly direction along the front range and its heavily wooded mountains. Chris was pleased because the murderer was actually leading Chris Colt closer to his home. This not only brought the chief of scouts closer to his loved ones, but it also was getting him closer to country that he now knew like the back of his hand.

What Chris Colt could not know, however,

was the ruthlessness of the man he pursued. Thinking that Chris Colt was no longer on his trail, the Apache Kid headed for one particular destination, the ranch that had been owned by the famous scout, Chris Colt, Coyote Run. The man had pursued him and wanted to kill him, but was unable to. Now, the Apache Kid would take more of Chris Colt's medicine when he would take Colt's beautiful wife whom he had often heard about.

As the Apache Kid led Colt closer and closer to the Wet Mountain Valley in which his home lay, Colt got increasingly suspicious and started to reason through the thinking of the twisted outlaw. The killer had to find out where the ranch was. He would stop some drunk leaving a saloon in Rosita, Westcliffe, or Silver Cliff and find out. The Apache Kid did speak English quite well.

When the trail led toward those towns, Chris Colt went on toward his ranch, hoping he would not be too late. The Apache Kid still had a day of travel on the chief of scouts, and Colt was certain now that the man's objective would be to violate and kill his wife.

Shirley Colt had gotten Brenna and Joseph asleep much earlier, and she worked on a new elkskin war shirt for Chris. She had learned leather work when she was held hostage in the village of Screaming Horse, Cheyenne chief.

It was a hard time in her life. Shirley had left Bismarck behind her, quickly selling her successful restaurant business and adjoining house to a local banker and his wife. She had heard that Chris Colt had been blinded in a grizzly bear attack along the Snake River, and she was bound and determined to make it to his side and rescue him. She decided she would make it there or die trying. Everything she owned was packed in a freight wagon, and she had joined a small group of freighters. One of them had tried to take advantage of her the first night out, but he was now just a pile of bleached bones on the Montana prairie. As the small group of wagons headed into the foothills, they were spotted by scouts from a small Cheyenne band.

Shirley Colt stared into the flames of her big rock fireplace, set the leather war shirt down on her lap, and thought back to the wild experience she had endured.

The next day, they started into the foothills leaving the relatively easy travel of the prairie behind them. Shirley was excited, as she knew that her love was also in the rough, mountainous country connected to this very land. Somehow, leaving the prairie and moving into land that was roughly similar in feature and connected by vast, winding chains of rocky peaks, she felt at least connected to Chris in a sense.

The way would be much rougher now, but that was inconsequential to Shirley. Her mind had been made to seek out, find, and care for her ailing man, and she was that much closer to her goal.

They had followed the Yellowstone and opted not to travel the Clark's Fork, as they first planned, but to continue due west toward the headwaters of the Yellowstone. Their goal was to make Fort Ellis and try for a military escort or even join a troop train to Fort Lapwai or Fort Walla Walla.

Screaming Horse had been in on the Battle of the Greasy Grass, or at least was joined with the giant encampment. The Battle of the Greasy Grass took place where the famous long-knife leader, Yellow Hair, Long Hair Custer, Son of the Morning Star, as the Crows called him, walked the spirit trail along with all of the blue-coated soldiers with him. The *wasicuns* called it the Battle of the Little Big Horn, but in any event, it was the beginning of the end for the people of the Lakotah and Chyela circles.

Screaming Horse's little band had journeyed to the giant camp and had only two warriors partake in the Sundance Ceremony in which Sitting Bull gave up so many pieces of flesh and had visions of "enemy soldiers falling into the camp." The old chief's band was from the Northern Cheyenne nation, and they had moved around from here to there after the camp moved and the many tribes and nations split up and went separate ways.

Screaming Horse's scouts had been seeing too many blue-coats coming into the territory and too many patrols since then, so they were now headed north to seek out and find Sitting Bull and Crazy Horse, who were rumored to be seeking refuge in Canada.

The wrinkled old war chief had actually arrived at the big camp on June 24th and joined the Chyela (Cheyenne) circle, but he and his handful of braves had been out hunting to the west of the encampment when the battle actually began. Only two of his men got back in time to fire some shots at Reno's retreating command, after Custer and his battalion were already wiped out. Screaming Horse was embarrassed and angry that he and his braves could only watch the other braves, who had won so many battle honors, as they celebrated and carried on through the night and for days after the death of Long Hair.

They had since been wandering from place

to place in the Montana Territory, almost hoping for a major skirmish with Long-Knife troops, so they could win their own battle honors. The wily old man knew that the time was short for the life of the plains as his people had known it. Through traders and loyal *wasicuns,* they had learned that a great cry rang up among the whites over the death of Long Hair, and his journey would certainly be avenged. The *wasicuns* were as many as blades of grass upon the prairie and any time a red man pulled one up and tossed it into the wind, ten more would take root.

It was on their way toward the Bear Paws, far to the north, that the chief's scouts reported to him that they had found a five-wagon train with three buffalo scalpers and one woman. The second wagon had a long rope tied to the third wagon's team and was leading the team in effect.

"Hokahey!" Screaming Horse cried in Cheyenne, "we will take the wagons, kill the *wasicuns,* and the white woman will be my slave. Wakan Tanka has surely smiled down upon us this day. My winter count had grown long, and the *wasicuns* have taken a hold of Mother Earth and claimed that she is theirs. We will make battle with these *wasicuns* and have a victory dance tonight."

Screaming Horse and his warriors swept down on the freight wagons and killed the white men, but they wanted to try to take the white woman alive.

Shirley Ebert was scared, but more than that, she was angry, very angry. Her eyes scanned the hills back and forth, but saw nothing. She yelled, "Come on, you cowardly dogs. You brave warriors who make war on women! Come and get me!"

Knowing the pride of many warriors of the plains tribes, she figured her taunts may make them keep from killing her, too. She was tough-minded, like Colt, and she could not even think about the death of her new friends right now. She had to survive. No arrows came.

She hollered again, "I am the woman of Wamble Uncha! If I die, I will die fighting like he would! Come, fight me, you cowardly curs! I am only one woman! Are you scared to fight one woman?"

Her head switched around from side to side, scanning all the terrain in every direction.

Nothing happened.

She heard a moan and looked at Buster. He had been one of the men with her and was apparently the only one still alive, although at that time, Shirley had thought all the men were dead. Incredibly, he suddenly stood straight up and looked all around, as if in a daze. Two arrows came from nearby hills and buried themselves to the feathers in the side of his chest. He collapsed and folded up like an accordion, his bloody corpse like a quarter sack of potatoes in the bottom of his wagon box.

Shirley aimed her Winchester at a large bush on the side of the hill that would be a likely ambush spot. Using searching fire, without knowing that was a cavalry technique, she fired dead center into the bush, then quickly fired to the left and the right of her first shot. There was a moan, and a warrior stood straight up on his tiptoes, hands clutching at the hole where his windpipe had been. He fell on his side, legs and arms twitching, and his convulsing body rolled down the hill, coming to rest against the front wheel of Bubba's wagon, who was another one of the dead freighters.

She picked out more bushes and trees and started firing in the same manner. It was certainly understandable why Chris Colt would love this woman. She was certainly cool while staring down death's fatal jaws.

Screaming Horse and three of his warriors had seen Chris Colt from a distance during the Battle of the Little Big Horn, but had not seen his woman. They had heard of the pair of *wasicuns* who many said should have been born Lakotah or Chyela, but they did not know them.

None of his band could speak any English, but he heard the name of Wamble Uncha and figured that this woman was maybe claiming to be the great *wasicun's* betrothed. She also, he concluded, might have been saying that because it was known that Wamble Uncha, the man called Colt, was great friends with Crazy Horse himself and was highly respected by even Sitting Bull. She may have been claiming to be his woman, or his sister, to win favor with her potential captors. In any event, he would not kill her. In case she was the woman, or sister, of Wamble Uncha, Screaming Horse did not want to suffer the wrath of Crazy Horse or any other of his allies who treasured that *wasicun's* friendship. The woman would be taken without her shedding blood and would become his slave, and if she was the betrothed of Colt, he could pay a high price and buy her back if he wanted her. The only problem with the old chief on that bloody day was that it looked like he would lose all of his warriors to her bullets if he tried to take her alive.

He slid back down the hill behind him from his hiding place behind a cedar on the first hill's crest. The wrinkled old man easily vaulted onto the back of his yellow-and-white pinto pony. He held a coup staff in his left hand and had a thick bullhide shield on his right arm. He cantered the pony around the base of the hill and came into view to her front. She aimed the Winchester at the old man. He raised one arm and gave some signals in sign language. In less that a minute, a group of warriors came out from behind the hills on horseback and surrounded her. They slowly walked their horses closer. Shirley fired, and the top foot of Screaming Horse's coup staff disappeared. He ducked and his horse reared, but dropping the staff, he held his hand up to his warriors and signaled them not to shoot.

He walked his horse slowly forward, and she held her rifle level and aimed at his midsection. Screaming Horse kept coming, and Shirley looked around at the other warriors, calculating the odds against her. Finally, she lowered the weapon and set it next to her by the wagon seat. Screaming Horse rode up to her and extended his hand, and she resignedly handed him her rifle.

As soon as he had it safely in his hand, a scarred brave named Quills-in-the-Face gave out a loud whoop and swept down on her, wanting to count coup or capture this woman for himself. However, before leaving Bismarck to head west to Fort Lupwai, Chris Colt had left his betrothed a variety of weapons for her safety. One was a big one-shot boomer that could possibly get her out of trouble, and it was going to now. Her hand swept down and yanked the Barns .50-caliber boot gun from her right leg. She cocked it and grabbed the stock with her left hand and blasted Quills-in-the-Face in midchest, his body flying backward off his horse as if yanked with a lasso. Screaming Horse shook his head because the blast from the gun went right by his ear, which was now ringing loudly. He looked back and saw a hole through Quills-in-the-Face that actually showed the ground under him. The hole was so large, the chief could see right through the dead warrior's chest. He looked at the *wasicun* woman with awe and renewed respect.

Screaming Horse grinned and stuck out his hand again. She laughed and handed him the Barns boot pistol. He stuck his hand out once more as if asking if she had any more firearms, and she pointed at all the remaining warriors surrounding her. He dismounted and climbed up on the wagon box, grabbing her by the wrist and dragging her down to the ground. She reached up under her skirt and yanked out a derringer, but he grabbed her hand before she could bring it to bear.

Several other warriors ran up and grabbed her, pinning her to the ground while she was searched for more weapons and while binding her hands behind her back by a leather thong.

She was then made to stand, and she defiantly stared into the grinning eyes of the old war leader. "Are you Sioux?" she asked.

Then remembering their word for themselves, she said, "Are you Lakotah?"

He pointed to himself and his followers and said, "Chyela."

She smiled, remembering their name for their tribe and she said, "Cheyenne."

The man pointed to himself and his followers again and said, "Cheyenne," then repeated the gesture and said, "Chyela."

She nodded in understanding, then looked at him and said, "Do you speak English?"

He gave her a quizzical look.

She said loudly, "Do any of you speak English?"

Nobody understood.

She said, "Man, me, Wamble Uncha."

Screaming Horse grinned in recognition again and said, "Wamble Uncha," and made a gesture with his groin while he pointed at her.

Her face flushed in embarrassment, but she shook her head affirmatively. She thought he understood now, so she felt she would be safe. The old man said something to his men, and they all laughed. He then slipped a lasso over her neck and held the other hand while he mounted again.

She was led off by a noose around the neck, for the second time in her life. The first time was by Crazy Horse. While the chief proudly led her off toward the lodges, she passed women and girls carrying baskets and three leading horses with travois attached, on their way to the battlefield to strip the bodies of the dead enemies and collect war trophies.

Several women smacked her with sticks and Shirley, despite the thong around her throat, kicked at them and spit at them as well. They taunted her as they walked on, but did seem to decide to keep a respectable distance between her and themselves.

Ten minutes later, they arrived at the lodges of Screaming Horse's band. The expedient village had been set up along the banks of a small mountain stream in a grove of quaking aspens. Several dogs nipped at Shirley's heels as she passed between the tepees, still in tow behind the chief's pony. She kicked them, too.

The chief stopped by the farthest lodge and slid off the paint. He took her to a post outside the tepee and tied her thong to it, then tightening the noose part of it around her neck. His wife came about ten minutes later and went inside the tepee. Shirley could hear the two arguing, it seemed, through the thick bison hides. Several dogs came up and sniffed around her, but seemed friendly enough. The woman came out of the lodge and threw several meat scraps to the dogs and Shirley. Shirley kicked one back at the woman, who just laughed and went back inside the tepee.

Shirley waited and watched. It got dark and the temperature dropped sharply. She was thirsty and very cold. Within two hours, all the braves and women and girls had returned to the village with much booty. They brought the wagon mules with them and most of the goods. She spotted a number of men carrying new Henry carbines, so her hunch about the hide hunters carrying weapons was correct. Before leaving on the trip with them, she was concerned that they might have been hiding weapons to sell to the Indians. She didn't care, though, as she had to get to the man who was now her husband.

Shirley Colt took a sip of tea and remembered that first night in Screaming Horse's village.

A large fire was built, and there was laughter, dancing, and celebration. After that, various painted warriors stood up, and she could tell that they were telling about their exploits and acts of bravery during the so-called battle. It was all these people had, she guessed. They had to know that the end of their way of life was coming. During the evening, women, children, and warriors drunken with enthusiasm would walk over to her and taunt her. If they got within kicking or spitting distance, however, they learned to show Shirley Ebert a little more respect.

Finally, the fires were just glowing embers and all in the camp had returned to their lodges. Dogs had curled up in tight balls, their tails wrapped around their noses. In many cases, the dogs slept around the big fire circle where heat was still being radiated. Some, though, slept outside the tepees of their masters. The night was cold, very cold.

Shirley lay curled up in the ball, her bound arms cramping. Her teeth chattered, and she felt frozen all the way to the inside of her soul. She knew she would not make it through the night, at least not alive. She would have to do something or die.

The old woman came out of the lodge, carrying an earthen bowl of steaming liquid. She looked around and shivered, then set the bowl down in front of the white woman so Shirley could bend forward and drink it.

Shirley looked up at her and smiled. The old woman ignored the friendly gesture and turned, walking back into the tepee.

Shirley, hands still tied behind her back, bent forward at the waist and stuck her mouth down into the bowl of steaming stew. She slurped it up like a dog, but stopped, hearing several dogs growling. Two dogs, teeth bared, growled at her, wanting the stew. The larger of the two inched forward toward the bowl, his nostrils flaring, smelling the pungent aroma. He was almost there when Shirley butted him with the side of her forehead hard enough to make him yelp and jump back.

The smaller of the two inched forward, but suddenly lunged for her, teeth bared. She butted him straight on with the top of her head, and he jumped back, blood running out of his mouth. His tongue started lapping it up over and over. One tooth was bent oddly to the side at a perverse angle.

Still, the two dogs, ribs showing slightly, tried to creep closer to the bowl, although they were more cautious. Suddenly, Shirley smiled and turned around, soaking her hands and leather bonds in the bowl of steaming broth. She soaked them for several minutes, keeping the dogs away with her feet. Shirley then turned around again and kicked the bowl over, the broth soaking into the cold ground. The two dogs rushed forward and started licking the spot where the bowl was spilled, and Shirley spun around once more and inched backward toward the curs with her hands outstretched behind her.

She felt a tug, then another, and looked back to see that the two hungry animals were now starting to chew on the smelly rawhide. She pulled while the two dogs bit into the leather thong, and she tried her best to keep her shivering down as much as possible.

Finally, after several minutes of the two chewing and trying to get as much of the stew-soaked leather into their gullets as possible, the rawhide rope snapped, and Shirley's hands were free. She rubbed her wrists and beat her arms across herself as quickly as she could.

After a minute, she removed the thong from around her neck and almost dived into the door of the lodge. The old chief and his wife were lying under a thick buffalo robe, and they both sat up bolt upright. Shirley's eyes met theirs, but she went directly to the fire and rubbed her body all over, trying to warm up. She picked up a bowl and poured herself some more stew from a pot still by the fire. She gulped the broth while the two just stared at her. Not a word was spoken.

The white captive spotted another thick buffalo robe across the fire from them and she, still staring at the two, wrapped herself in it and curled up close to the fire. They looked at each other, than back at her, finally laying their heads down and going to sleep.

They must have reasoned that she had nowhere to go anyway. The wife realized that the *wasicun* woman was probably thankful the old man owned her instead of some young buck full of lust. The chief's wife had heard that the captive was the woman of Wamble Uncha, so she knew where her heart must be.

Shirley pulled the buffalo robe up over her head, then with her eyes finally hidden from all others, she silently wept, long and hard. She finally stopped and thought, she had survived so far and must continue to do so. She knew that Chris would find her somehow, some way. If anybody could, it was Christopher Columbus Colt.

Tears spilling down her cheeks, Shirley Colt walked to the stove and poured herself another cup of hot tea. How many nights had she sat here, alone by the fire? But she would never complain. She had gone into this marriage with her eyes wide open. If she was to be the wife of Chris Colt, she would have to always understand that she had to share him with a mistress. That "other woman" was the untamed frontier of the

American West. Men like Chris Colt were the leaders in handling this lawless wild place, and Chris had a part in carving out American history. Shirley knew that and was simply thankful for the time she did have with her husband. After what had happened, she wished he were here now, but she had learned to be patient.

Sitting down with her tea, she thought back to an incident that was one of the turning points during her captivity.

Winter had come, and she was already learning to outwork her captors. They were moving and at that time Shirley fell and pulled a thorn out of the side of her calf. It had been buried beneath the deep snow. She stood again and tugged on the heavy travois, walking toward the winter village site Screaming Horse had decided on in the Valley of Many Smokes, the Yellowstone Valley. In the spring, when the killer mountain snows and blizzards were gone, he would lead his band to Canada and marry up with Sitting Bull.

Screaming Horse's sister lashed Shirley across the back with a switch, and Shirley turned, teeth clenched, and dived headfirst into the woman's midsection, knocking her backward over a log. The woman, struggling for air, tried to stand, and Shirley's kick caught her full in the face, bloodying both lips. The Cheyenne braves laughed as Shirley brushed herself off and picked up the end of the travois and continued on.

She would do what she had to do to survive, she thought, but she would be respected while she survived, no matter what. Shirley wondered where Colt was and when he would come to save her. She could not give up hope.

It paid off for her, too, because Chris had eventually come and paid the chief for her with a whole herd of horses, when the old man was asking for five ponies to buy her. After having been kidnapped and raped by Will Sawyer, then captured and held by Screaming Horse, Shirley was promised by Chris Colt that he would never let anything like that happen to her again.

The Apache Kid rode down the long driveway to the Coyote Run ranch buildings. It was dark and all would be asleep. He heard that Colt's widow had hair that looked like it was made from the dark embers of a fire, when the flames were gone and it was getting sleepy late at night. That hair would decorate his clothing in just a short time.

The ranch yard was just ahead when Chris

Colt, on War Bonnet, rode out of the shadows and blocked the driveway.

Chris smiled softly when, from out of the shadows, he heard the voice of old Tex Westchester, "Don't worry none, Colt. Ef'n ya should miss him, I got a bead on him with mah long gun."

Another deep voice said, "So do I, brother."

Colt smiled more broadly and kept looking at the Apache Kid while saying, "Hello, Joshua, Tex, good to be home. You, you've raped your last woman."

The Apache Kid's face was expressionless, but under the quiet surface panic was raging. He wanted escape because he knew he was a dead man, and he was not true to his tribal beliefs and mores. He would not be walking any spirit trail and meeting with dead family members or hunting lots of game along beautiful streams. He would be lost forever, and he always meant to correct things before he died. Now, it was too late. He would have to think of something.

Chris Colt was looking at the white man's saddlebags of the Apache Kid. He wanted to make sure he knew which side held the remaining sticks of dynamite. Colt saw fuses sticking out of both saddlebags. The man was right at the end of Colt's gun range.

Chris whispered. "Take cover, boys."

He swung one leg over War Bonnet's neck

and said, "Go home, boy." The big horse took off for the barn.

Colt reached into one pocket, still staring at the killer, and pulled out his cigarette papers, divided them in half, and rolled both halves into little balls, which he jammed into his ears.

Colt said, "No man comes after my wife. Draw your weapon and kill me if you can."

The Apache Kid slowly pulled his rifle from his saddle scabbard, but he had to bring it up and cock it. This white-eyes couldn't possibly be that fast, he thought. He had a chance. The Apache Kid swung the rifle up.

Chris Colt's two Peacemakers came out in one smooth draw, and they bucked in his hand.

Shirley Colt spilled her tea as she heard the giant explosion outside. Both of her children started crying, but she couldn't quiet them right now. Grabbing another Colt revolving shotgun, she burst out the door and turned down the driveway, lantern in her hand. She saw a giant smoke ball, and Joshua and Tex were helping someone stand up. He was covered with blood from head to foot. It was her husband.

Shirley dropped the shotgun and ran forward, screaming, "Chris, oh Chris!"

Joshua, realizing her horror, said, "It's okay, Shirl, it's not his blood. He's okay."

Colt shook his head and saw his wife. He smiled and held up his hand, then ran off to the side of the driveway and dived into Texas Creek. Wiping his face and hair underwater, he assumed the blood was rinsed off in the fast running stream. Colt crawled out and walked up to Shirley, smiling. He grabbed her up in his arms and kissed her long and hard.

Stepping back, she said, "Chris, what happened?"

Colt smiled at her and said, "The Apache Kid was here. He's gone now."

She saw pieces of human tissue and horse lying all around. There was blood everywhere, and Shirley choked back the sickening feeling in her stomach.

She said, "Gone?"

Chris said, "Yes, like most men, he just wanted to make his mark on the land. I helped him out a little."

Tex chuckled behind them as Colt put his arm around her and escorted her back to the ranch house. Inside, they drank coffee, along with Tex and Joshua, who were invited in. Chris held both of his now wide awake children on his lap. He said, "Have you heard from Man Killer? I figured he would be back by now."

The three gave each other strange looks
and Chris knew immediately something was
wrong.

Joshua said, "You haven't heard. The night
before you two left, Chancy Banta was forced
into a gunfight by two gunslicks named Buffalo Bob Smith and Durango Hobbs. He was
killed. Beaver was found dead in his cabin,
too, a hole in his head at close range.
Jennifer Banta is on her way to Australia
with her aunt and uncle, and nobody be-
lieves she went of her own accord."

Colt said, "What did Man Killer do when
heard about it?"

Shirley said, "It was very strange. He didn't
speak to anyone. He went off into the darkness and reappeared outside the house,
wearing war paint and riding one of his
horses, but not Hawk. He left him here. I
asked him what he was doing, and he said he
was going to Australia. He turned and rode
off very slowly."

Colt smiled.

Shirley said, "I was going to try to tell him
he could never make it to Australia, but I remembered that he has been trained by you,
and I wouldn't dare tell him he couldn't hit
the moon with a Sharps .50."

Joshua said, "What can we do?"

Colt said, "We will smile at how much bigger his muscles are and how much taller he is when he gets back from Australia."

Shirley said, "Why did he leave Hawk here?"

Chris said, "Because he knew he couldn't ride the horse across the ocean, honey."

"Do you really think he'll be gone that long?"

Colt said, "Shirley, it takes months just to cross the ocean in one direction. He has to get to California first, then cross the ocean, then find Jennifer somewhere in Australia, which makes Texas seem like a little dot on a map, then rescue her, bring them both back across the ocean, then make it home. I think it will be a little while before we see Man Killer again."

"But, how will he get there? What is he going to do?" she asked.

Colt chuckled.

"Chris, answer me."

Joshua interjected, "Shirley, did you ever look at the way Jennifer and Man Killer looked at each other?"

Shirley grinned and said, "Yes."

Joshua said, "Now, let's say you were kidnapped and taken to Australia, and Chris was an Indian brave instead of being white, but he felt the same way about you that he does now. Would he come after you and make it there?"

Shirley said, "Of course."

Joshua said, "But I said he was red, not white. How could he?"

Shirley said, "Chris? He would find a way. He would get there before I arrived. You know what he's like."

Joshua winked at Chris and said to her, "As Brandon Rudd would say, 'I rest my case, your honor.' "

Shirley thought for a second and said, "I guess he *will* find a way."

"Chip off the chopping block," Joshua confirmed.

The last place that Buffalo Bob Smith and Durango Hobbs were spotted was a small town near Bingham County, Utah. Man Killer boarded a freight with the horse and rode the rails most of the way. Riding cross-country, he noticed such a difference in the mountains. In the Wet Mountain valley, it seemed the mountains rose with many sloping ridges like great sentinels up in the blue sky. In central Utah, however, the mountains seemed to go straight up into the sky. They were more like the steeper San Luis Valley side of the Sangre de Cristo range, but even steeper. There didn't seem to be as many foothills, either.

It was late at night when Man Killer rode into the small mining town and headed toward one of the two saloons. Both were packed to overflowing, and loud raucous, tinny music emanated from old pianos being played in both saloons. The yelling, music, and laughing was easily heard through the canvas-topped slab wood buildings. Man Killer entered one saloon, and the music stopped, as did the laughing and talking. Everyone looked at the Indian sporting a Colt Peacemaker in a low-slung holster, another belly gun tucked into the front of his belt, a faded red shirt with white polka dots and bone hair pipe choker necklace over it, fringed leather trousers, moccasins, long, braided hair with a single eagle feather slanted down in the back, and most startling of all, a face covered with black, red, and yellow war paint.

A voice in the back said, "Looks ta me like a red blanket nigger is lookin' ta git his neck stretched."

Murmurs of agreement echoed throughout the room, but Man Killer ignored them. He walked up to the bartender and tossed a coin down on the bar, saying, "Water."

The bartender laughed and looked around, but something in Man Killer's eye made him very quiet and serious. He set a pitcher of water and a glass in front of the scout, saying, "No charge. Just drink it and leave."

Man Killer lifted the pitcher to his lips and drank from it, water running down his chest. The whole time his right hand hovered over his gun. The others in the room stared at him in utter silence. Most of these men were miners. Man Killer set the pitcher down and wiped his lips with his left sleeve.

He said, "Buffalo Bob Smith and Durango Hobbs."

One man in the corner had the look of a gunfighter, and he now stood in a crouch and snarled, "You talk about uppity redskins. He comes into a white man's bar and boasts he's hunting two men. They'll skin your ears back anyhow."

Man Killer turned and said nothing. His left hand hovered above the belly gun, while his right stayed over his holstered gun.

Another man across the room said, "Ya better watch yer mouth, Pilgrim. That redskin'll pin yer ears back fer shore. Ya know who thet is? Thet's Chris Colt's sidekick, Man Killer, and he's rattlesnake-tough."

There were more murmurs, but the gunfighter snarled, "I don't care. I ain't seen the day no blanket nigger kin draw down on me. Draw!"

With that, the man's hand dropped to his .44. His fingers wrapped around the walnut handle, and he grinned at the same time, knowing he was going to add another notch.

But something went wrong. Something slammed into his stomach and propelled him backward onto the poker table behind him. A beer mug bruised his spine, and he yelped in pain. The table tipped, but he did a complete back flip with the table and came up on his feet, the momentum carrying him back and slamming him into the wall. He looked down at the giant red pool on his shirt and stuck his finger in the hole in his chest. He looked up at Man Killer and saw smoke coming out of the Indian's gun barrel.

Man Killer thumbed the empty shell from his cylinder and loaded a fresh bullet, saying, "Now, you have seen the day."

The would-be gunfighter said, "Huh?"

He fell forward and saw the top of the poker table rushing at his face. He felt his nose break as his face hit the table, and his neck jerked back with a snapping noise. Neither injury hurt, though, and he felt strange when his face slammed into the floor, because he saw the floor coming at him without his eyes blinking. He lay there, listening to people talking about his death, but he couldn't move. He didn't really die, in fact, until the undertaker placed him in the old pine coffin and stood him up in the mercantile store window. The whole time, he kept trying to scream, but nothing would work, but his brain.

Right after the shooting, a large bearded man walked in the door. With an enormous belly hanging over his belt, he hitched up his pants and Man Killer saw the star on his shirt.

The man looked at Man Killer, saying, "I'll take those guns, Injun."

Man Killer said, "No, you won't."

The bartender said, "Flint asked for it, Marshal."

The marshal said, "No matter. I said to hand over the guns, or I'll take 'em." He felt he had something to prove now. He had been challenged. The big lawman said, "I won't say it again."

Man Killer said, "I'm looking for Buffalo Bob Smith and Durango Hobbs."

The marshal said, "They headed for Virginia City. Now, the guns."

Man Killer turned, walking toward the door.

The marshal hollered, "Hey, you!"

The marshal started to draw his gun, and Man Killer apparently sensed it, because he suddenly wheeled, lips curled back over his teeth. The young warrior was just not in the mood for any more trash from the mouths of any more white men. There was his holster Colt in his right hand and belly gun Colt in the other, both guns cocked and pointed at the belly of the marshal.

Man Killer said, "If I was a white man, you would listen to what I say and to the witnesses and smile, but because I am red you want to try to violate my rights. The Constitution of the United States of America says that all men are created equal, but you do not believe this, Marshal."

With that, Man Killer uncocked his pistols, spun both guns backward rapidly, stopped the spin with his middle fingers, and spun them forward, stopped it again and spun them backward again, with the right spinning into the holster and tucking the left into his waistline. He crossed his arms over his chest and looked at the marshal with a defiant half grin.

The scout said, "I am looking for two killers outside the law, but you treat me like *I* am. I am also a warrior, so now, I give you a chance. My arms are crossed, Marshal. You have a gun pointed at me and cocked. Just pull the trigger and maybe I will die, but I think you will, too. Let's learn, Marshal. Kill me."

The marshal thought about it, but hesitated at the intelligent look this young Indian gave him. He must have an edge, the marshal thought.

Man Killer taunted, "You want to impress your townsmen drinking here? Go ahead. Just pull the trigger."

The marshal wished he had taken the day

to go fishing for brook trout. He really enjoyed the taste, and he knew many nice pools where some good ones liked to while away the afternoon hours in the lee of a large rock. Giant, glistening beads of sweat popped out all over his forehead. He thought about what to do to get out of this situation.

Man Killer knew the marshal needed some more convincing, and he was so angry and fed up with his treatment right now, he just did not care. He was ready to fight anybody. He said, "I do not have all night for this. I will count to three and kill any man pointing a gun at me. One . . . two. . . ."

The marshal didn't even have time to think it over. He quickly shoved his pistol in the holster, and Man Killer just stared at him with his arms still folded over his chest.

A cowpuncher in the back of the saloon stood up, beer in his hand, and said, "Marshal, I cain't believe yer gonna let a dirty Injun make ya take water. Injuns ain't never thet fast with hoglegs, nohow. He was jest lucky afore. He couldn't even."

Boom!

The explosion of the gun was so fast and unexpected, the man's beer mug exploded into a million pieces, and the man was covered with beer and broken glass. He let out a scream, and the other saloon patrons pointed at him and laughed. His face was bright red

with embarrassment and shame. He was totally shocked to see the six-shooter in Man
Killer's right hand. It seemed to have come
from nowhere in the blink of an eye.

Now the Indian spun it back into his holster and crossed his arms again. "Get me another beer."

The man ducked his head and walked over
to the bar and grabbed a draft for Man Killer
and handed it to the scout.

Man Killer said, "The marshal was just trying to do his job, but forgot that he should
respect all people no matter what color their
skin is. Right, Marshal?"

"I guess yer right, young man. Sorry about
thet."

Man Killer said, "I will leave your town
now." He went out the door without further
incident. The lawman turned back toward
the bar with a very red face. He glanced
around the room and met many suppressed
laughs. Several men started chuckling out-
right, and he spun around. Instead of stopping, everyone roared with laughter, and he
stormed out of the bar. Man Killer was already in the darkness, riding south of town.
The marshal went back to his office and the
bottle he had hidden in his desk. He was a
simple miner who had not made it, so he
picked up the job of town marshal, but he
knew nothing of the law. What did he care,

he thought. For some reason, that night was the first of many nights he would drink much more than he ever did in his life.

In Virginia City Man Killer went into the first bar he saw, not wearing war paint, and was served without question. Nobody would talk, but Man Killer was a scout and could read sign. He read it all over the bartender's face.

He then disappeared, but many people talked about the strange, handsome Indian who had wandered in looking for the two gunfighters. Nobody could figure out what had happened to him, but he was not seen again. Buffalo Bob's and Durango's drinking buddies kept watching for him and kept the two men posted in the room where they stayed at the Virginia City Hotel.

At the end of a week they showed up at the saloon again. They both bellied up to the mahogany bar and ordered glasses of rye. It had been boring spending the week in the hotel room, but they knew who the Indian was and didn't want to tangle with him. The thing that surprised them, though, was that nobody mentioned the Indian wearing the big sword.

Buffalo Bob Smith had earned his name in Montana. He had killed one buffalo in his entire life, but he had earned his nickname when a gang he was with decided to take a break and bathe in a tributary of the Canadian River after a week of running from a very angry posse. Once they all undressed to jump in, one of the gunslingers noticed that nature had been more than generous with Bob Smith when he was given certain body parts. The men started teasing him, and he was given the name Buffalo Bob after that. He was tall and wide, but his prowess was not in fist fighting. He had nerves of steel and had taken several bullets during gunfights, but still took careful aim and fired. He was careful when making his draw, too. His draw wasn't all that quick, but he was steady, whereas most men in gunfights hit everything but the man they are shooting at, they are so nervous.

Durango Hobbs was from Philadelphia, Pennsylvania, where his mother had been a brothel madam, and he had no idea who his father was. He had been molested by two of the prostitutes working in his mother's crib when he was only ten years old, and he hated and distrusted women after that, especially his mother. The only sexual thoughts he ever had after that were about men, but he would quickly try to push them out of his mind and never could figure out what was wrong with himself. Several times he became almost close enough friends with several men to tell them about his feelings, even Buffalo Bob, but he could never bring himself to do so. He had a burning anger inside, so he learned to use guns and shot anybody he felt like. His first killing was the only man with whom he had ever had any sexual contact. Ashamed after his actions and never wanting anyone to learn about it, Durango, whose real name was Elmer, unloaded a Navy .36 into the man in a seedy Philadelphia hotel room after a night of drinking. He then fled the city of Brotherly Love and headed west. He was always looking for new challenges. A good-looking man, he loved to get into a gunfight in a town street, with all the womenfolk watching, and then figure that they were all wanting him but not even able to approach him.

Both men were surrounded at the bar by three other toughs who had joined in with them and the five were, in essence, the beginnings of a new gang of outlaws. A rope slipped over the roof of the saloon, and a figure quickly came down the rope in the darkness. It was Man Killer. Now he wore a breechcloth, his guns, choker necklace, two arm bands, moccasins, eagle feather, and bowie knife. The upper half of his face was painted black with a yellow stripe running straight down the middle and two diagonal stripes running out from each side of his bottom lip down his chin.

He stepped into the saloon, and again all noise stopped immediately.

One of the toughs tapped Durango and said, "There he is."

Durango looked at the man, then over at Buffalo, saying, "That's not him."

One man in the back of the bar hollered, "Injun!" He jumped up, drawing a well-polished and oiled Russian, but a bullet from Man Killer's right-hand gun took him in the right shoulder and sat him down in his chair inadvertently, while the gun flew into the well-used spittoon. A friend patched the man's shoulder while he cursed his luck over the ruined pistol. Man Killer, in the meantime, spun his pistol backward into his holster after reloading and looked at Buffalo Bob and Durango. They stepped away from the bar and their three friends braced themselves to either side of them.

Man Killer said, "Buffalo Bob Smith and Durango Hobbs, you killed my friends, Chancy Banta and Beaver, a mountain man, in Westcliffe, Colorado. They were old men and did not have a chance." To the three toughs, he said, "You three do not have to die. I am Man Killer. I have spoken."

One of the sidekicks to the two killers started chuckling. He said, "Beaver, huh? You mean ole Banta's brother Larry? I s'pose, Injun boy, ya think yer gonna smoke all five a us, huh? Ya know how many bullet holes we'll put in ya?"

Man Killer said, "Probably many bullets, but I will live long enough to kill all five of you. It hurts to be shot, but what is pain. I will lie in a doctor's office and moan for a week, but I will not die. You will. My guns speak good. I was taught by my brother, Chris Colt."

He saw Colt's name take effect, and that was what he had counted on. His matter-of-fact conversation about being willing to be wounded had an effect, too, especially after everyone admired the large, rippling muscles and many scars all over his young body. Man Killer also now had the answer to the mystery of Beaver. Every man in the room knew the man was young, but he was a warrior, a live one. All those scars had been wounds at one time, and they healed. His bold bragging didn't seem hollow.

Durango wet his lips. Buffalo Bob stood unmoving, figuring his odds and wondering if he could position himself so the Indian would fire at one or two of the others first.

Man Killer read each man's eyes. His best hand was his right, and he would take Durango with that gun. He would be the fastest. Buffalo Bob was the careful one and always made his first shot count, so Man Killer made a mental note to sidestep when his gun came out. He would take the two smaller men on each side of the principals first because they looked fast. He figured Buffalo Bob might get the first bullet into him, but he had to keep shooting even while falling. The fifth man wasn't wearing his gun properly for any kind of quick draw, and his holster wasn't very worn. His face and hands looked like he was a brawler, so he might get Man Killer with a lucky shot, if at all.

The scout addressed Buffalo Bob. "Before you die, tell me. Who hired you to kill those two men?"

"They both was kilt in clean fights, but they was an old John Bull guy who dint like them nohow, he happened ta mention."

Man Killer stood, waiting, keeping a calm, but ferocious outward appearance, something quite easy to do with his face painted as it was. He knew the "John Bull" had to be Horace Windham.

A voice from outside said, "Wait, boys. If ya'll having a ball, Tora and me would like to dance."

Justis Colt and Tora walked in the door and walked up next to Man Killer, to his immediate right. Justis said, "Howdy, Man Killer. Buffalo Bob, Durango. Howdy, boys. Remember us? We owe you. Wanna surrender and go back to Texas to turn yourselves in?"

Durango laughed and said, "Sure. You gonna talk or shoot?"

Justis winked at Man Killer and said, "Good point."

Both men drew their guns and started firing. Man Killer put two bullets into the left breast pocket of Durango Hobbs and saw Buffalo Bob fall to two similarly placed bullets from Justis. A metal star stuck out of the forehead of the man to Durango's left, and Man Killer saw Tora move forward with a flash, and with a slash, his sword came down and split the face of the same man. Then he immediately slashed sideways and cut halfway through the screaming man's torso.

A bullet burned Man Killer's cheek, and he felt blood. He and Justis both shot the man immediately. The brawler put a bullet into Justis's left thigh and the ex-lawman's leg buckled. Man Killer grabbed his arm and yanked him behind and fired three shots into the man. The brawler fell and started to rise back up, taking aim. Justis and Man Killer both desperately tried to reload, but Tora rushed forward and stabbed the man through the heart with his Samurai sword. The sword stuck into the wall behind him, and Tora let go of the handle, leaving the man pinned to the wall in a half-standing position. He drew his shorter Tanto sword and stood guard over the two gunfighters, but there was no reason. The five men were dead.

The bartender ran out the door to summon the marshal, and two ranch hands walked over and one wrapped a bandage around Justis's thigh. A dance hall girl grabbed a towel from behind the bar and started dabbing it on Man Killer's cheek. But the bullet had cut deep, and Man Killer's shoulder and side were covered with blood.

One of the punchers said, "Ranger Colt, that was some slick shootin' from both a ya. I seen ya down ta Austin way and heerd a ya many a-time."

The marshal came in and interviewed the men and witnesses, letting the three go. Numerous patrons came outside to watch Man Killer ascend the rope, retrieve his belongings, and clean his expedient rooftop campsite. Everyone started talking about how he had stayed on the roof for a week, keeping a vigil over the saloon without a soul knowing he was there.

The lawman said, "You mean you have been up there ever since the night you left?"

Man Killer said, "I had to sleep somewhere."

A young deputy said, "Thought Injuns never broke their words. I heerd you said you was leavin' town last week."

Man Killer said, "I did. I came back an hour later."

Justis said, "If you gentlemen will excuse us, we would like to visit with our friend now."

The marshal looked at Man Killer and quickly said, "Yes, sir, help yerself."

Man Killer spent the night with Tora and Justis, then departed the next day at daybreak. Justis told him to head to San Francisco to find a ship traveling to Australia. Although Man Killer had earned plenty of money with his horse herd of Appaloosas and his small share of ownership in the ranch, he had taken only pocket money when he left, angry, hurt, and determined to exact revenge. He was even more determined to find and save his love, but his pride kept him from accepting the money Justis offered or wiring home to have some sent. He would figure out a way. A doctor came to Justis's room and treated and sewed up Man Killer's cheek, but the scout knew he would have another scar, this one more visible. Justis had had a Navy .36 bullet pass through the fleshy part of his thigh. It temporarily paralyzed his leg when the bullet struck a nerve, but he could walk after an hour and would be sore for a few weeks. He should heal nicely, the doctor had said.

* * *

San Francisco was big and wild, and Man Killer was surprised at the hills in the city. He, having learned from Chris Colt, went straightaway for a saloon on the western outskirts of town and got service this time and a lot of stares. In a corner a commotion started, and Man Killer saw three big miners who had jumped to their feet and were facing a large sandy-haired man with an impish smile on his rugged face.

One of the three roared, "Yer a damned card sharp! Ya oughta be run outta town on a rail, damn ya! But I'll fix ya. We all will! We're gonna tear yer meat wagon down."

The sandy-haired man said, "Say blokes, I don't even know yer games, ya know. Let's just take us a walkabout and cool off, eh?"

Man Killer immediately identified the speech pattern.

The three men took a step forward, and the one on the left yanked the poker table angrily and sent it flying sideways. The Australian kicked the chair in front of his right foot directly into the knees of the largest one, then he came off his chair with a lunge, his beefy fist slamming into the cheek of the one man in the center.

The third man started forward and stopped short, as did the others when a giant bowie knife twisted through the air and stuck in the wall directly in front of the big man's face. The big man turned and stared daggers at Man Killer.

The scout said, "He is my friend. I do not think three should fight one."

The man by the knife said, "We can fight two as easy as one, redskin."

Man Killer said, "You do not want to do that."

The second man, rubbing his kneecap, said, "Hell we don't, boy."

Both of those men stepped toward Man Killer, while the Australian smiled in wonder. The scout braced himself, and thought, oh, oh, I *am* in trouble.

Man Killer held up his hand and said, "Wait."

Both men stopped. The third had gotten up and stood by the Australian, just watching. Man Killer picked up a bottle of whiskey from the bar and walked over in front of the largest man, setting the bottle down in front of him.

He said, "Have you ever seen a man punch so fast he can knock the top of a whiskey bottle off without spilling any or breaking the rest of the bottle?"

The big man said, "Naw. No way."

Man Killer got ready to punch it, but the whole time was remembering the earlier trick that Chris Colt had pulled on Boston Bill Brannigan with the board. He punched, stopped his fist just short of the bottle, grabbed it by the neck, and smashed the largest man across the face with it. Glass crashed everywhere, while blood spurted in every direction. The man by the Australian stuck his chin out, openmouthed, and the man from down under lifted him over the bar with an uppercut to the jaw. The third man came at Man Killer with a rush, and the scout dropped to the floor, hooking one foot in front of the man's shin and the other behind his calf. He scissored both legs as hard as he could, and the man went crashing onto and over a table, spilling headfirst into the edge of the bar.

The man who had been hit in the face with the bottle staggered around, holding his bloodied face with both hands, and the Australian and Man Killer both swung, their fists hitting the back of the man's hands covering his face at the same time. He flew backward over the bar and out of sight behind it.

The Aussie looked at the scout and both men started laughing and shook hands. "Thank ye, mate," he said, "but we oughta get outta here, don't ya think?"

Man Killer looked at the moaning men and said, "Good idea."

They started to exit, but the bartender said, "Hey, whose gonna pay fer the damages?"

Man Killer said, "They started it. Ask them."

The bartender walked out from behind the bar with a lead pipe in his hand and patted his palm with it. Man Killer smiled at the barkeep while he pulled his bowie knife out of the wall, tested its balance a second, and sheathed it.

The bar man cleared his throat, walked over to the moaning miners, and bellowed, "Okay, wake up. Ya got a mess to clean up and pay for."

Man Killer and the big Australian ducked out the door, chuckling. Outside, they mounted up and trotted their horses into town.

The foreigner said, "Ya know, mate, I din't wanna be in hoots with those boys, but they pushed the matter a bit. I am beholdin' to ya, mate." He laughed. "That one battler sure went ass over tits across the mahogany, he did, mate, din't he?"

Man Killer started laughing, and the other joined in.

They rode on for another fifteen minutes and found a quieter saloon and tied their mounts out front at the hitching rail. They talked for some time about each other's backgrounds and experiences. Inside, Man Killer ordered two orders of steak, potatoes, stewed tomatoes, and coffee.

After the meal, he explained about Jennifer and Horace Windham. The two talked well into the night because Man Killer wanted help from this man. The adventure he was about to embark on was the most dangerous he had ever attempted.

Chapter 6

>>>>>>>>>>>>>>>>

Down Under

Man Killer looked up at Looking Glass as the chief started to walk out of the tepee. The young scout saw the cavalryman's bullet headed at the older Indian's face and jumped up.

He hollered, "No!" as he sat up and looked around in the darkness.

Several rats scurried nearby in the hold of the moving ship, but Man Killer paid them no mind. He thought for a few seconds to orient himself. His head ached horribly, and he felt dizzy, but that would wear off with time. He would just put up with the throbbing headache until it went away.

Man Killer was so influenced by Chris Colt that for days now he was always thinking about what a man the famous Chris Colt was, his mentor, and what a warrior. He thought about all that man had gone through to express his love for that one special woman in his life. So many men, especially in the West, were so afraid to let a woman know how they felt about her if they were in love. It was the same with many Nez Perce warriors, even though the concept was slightly different for them. Nevertheless there was true love between some Nez Perce men and women. It seemed to Man Killer it was like a gunfight. It might be frightening and even make a man sick in the stomach, but why not be up front with it? Tackle it head on. That's what Chris Colt had taught him, by example.

Man Killer found a bucket of dirty water, but he drank from it and poured some on his aching head. He felt in his hidden pocket and found the makings and built a cigarette. He smiled, even in his pain, and thought about the initial meeting of Chris Colt and Shirley Colt. He had heard the same story from both Chris and Shirley, but from each one's point of view.

Colt had his initial run-in with Crazy Horse when the war hero's party killed the Sawyer brothers, and the Oglala rewarded Colt with War Bonnet because he admired the white man's courage so much. Colt made it to Fort Lincoln not long after that and reported to Custer.

The next morning, he was out of bed before daybreak and saddled up War Bonnet, deciding to look around nearby Bismarck. The town was about the same as other frontier towns with false-front buildings and a few brick ones and a helter-skelter system of streets that just kind of evolved as the town grew in size.

He saw a restaurant called the Frontier Cafe oddly enough, and it boasted a big sign in the front window advertising home cooking. That sounded like something Chris could appreciate as much as the sleep he got.

He was really feeling healthy already. His head no longer hurt, and he felt rested. Well, he felt good until the auburn-haired waitress–restaurant owner–cook walked into the room to wait on him. He thought he was going to suffer a seizure, as his breathing came out in gasps almost, and his heart pounded heavily in his chest. In fact, he thought it might explode.

The top of her full head of golden red hair would touch him right about the chin, and the simple gingham dress she wore could do nothing to hide the curves of her body underneath. Her lips were full and her cheekbones high, and she had a very proud uplift to her chin. But a warm smile could make anyone feel welcome. What caught Chris Colt's breath, though, were her bright green eyes. They penetrated through his stare and went right inside his head, traveling all the way deep into his soul. He felt he could have closed his eyes tightly, and those green eyes would have still shot right through him.

"Coffee, sir?" she asked with a voice like crushed velvet.

"Thank you, ma'am," Chris said, nodding.

He wished he had taken a bath. He wished he had brushed his teeth longer and combed his hair. He wished he didn't feel as though he was about to tangle with a war party of angry Apaches.

She poured him a cup, and they stared at each other, smiling uneasily, and she accidentally poured too much in the cup, the hot liquid making Colt jump up and bump the table into her, spilling the entire pot of coffee. She screamed and grabbed a napkin, trying to clean up the spill, and Colt grabbed another one, also trying to wipe up the coffee.

"How clumsy of me," she cried. "I'm so sorry, sir."

Chris said, "You? It was totally my fault. I'm sorry, ma'am."

They stopped wiping and looked up at each other, first grinning, then both breaking into an embarrassed laugh. They ended up sitting down at the next table and just laughed. It was infectious, and the more they giggled, the harder it made them laugh.

Finally stopping, Chris said, "This your place, ma'am?"

"Yes, it is," she replied, sticking out her hand to shake. "My name's Shirley Ebert. Are you new in town? Are you staying?"

"Yes and no," he replied. "I'm the new chief of scouts for General Custer at Fort Lincoln. My name is Colt, ma'am, Christopher Columbus Colt, but folks call me Chris."

"Any relation to the famous Colonel Colt?" she asked.

"My uncle."

"Well, Mister Colt."

"Chris, please," he said.

"Fine, call me Shirley," she responded. "Can I get you some breakfast, Chris?"

"Yes, ma'am," he said, "I am ready for some home cooking."

"What would you like?" she asked.

He looked into her eyes and didn't answer for a second, and both of them blushed again.

Chris broke the silence by saying, "It's up to you, Shirley. You decide."

"Okay, I'll surprise you, and it's on the house," she said, "since I almost scalded you with hot coffee."

Chris laughed and blushed again, saying, "Shirley, it would have been worth getting scalded, just meeting you."

He shocked himself with the statement

and felt like he shouldn't have said a word. He really blushed now, as did Shirley, but she also gave him a smile and a look that promised volumes of love poetry in just a glance. She quickly left the room, and Chris wondered if he had offended her.

Man Killer thought of this statement and smiled as he remembered telling the young teenaged Jennifer Banta that he would marry her someday, as he rode away from her ranch to scout for the Ninth and Tenth Cavalry. He remembered how he sat his horse back straight and walked away proudly after making the boast, but how embarrassing it had been, too. He worried for a long time if she thought he was a fool, but she had assured him he certainly was not, and the two of them were almost no longer teenagers. He thought more about the initial meeting of Chris and Shirley.

Man Killer's mentor heard footsteps on the board sidewalk outside the cafe, and the door opened suddenly. Three cowboys walked in, but each wore his gun low and looked more like a gunslinger punching cows, than a cowboy who could handle a gun. They were followed by Goliath himself. The giant behemoth who walked in the door had to be Will Sawyer. He was every bit of seven feet in height and looked as broad in the shoulders as he was in length, toes to hair. He wore a Colt .45 Peacemaker in a low-slung holster and was filthy with a long unkempt beard.

He looked over at Chris and said, "You the one that owns that red nigger horse outside?"

Chris said, "That's my horse at the hitching rail, Sawyer."

Will angrily said, "How do you know my name?"

"Lucky guess," Chris said with a smile.

Colt knew by his attitude that this man came in wanting to prod him and had probably heard all about the various troubles Colt had had with his brothers.

"Who are you?" Will asked.

Chris took a sip of coffee and said, "I believe you already know my name."

Sawyer responded, "Yeah, I know who you are: Colt, the cowardly son of a bitch who ran out on my brothers and let them get massacred by the redskins."

Colt looked over at Will and said between clenched teeth, "Sawyer, I know you must be distraught over the sudden death of your brothers, so I'll let that slip, but nobody questions my courage or honesty, nobody."

Sawyer stood up and said, "You sawed-off son of a bitch. Nobody but nobody ever talks to me like that. I'll call you and anyone else anything I want. You wanna do somethin' about it?"

Chris said, "Not really. I just came here to enjoy a quiet breakfast."

Sawyer walked forward a little and said, "Wal, in fact, we don't cotton to no red nigger lovers around here, and yer a liar and a coward. Now git out of this restaurant."

"No, you leave, Will Sawyer, right now," Shirley said, as all eyes turned toward her in the doorway to the kitchen.

He just stared at her, hands on his hips.

She continued, "This is my business, and you might bully people all over this county, but you aren't doing it in my business. Understand?"

He walked toward her, but she stuck her chin out defiantly, folding her arms in front of herself.

Still trying to clear the cobwebs from his head in the rocking hold of the ship, Man Killer grinned to himself, in spite of his headache and queasy stomach. He thought of Shirley Colt, and the fire that coursed through her veins. Now, there was a woman, he thought, and if he could have Jennifer turn out to be half the way Shirley Colt was, he could be very happy. He could picture her defiance in the face of the seven-foot bully who scared everyone else to death. Man

Killer remembered Chris's grin as he bragged about Shirley, and Shirley's grin as she did the same about Colt.

While Sawyer walked across the room, he said, "Nobody talks to me that way, man or woman."

He was stopped in his tracks by Chris Colt's deep quiet voice. "If you even look at her cross-eyed Sawyer, it will be the last thing you ever do."

Will Sawyer spun around in a gunfighter's crouch, ready to draw, but he was staring down the barrel of Chris Colt's weapon. The muzzle looked like a cannon from the business end. He moved his hand away from his holster as if it were holding a diamondback rattlesnake in it.

Will said, "That ain't fair, you coward. You got the drop on me."

Chris laughed and said, "Fair? Tell me, Sawyer, how many seven-footers have you ever picked on?"

Sawyer just stared flames of hatred at the ruggedly handsome scout.

Colt said, "Now, you and your pals there, unbuckle your gunbelts and let them drop to the floor. Shirley, step back into the kitchen where it's safer."

"No," she said and stood her ground.

He smiled at her, then looked back at Will

Sawyer, who said, "Yer real damned big with that six-shooter, Colt. I wish I could git my hands on ya'. I'd show ya."

Chris said, "Well, it's obvious to me that you've been planning on trying that, so we are going to go outside, and I'll let you try it."

Sawyer looked at Colt and gave out a big laugh, saying, "What? Are you kidding me? Are you really going to be crazy enough to fight me? Do you know I'm seven foot one inch tall and weigh three hunnert and sixty-five pounds?"

"No, I didn't know that," Chris replied. "I'll have to pay more attention to how big they make the piles behind the livery stable from now on."

Nobody laughed, least of all Shirley who looked like she was ready to cry. Finally, she spoke, "Chris, please? You can't fight him. He's a monster. He killed a man in a fight with his bare hands."

Sawyer and his friends chuckled.

Will said, "Now ain't that sweet, boys. She's all worried about Colt's health."

Chris said, "No, I'm worried about her being treated with respect, so when we are done, you will apologize to Miss Ebert for the disrespect you've shown her."

* * *

Man Killer grinned to himself. Chris had not really told him about the fight itself. He was too modest, but Shirley sure had.

Inside, behind the stone cold-face, Chris was scared to death. This man was a behemoth, and he loved to fight and kill. He taunted the giant on purpose. He wanted to make him angry. An angry man fights like a fool. He also wanted to make him unsure. More than anything, though, Chris Colt was at that point he sometimes reached when he just didn't care about the odds. Sawyer had insulted this beautiful, wonderful woman, and Chris just wanted to rip his head off. He wondered why he considered her wonderful when he just met her and didn't even know her. The beautiful part he didn't question. She was, by far and away, the most gorgeous woman he had ever met.

Will Sawyer spit on his hands, which were the size of hams, then he rubbed the palms together. He rolled up his sleeves and said, "Ya' jest tryin' to show off fer Shirley here, or are ya' really gonna go outside and fight me? C'mon, Colt, I'd love it."

Chris signaled the others out the door of the cafe with his gun and followed them. Shirley ran up behind him and pulled on his sinewy right arm, spinning him around. Colt looked into those entrancing green eyes and almost melted.

"Please don't?" she pleaded.

Chris didn't know why, but Sawyer and his cohorts were outside. He just smiled at Shirley, swept her into his arms, and kissed her passionately. When he stepped back, she had tears running down her cheeks, but she was smiling bravely. He removed his gunbelt and handed it to her, as well as handing her his Colt.

Chris said, "If any of them go for a gun, shoot him."

Shirley said, "If I can't talk you out of it, and you're bound and determined to do it, I want you to go out there and kick Will Sawyer's ass."

Chris winked and turned, stepping out the door. A fist the size of a Thanksgiving turkey smashed into his lips and drove him backward through the door.

Man Killer had heard a blow-by-blow description of the fight from Shirley and how Chris had amazed everyone by defeating this Goliath by sheer courage, wits, and fighting ability.

In the end, Colt actually did get the dazed and semiconscious Will Sawyer to apologize to Shirley. After that, Colt had amazed the townspeople and Shirley even more when one of Sawyer's compatriots forced a showdown with him. Colt did what he could to avoid that fight, as well, but the man thought he was good. He found out the hard way that shooting at a *man* with a gun was much harder than shooting at branches and targets that can't shoot back.

Chris was sad. He hated to kill anybody, but the man had asked for it, and Chris had no choice. It didn't matter, though, as he still hated to kill anyone, no matter what the reason.

Man Killer understood that. He, too, hated killing another man, but in a wild country it had to be done often, too often.

After the sheriff had cleared Colt, Shirley took him into the restaurant and fed him, then doctored up his wounds, including bandaging his broken ribs.

Remembering that part of the story made Man Killer touch his own tender ribs, puffy eyes, and split lips, and he thought of the fight he had at the Pacific Pearl bar and moaned. He lay back on a bag of potatoes and moaned, blowing smoke from his cigarette to the ceiling. Thinking of his own predicament, he remembered what Shirley had

said about her amazing introduction to Chris
Colt. She had locked the doors of her cafe
and sat down, watching while Chris ate.

Shirley told Chris, "You must think I am
very forward. I just met you. We kissed already. I closed my restaurant and am sitting
here alone with you. This has never ever
happened to me in my life."

"Me either," he said between bites, "and I
don't think you're anything like forward."

"What *do* you think?" she asked.

He said, "About you?"

Shirley nodded.

"I think you're absolutely wonderful, Shirley."

This time *she* blushed, but Chris was familiar and confident about her now.

He went on, "In fact, you are the most
beautiful woman I've ever met in my entire
life."

Chris couldn't believe he told her that, but
he was too honest, and he really believed it.

Shirley just stared into his eyes for a few
seconds. His food was almost devoured,
which was a very good thing, because Shirley
moved around the table and swept his plate
and cup and silverware to the side and sat
down in his lap, kissing him with all the passion that was in her. He responded in kind.

Chris dropped his head when she returned to her seat, and he looked down at the floor.

"What's wrong?" she asked.

"Have you ever been married?" Chris asked.

"No," she replied, "Why?"

He said, "I lost my wife and daughter to Crows a while back. It'll probably take me a long time to get over it."

She responded, "I know about it. Did you love her?"

"Yes, I loved her very much," Chris replied, "How did you know about them?"

Shirley laughed and said, "Chris Colt, don't you realize what a hero you are here, all over? You're becoming a legend. Everyone knows about the tragedy, and you probably will never get over it, but you don't strike me as the type of man who will let tragedy make you stop living."

"I'm not," Chris said, "but I don't want any feelings I develop to be disguised by the pain."

Shirley said, "Then don't let them. You're a man, a real man."

Chris smiled and walked around the table, sweeping her up in his arms. He pulled her close and held her in a long hug. He then tilted her head up, swept her hair back slowly, and kissed her softly and tenderly.

They stepped back from each other and just stared deeply into each other's eyes.

Man Killer pictured that little scene between the two star-crossed lovers and imagined reenacting it with Jennifer somewhere in Australia. He thought about the loss of Chris's first wife and daughter and the two times Shirley had been kidnapped. Was he exposing Jennifer Banta to this same type of life-style? Would she be killed? He felt even more determined to rescue her.

Man Killer thought about the bar that Christian Bruce, the Australian had led him to. It was called the Pacific Pearl, and the Australian, after much protesting, had actually told Man Killer how to get himself shanghaied on one of the ships to Australia. That's where the poor unfortunate souls ended up who were shanghaied at that particular bar.

Man Killer had gone into the place and simply started drinking, knowing he couldn't hold whiskey very well, and he would end up in a fight.

Earlier, knowing the incredible undertaking he was about to embark upon, Man Killer packed his guns, bowie knife, and a few important mementos and shipped them via Wells Fargo back to Coyote Run. He was crazy, he knew, but his love for Jennifer was so strong he had to do something and do it now. He didn't even consider asking for anyone's help, such as having money wired to buy ship's passage, which he doubted he would be granted anyway. He had taken off as soon as he heard what had happened, with malice in his mind. He would go for the woman he loved and do whatever it took to get there. He had also reasoned that, if he were shanghaied and taken to Australia, he might not be traced as well as if he had shipped there, in case he was sought for the killing of Horace Windham. That was an event certain to happen, he was sure.

In the corner of the bar three sailors kept giving Man Killer dirty looks, and that was all the excuse he needed. He kept drinking, and his mood got uglier as he did so.

One of the men was named Billy Brambles, and to Man Killer he looked to be the size of Barrel Sawyer, the man the Nez Perce killed in the knife fight at Fort Union. The other two were Scotty Lawson and Lem Hitchcock. Hitchcock, a freckled redhead, was the smallest of the three and always the one to get them into fights. He usually stayed back while the two larger men beat on people, then jumped into the fray when the larger ones were softened up.

Man Killer, as he continued to drink, developed a silly look on his normally handsome countenance. His lips curled up in a bit of a smile, and he looked around the room, breaking into a giggle when he saw anything, no matter how insignificant, that struck his fancy.

At the same time, the mean redhead kept looking over at the Indian with the stupid grin on his face, and his mood got uglier.

Finally, Hitchcock said, "Hey you, you blanket-nigger! What are you looking at?"

Man Killer started giggling and said, "Something like an ugly man but much, much smaller."

Several patrons in the bar chuckled along with the drunken scout, but Hitchcock's freckled face got much redder. Hitchcock looked at his companions and said, "Did you hear what he said?"

Brambles said, "Yeah, don't pay no attention, Lem."

Hitchcock said, "Yeah, but I don't like the way he's been looking at us."

Scotty said, "Mon, you doon't like the way anyboody looks at us, ever."

Hitchcock jumped up and said, "Stop staring at us like that!"

Man Killer started laughing again, holding his sides, and said, "I cannot help myself."

Lem said, "Why not?"

"Because you look like a carrot sandwich. Sitting between your friends there, you look like a tiny carrot between two big fat biscuits."

With that, Billy slammed his chicken-sized fists on the table and stood up, weaving a little as he reached his full height, which Man Killer noticed was considerable. His partners, taking this as their cue, also jumped to their feet.

Man Killer pointed at them as they walked forward and grinned at two cowpunchers at the next table and said, "Oh-oh."

The two men laughed heartily and were joined by other patrons. This seemed to anger the sailors even more.

Man Killer continued to sit at his table as the three sailors stood towering. Billy Brambles, his arms folded over a wagon-sized chest, stood in the middle. The red-topped instigator stayed back slightly behind the other two.

Bill said, "Stand up, redskin. We're going to teach you some manners."

Man Killer looked at the duo at the next table and started giggling and made a circular sign with his index finger indicating the man was crazy. He said, "Are you sure you three can beat me? Maybe you should go get the U.S. cavalry. I have some land they can steal."

Billy Brambles said, "That does it, matey. I was going to give you the chance to apologize, but nobody makes fun of the American military."

Man Killer says, "I am part of the American military."

Brambles, who wasn't a particularly fast thinker anyway, was puzzled and said, "What part?"

Man Killer said, "I am a Nez Perce warrior."

Brambles said, "So what?"

"We are warriors, and we live and were born in America. Where were you born?"

Brambles said, "London, England, but my folks moved here when I was but a tyke."

Man Killer chuckled and said, "Oh, were they born here?"

Brambles getting angrier said, "No, but—"

Man Killer interrupted, "My father was born here, and his father before him, and his father before him, and his father before him. You are foreigners. Leave my country, and go home where you belong."

Man Killer found his joke hilarious and slapped his leg, howling with laughter. He laughed alone this time.

Hitchcock said, "No red nigger Injun is gonna make fun a the U.S.A. when we're around! The U.S. cavalry can whip anybody!"

Man Killer stopped smiling and said, "Especially if it's Nez Perce women and children."

Billy said, "That it!"

With that, he grabbed Man Killer and lifted him bodily out of the chair, just as the grinning scout was swallowing more whiskey. Man Killer started to hit him with the bottle, but Scotty yanked the bottle from his hand. Man Killer spit a stream of whiskey from his lips right into the eyes of Billy Brambles, who screamed in pain and dropped him, while grabbing at his eyeballs.

Man Killer saw a punch coming at his head from Scotty, and he quickly ducked, the beefy fist slamming into the cheekbone of the blinded behemoth. Billy made a wild backhand swing that caught Scotty on the point of his chin, and he flew backward over the table with the two punchers.

Man Killer used this opportunity to quickly jump up on his table and launch himself over the head and shoulders of Billy to land on Hitchcock's face. His momentum carried him and the redhead backward over another table, Hitchcock's head slamming into and denting the brass spittoon by the stove. Man Killer poured its contents on the man's face and jumped up to face Billy, who was rushing at him now, fists balled.

The bartender got a nod from the ship's mate on the *Wallaby*, a three-master trade ship out of Melbourne, a city that had already passed Sydney in size with over a half a million people. Bruce had told Man Killer it was on the southern tip of Australia, but, more important, it was in the area called New South Wales which took up the south-eastern sector of the continent and was the area where Horace Windham's cattle ranch was located.

Man Killer was breathing heavily, but laughing, when he ran to the bar and gulped the drink with a Mickey Finn slipped in. Christian Bruce had warned him that he could be killed and that he even heard of one bloke dying from the wrong additive in a drink. The scout knew there was a good chance he could be killed or even end up on a totally different continent, but it was a chance he had decided to take before even coming into this bar.

Billy rushed at him with a roar as Man Killer quickly downed the deadly drink the barkeep had poured out, and secretly doc-tored, for him. The big seaman ducked his head, hoping to smash the much smaller dark-skinned foe with a vicious butt to the middle of Man Killer's chest. At the last sec-ond, the scout dropped to the floor and Billy rammed into the bar with a full head of steam. It seemed like the whole building shook as Man Killer jumped to his feet and suddenly the room started spinning. He saw Scotty's right fist coming at his face almost in slow motion, and he remembered laughing at the image of Hitchcock sitting up with the dark brown contents of the spittoon draining off his face. That was the last image Man Killer saw as everything went black like a bottomless pit.

He lit a match and looked around in the hold of the ship while rats and cockroaches scattered in every direction. He wanted to see what the ship was carrying. It might give him a clue if he was going to Australia. He knew that this particular ship carried wool to the United States from the big sheep-raising area of New South Wales. He found a metal pry bar and started opening some of the crates in the dank hold. He found a lot of mining equipment, which gave him hope, because he had learned from Christian that gold had been discovered, years before, near Melbourne and the mines had petered out somewhat, but there still was some mining going on.

It was hard for Man Killer to keep his footing because of the ship's rocking, but surprisingly, Man Killer was so far experiencing no seasickness. Christian warned him about it, but also explained that some people got it and some didn't. Following the lead of Chris Colt, Man Killer had already determined, even before going to the Barbary Coast dive, that he would not ever become seasick.

He did have a hangover, but the rocking and swaying really didn't affect him. His head hurt like the dickens, and he had a stomachache, but he could tell by the taste in his mouth and the coating of his tongue, it was from the liquor consumption. Man Killer, though, was single-minded in his task, which was to rescue his love, Jennifer Banta, and all he would do in the months ahead would be to that end.

The sun was unforgiving in the Port of Melbourne. Man Killer had learned, over the previous months, how to be a seaman, but it was not something he desired. He had no friends on board but all respected him. The warning had been given to him and the other three who had been shanghaied, about trying to jump ship and hide in Melbourne. The captain knew that this quiet, strange, and ferocious Indian had something on his mind the whole trip, and he knew he would make his escape attempt in Melbourne. His questions, if ever, were about the city, the terrain surrounding it, and ranches. He even thought the cagy redskin had gotten himself shanghaied on purpose, if anybody could ever have been crazy enough to do that.

The captain also remembered the start of

the voyage, just thirty days out from San Francisco, and he had told his first mate, Wally Bristol, "to notch the red bloke up a mite." He was somehow frightened by the quiet Indian, and he often had the first mate intimidate prisoners by making up a reason to get angry at them and then threaten them with a knife. Some, the tougher ones, were to get a slash across the chest or stomach, but not too deep, just enough to give them "religion" and let them know where the power lay.

Man Killer had not flinched when Wally slashed across his muscular chest with the sharp knife. He smiled at the large first mate, looked down at the blood, and rubbed his fingers through it, then licked the blood off his fingers. He then spit the mouthful of blood into Wally's eyes and attacked the big man with the speed of a "lightning bolt over the outback" while the big man wiped the blood from his eyes.

The Indian's hands were so quick, the captain could not believe it, as he punched and pummeled the bigger man into submission, then bodily picked him up on his shoulders and tossed him into the blue Pacific. All shuddered as they heard the man's agonized screams. The sharks were immediately attracted to him because of the blood streaming from his mouth, nostrils, left ear, and the cut over his left eye, all from Man Killer's powerful fists and elbows.

The scout then grabbed the first mate's knife and walked up to the white-faced captain and handed it to him.

Man Killer spoke softly so nobody else in the crew could hear him. "I needed a ride to Melbourne, and I have worked to pay for it, but do not have any other man try to fight me, or you will wear a knife such as this in your belly."

Man Killer turned and walked away, joining another kidnapee at repairing a torn sail. The captain felt a chill up and down his spine. He had been threatened before, but this was different. This man was only being mistreated because he allowed it to happen. He had, up until that point, outworked every other hand on the crew and kept to himself. He exuded leadership, and all seemed to be constantly trying to make up to him, but he wanted to keep to himself. He would occasionally sit and listen to crew members, talking, sharing a smoke with them, but he seldom spoke himself. When he did, all listened. The captain was also shocked at the red man's command of the English language. He thought American Indians would remind him totally of the aborigines down under, but this one sounded like an educated school teacher when he spoke.

The captain called all hands together on deck and said, "Mates, we're about to put up at dock. I give ya the warnings about any bloke who tries to jump ship on me."

Man Killer felt a gun against his spine and looked back. Benny Bly, the new first mate, had an old Starr double-action Army .44 against his ribs. Another mate slapped shackles on Man Killer's wrists, then nodded at the captain when they were secure. The ship's officer seemed totally relieved when this occurred, and his whole demeanor seemed to change instantly. He seemed much more confident and in charge.

"Sorry about that, mate, but I know. The whole ship knows you was plannin' to leave us in Melbourne, and good hands are hard to find. We're gonna head up ta Sydney and pick up some abos at the Loo, when we leave 'ere, mates. When we get safely out ta sea, red man, whatever yer name is, I'll turn ya about, and ya kin go back ta work, if yer a good boy, see."

Man Killer stared at the captain and said, "My name is Man Killer of the Nez Perce nation, and you, captain, will soon see your ancestors."

The captain laughed, "Man Killer is it, eh, bloke? Now, there's a name, mate."

The captain chuckled again, but nobody laughed with him. He felt another chill down his spine when he thought about the unusual name.

Man Killer knew just what the captain was talking about. The Loo was a part of Sydney harbor actually called Woolloomooloo. The outrageous captain apparently was going to try his hand at slave-trading now, picking up aborigines at Sydney and taking them to who knew where, but Man Killer had other plans.

He felt the sharp pain behind his ear and then slipped into a very comfortable blackness.

Jennifer Banta was wearing shackles on her wrists and ankles, and a gag in her mouth. Tears streaked down her cheeks, and there was a pleading look in her red-rimmed eyes. Man Killer looked up at a puffy, blue cloud, and it swirled around until the cloud became a face. The form of the visage kept sharpening and became Chief Joseph. His face came down out of the clouds and smiled softly at Man Killer.

Joseph said, "You must save her, my son."

Man Killer said, "I can't, my chief."

The chief's face suddenly changed into Chris Colt, and he, too, smiled and said, "You can do anything if you want to bad enough, Little Brother."

Jennifer suddenly changed into a white dove and started to fly away, but one of the ankle shackles became a leather bond, and it played out as the dove flew away.

Man Killer screamed, "Look out!"

The bond caught and snatched at the bird's little leg, and Jennifer's voice came from its beak, crying, "Man Killer, please come and save me! I love you! Please help me!"

He saw Horace Windham with a double barrel ten-gauge shotgun, and he aimed at the dove flying around desperately trying to break free.

He swung the end of the shotgun around, trying to get a bead on the little bird, as it kept screaming, "Man Killer, save me!"

Horace started to squeeze the trigger, and Man Killer screamed, "No!"

He sat up, panting heavily, and looked all about him. He saw he was again in blackness. He was shackled in the same dank, dark hold where he had been left when he was shanghaied so many months before. This time, though, Man Killer was prepared. Three months earlier, on one of his many nightly excursions around the ship, he had made another silent visit to the captain's chambers. While the bearded old Australian snored, Man Killer probed around his room, looking for things, anything that might help him in the future.

In a small drawer in the captain's desk, the scout found an extra set of keys to the shackles, which he carried from then on, only having to move them from their hiding place when he had to relieve his bladder.

He now worked the key out from under his breechcloth and quickly unlocked the shackles. The first thing Man Killer did was to reach up and feel the painful bump under his right ear, where the blackjack had hit him. No matter, he thought, just some more pain to ignore for a few days. He had to find Jennifer, but in the process, he would ensure that the *Wallaby* would never become a slave trader.

Man Killer felt his way along the wall and over to the ladder. His hands went up the sides of the hard, dank wood, and he quietly went up the rungs, feeling them with his soft-soled moccasins. At the top he placed the back of his head against the hatch cover and raised it up slowly. The scout peered out from under the hatch and watched, listening. The ship seemed all but deserted. He kept a vigil for a full five minutes before attempting to crawl out of the hold.

Finally, satisfied that most hands had left the ship, Man Killer crawled out the hatch and slipped under the shadow of a lifeboat. He did not see the eyes that watched him from the time that he first eased the hatch open. Man Killer heard the cocking of a cap and ball gun.

A booming bass voice said, "Awrighty, matey, you'll be comin' out from unner the boat now, or I'll blast a porthole in yer bloody port bow."

Man Killer crawled out slowly, his hands raised. Standing in front of him was a smiling sailor with a broken nose and two front teeth missing, a man he had not cared for at all.

Smiling with pride in his valuable capture, the man yelled past Man Killer, "Hey, Cappin, I caught me the bloody redman, I did!"

Man Killer turned to see the captain, Benny Bly, and most of the crew, just walking off the end of the dock and headed for the seaside dives bordering the water's edge. Moonlight rippled off the dark South Pacific waters, and it created an eerie effect, combined with the lights from the city.

The whole crew started back toward the ship, and Man Killer heard the ship's owner holler back, "Good job, mate. E's been too much trouble, ya know, so we'll tap 'im on the head with me bloody waddy-stick, load 'im with chain and ball, and let 'im escape down below, ta bloody Davey Jones's locker!"

The gap-toothed sailor laughed heartily at

this, and Man Killer knew he had to do something.

The captain yelled, "Don't let 'im trick ya, Manny, or it'll be yer bloomin' hide! If he blinks his bloody eye, shoot him!"

Manny smiled at Man Killer and quietly said, "By golly, mate, I think ya blinked yer eye."

Man Killer had been eyeing a gaff hook on the deck, and he now dived forward into a somersault, the gun exploding and the bullet cracking by his left ear. In midroll, his hand closed around the handle, and he came up swinging the hook with all his might. He buried it in the man's chest and pulled on it, bringing him up eyeball-to-eyeball with the now-screaming, dying sailor.

The Indian heard the captain in the distance yelling, "Manny! You bloody fool!"

Man Killer whispered, "You chose the wrong side, Manny," and the sailor died on his feet, then collapsed onto the deck.

A shot rang out from the dock, and Man Killer looked up, holding the empty pistol in his hand and aiming it. The crew members all ducked, not knowing how, or if, he was armed. They were close to the bottom of the gangplank however.

Man Killer crouched low and made his way quickly to the captain's cabin, where many weapons had been stored. He opened the

door and was surprised to see a shocked
deckhand spin around, a bottle of rum in his
hand. The man was nipping on the captain's
rum while the other was on shore loading up
on more. The scout ran forward and put a
shoulder into the man before he could react.
The sailor hit the outer wall of the cabin and
bounced off, only to be viciously head-butted
by the Nez Perce brave. The man's teeth
cracked together, and blood sprayed out
from his nose. He slid to the floor while Man
Killer grabbed the handle of his knife and
pulled it from its sheath.

He looked around the cabin, but all the
weapons were gone. He grabbed the lantern
and slammed it against the wall, flames
pouring up the dry wood. Armed only with
the rum-stealer's knife, Man Killer ran from
the cabin and made his way along the deck
again. He crouched below the starboard gunwhale and crept along, as the crew cautiously
made their way up the gangplank.

They were near the top of the gangplank
when they looked up at the blood-curdling
sound of Man Killer's war cry. Knife in his
right hand, he crouched over the gunwhale,
leaped onto the railing, and dived over the
heads of two crewmen, his arms wrapping
around the captain's neck as the two of them
went off the far side of the plank, out into the
darkness, and finally splashing into the wa-

ter below. All the hands watched over the edge of the gangplank, four of them aiming guns at the water.

They watched and waited, but nothing happened. A minute passed.

One of the hands said, "I think they're both dead."

Benny said, "The cappin better not be, boys. E's got me bloody wages."

They kept watching. Ten more seconds. Twenty. Thirty. Five more seconds, the captain came up out of the water, gasping for air, as his men cheered. He smiled briefly, then a look of fear swept his face. A copper-colored arm and hand came out of the water and swung in a high arc, the blade going into the man's chest at water level. He screamed and went under, blood swirling up where he had just been.

The men stared down at the water in disbelief, and suddenly Man Killer burst up through the bloody foam, gulping in air. His hand was up and it whipped forward and up toward the men on the plank. The big knife spun over three times and imbedded itself to the hilt in Benny Bly's windpipe. He clutched at his throat and tried to scream, but couldn't. The crew members helplessly looked at him, and the flames now licked up at the sky behind him. He staggered around, eyes wide open in sheer panic, and simply stepped off the other side of the gangplank, disappearing into the water below with a splash.

Just then they heard a scream, and the man who had been in the captain's cabin jumped over the starboard bow, the back of his homespun blouse ablaze. The other crew members suddenly decided that there were plenty of other ships to serve on.

Man Killer swam as far as he could underwater until he thought his lungs would burst wide open. He came out of the water and gasped in a lungful of air as he did a quick whale roll. He was relieved that no bullets followed him through the water, so he rolled over on his back and surfaced again, opening his eyes and looking back. The crew was gone. This water was strange to him, as it didn't have the sweet taste he was used to swimming in back home in Oregon. It was salty and so distasteful that he fortunately didn't try to swallow any.

Man Killer swam along the water's surface until he found a ladder hidden by shadows, going up the side of another dock. He climbed out and up. It wasn't long before he had passed down an alleyway and went up the fire escape of a large structure.

Man Killer looked back from the rooftop of the large tenement building and could see the flames from the *Wallaby* licking up at the sky. The captain, he knew, owned the ship and that was all he owned, except for the flaming cargo he had stupidly not unloaded yet, so anxious were he and his crew to have one night on the town first. That cargo of expensive mining equipment would soon be rusting at the bottom of Sydney harbor, a costly burial marker for a greedy, unprincipled man.

Man Killer made his way nearer the edge of the building, looking below for lawmen in pursuit. He watched the many people running toward the fire and wondered about white men and how silly they seemed to be. He didn't understand why, like sheep, they wanted to live so close to one another, yet scream at, and about, one another as if they all wanted to live as Beaver had. If anybody needed help, many times, people stayed in their homes, but just yell the word "Fire!" and people swarmed over the area like an army of ants.

"Thought you'd 'ide up 'ere, mate, did ya' now?" the voice from behind said softly.

Man Killer froze and turned, raising his hands as he stared down the muzzle of a Colt Russian .44 in the hand of a man who looked to be a constable.

The grinning lawman said, "Ya know, mate, when certain ships come in, I always come up 'ere, 'cause the blokes like you what wants to jump ship always seem to think they was the only one what thought a goin' to the rooftops to get away. Say, what are you anyhow, mate, a blackman? Ya don't look it at all, mate. Git walking there."

Man Killer turned and continued walking near the edge of the five-story building, where the constable had gestured.

The man behind him said, "Ya know, mate, a constable don't get paid much, ya know. Manys a captain'll pay a pretty penny fer a ship-jumper. In fact, mate, when one sets his ship afire, I bet a copper or two that the captain'ld pay a 'ell of a lot more fer a dead ship-jumper."

Off to Man Killer's left was a pole mast sticking straight out below the third-story window on the opposite building, with a clothesline hanging under it. Man Killer dived as the first bullet burned his left calf muscle.

He fell headfirst two stories, and his powerful hands and arms absorbed a little of the shock, but still he slammed into the pole and his wind left him with a rush. He swung underneath it from the momentum, and he squeezed for all he was worth, but slipped right off, and his left hand grabbed the clothesline, the building and tearing loose.

Holding the line, Man Killer fell farther before the pole end of the rope gave way, and he fell down back-first. He landed on a pile of wooden crates outside the door of a warehouse and rolled off, a second before another gunshot, from above, splintered the wood by his head.

Man Killer ran through the darkness as he heard the constable blow his whistle and the signal was picked up by others. Two more lawmen appeared in front of him, and he spun, running down a side alley. Their whistles sounded the alarm, too.

He heard the voice of the one on the rooftop, shouting, 'E's a bad one, mates. Pulled a hidden gun on me. Shoot 'im down like the mangy cur what 'e is!"

The two constables were soon joined by one and then another as the chase continued on down street and alley for another ten minutes. Finally, the winded Indian came out on a main cobblestone street and saw a commotion ahead of him. There were some shouts, and he saw a gray-haired black man in a tuxedo yelling in a black surrey, drawn by a pair of matched blood bays. The man stood up and seemed to be screaming in fright as the panicked horses galloped toward Man Killer at top speed. He kept running at them, the four constables close behind him. A shot whistled past his ear and then another. He couldn't believe the men would shoot at him and risk hitting the man with the runaways.

The horses were closing fast and were just a few bounds off when Man Killer suddenly dropped to his stomach and covered his head with his forearms. The steeds bounded over his prostrate body, and he quickly rolled onto his back and let the carriage pass over him. He reached up and grabbed the axle cover in the back. Dragging on his buttocks and heels, and kicking his legs up behind the buggy, he pulled hard with both hands. He swung upside down into the luggage boot at the back of the surrey just as they passed by the spread apart constables.

He heard the black man yell, " 'Elp me, sirs! A runaway! Help!"

Shots rang out after the buggy as it careened down the street and slid around the corner to the left. Man Killer made his way to the front of the buggy and there found the black man, still standing, but very much in control of the lathered horses. He gave Man Killer a wink and didn't slow down until they were well outside the city in the wilderness. He pulled the buggy over into a grove of white gum trees and hopped down. Man Killer followed suit.

Suddenly, numerous painted aborigines, sporting spears, spear-throwers, knives, and boomerangs appeared from the darkness.

The old man spoke to them in a tongue Man Killer did not understand, then turned to him and said, "So, what are ya', mate, a redman from America?"

Man Killer said, "Yes, I am Man Killer from the Nez Perce nation."

He waited while the tuxedoed man translated his words, and he distinctly heard "Chief Joseph," which brought acclaim and smiles from the assembled warriors.

The man turned around, saying, "Ya know, mate, in the New World your people are treated like we are here."

Man Killer said, "You are aborigines?"

The man nodded. He went on, "Why are you here, mate?"

Man Killer said, "The woman I loved was kidnapped by her uncle, Horace Windham, who has a large ranch near Melbourne. I have come to kill him and save her, but we are many miles from there."

The driver said, "Naw, mate, it's just a short walkabout for people like yours and mine. We'll get you there. Ya know, when ya set that ship afire, ya gave us the chance to rescue many of our people who were being held in a warehouse by there. They were to be taken on that ship to be sold as slaves. You saved them, mate. Horace Windham was the bloke who had every one of our people rounded up. We'll help you all right. First, you'll need some food and rest, and a chance to learn about our weapons. Go with my lads here, and they'll look after ya, mate. Then, we'll all pay Horace Windham a visit. His hands like ta play some games we don't care for, mate. We'll give 'em all their comeuppance, ya know."

Jennifer looked out at the red prairie and was somewhat reminded of the prairie out beyond Pueblo and Bent's Fort. The big difference was the red sand and soil in the area directly around the ranch buildings from the rich iron deposits. The red dust got on everything.

She had been watching the papers every chance she got for some small sign of Man Killer, but the only recent news was about a killer aborigine who had murdered some whites and set a ship afire, weeks ago, in the Sydney harbor. Jennifer prayed for a miracle. She prayed for Man Killer.

She could not believe that her own uncle had been trying to court her behind his wife's back, then she wondered if it really was behind her back. The woman had wealth and prominence with their large cattle ranch. She had numerous outbuildings and thousands of head of cattle and a giant ranch house surrounded by beautiful white-trunked, twisted gum trees. Maybe Beatrice didn't want to upset her own apple cart, so she kept quiet and looked the other way.

That had to be it, Jennifer thought, and felt silly that she had overlooked her own aunt being that way for so long. The woman had even sanctioned Jennifer's kidnapping, although that term was never openly used to describe Horace's forcing her to Australia with them so as to overcome her own grief.

Jennifer knew what his plan was. She knew now that the man was evil, very evil, and was never satisfied with any amount of wealth or power. He wanted her—he was obsessed with her. And he wanted power and prestige. Maybe he thought he would gain class and some youth if he could possess her, but that would never happen. She knew that he wanted the family fortune she had inherited, so first he would take her for his own, then probably get rid of her poor, spineless aunt. He had to have some scheme to get Jennifer's money. It didn't matter what it might be, for he would get none of it. He also had been touching her and had expressed his desire for her physically, so he had crossed the line. She felt, she knew, he would soon take her by force, but she would never give in.

Jennifer looked out the window at one of the hands driving some horses from one fenced pasture to another, cracking a large whip over their backs. Tears flooded into her eyes as she thought once again of Man Killer,

the man of her dreams. What was she doing
in a country so far away? Would he come and
save her? She had only one hope that kept
her from going into the deepest depth of de-
spair. Her handsome Indian warrior would
come charging up on Hawk and rescue her
from this living hell. Then she thought once
again how silly she was being. Man Killer was
an Indian. How could he possibly find her,
let alone rescue her? He couldn't even get
served food, goods, or services at many
stores and restaurants.

She was wealthy now that her father and
Uncle Beaver were gone, a millionairess, but
she never had any money. She had a family
fortune, but she could not get any money
even to bribe a ranch hand to help her get
away. She couldn't ever get into Melbourne,
Sydney, or Canberra to try an escape or at
least smuggle a message to Chris Colt or
some of her relatives back home. Horace
had, however, promised to take her to the big
cities and buy her beautiful gowns if she
would just sleep with him.

Jennifer shivered at the thought and
started crying again. She finished polishing
the silver and put it away in the drawer of
the china closet. What if she could steal it,
she thought. It was worth money, but all the
hands were totally loyal to Horace, and they

all looked at her with the same type of look her uncle did.

Jennifer's worst fears came true that night. She had, as she had done for close to a year, cried herself to sleep. The door to her room opened quietly, and Horace stood there, lantern in one hand and a snifter of brandy in the other, with the neck of the bottle hooked under his index finger. He had been drinking already.

"Sweetheart," Horace said, "tonight's the night. I have it figgered aout, gaerl. You can't go anywhere unless I let ya, and if ya scream, I'll have to kill my poor wife of so many years. I've tried to be patient and let you know I'd gladly show my love for ya, but tonight I will no longer wait for you to give me what I want."

She jumped out of bed and threw her robe on. Her teeth were clenched, and she hissed, "You forgot one thing, dear Uncle Horace. If you so much as touch me again, I will kill myself. How do you suppose that will sit with Man Killer when he finally comes for you?"

Horace started laughing.

He said, "Man Killer, that little red abo. Ha, is that why ya have been holding out on me, gal? He's halfway around the world, and besides ya ain't going to kill yerself, because yer a survivor, just like me."

He stepped forward, and she started backing up, her eyes scouring the room for a weapon. He tumbled over the footstool and hit his elbow on the dresser, shaking his arm and cursing.

Beatrice's voice sounded out from downstairs, "Horace is that you? Is everything all right? Jennifer?"

Horace grinned evilly at Jennifer and yelled, "Put a hold on yer tongue; go back to bed, woman, and be quick off the mark about it!"

There were a few seconds of silence while Jennifer held her breath and listened, but her heart sank when she heard her aunt's meek voice say, "Yes, dear," and a door downstairs slammed shut.

He kept on after Jennifer, and she hunched her shoulders, backing out the double doors onto the big stone balcony. Her room was on the third floor, and it was a long way down. He knew he had her now, and he reached out, grabbing her shoulders violently.

She screamed, "No!"

She shoved him back at the same time, and her gown and bedclothes tore, exposing her left breast. Her uncle stared at her now, and a wild, crazy look came into his eyes. He stepped forward and Jennifer screamed again as something large dropped from the roof, landing between her and her uncle.

Horace backed up, eyes open in horror, as he stared into the war-painted face of Man Killer, a large aborigine spear in his left hand.

Jennifer, behind him said, "Oh Man Killer! Man Killer! I knew you'd come."

Man Killer was filled with a fury like none he had ever known. He walked forward, and suddenly Horace pulled a derringer out from under the folds of his coat and pointed it at the Indian, but the scout never stopped. He kept walking, and Horace kept backing up, his hand shaking.

Horace said, "Stop, or I'll shoot!"

Man Killer didn't stop, and the gun exploded in the room. Man Killer flinched, but kept walking forward, blood streaming out of a bullet hole in his upper right chest. Jennifer screamed again and cried behind him.

He kept walking, raising the aborigine-made spear, and the gun boomed again, pieces of muscle tissue and blood tearing off Man Killer's left shoulder, but he kept on, and Horace suddenly stopped still in the doorway. His eyes opened wide, and he tried to speak. His eyes rolled up in his head, and he suddenly fell forward, dead, a large knife sticking out of his back just below the left shoulder blade.

Standing behind him in the dark hallway

stood Beatrice Windham, teeth clenched tightly and jaw stuck out firmly. She looked at her dead husband's back and said, "This time, you went too far, Horace Windham. My poor dead sister's little girl. You went too far."

Man Killer turned, blood running down his right pectoral muscle and left arm. Face painted black and yellow, he smiled at Jennifer, who had tears running down her cheeks like a waterfall.

She said, "I should have known that the aborigines would take you right in and help you if you could just make it over here."

They heard the scream of a ranch hand outside, then another one.

Man Killer said, "They know how we feel."

"I knew you would come. You're hurt."

He smiled and said, "It is just some pain to put up with for a few days. It will go away."

"Oh, Man Killer," she said, "I love you so."

She rushed forward into his big arms, and he lifted her off the ground and kissed her as though there were no tomorrow. Beatrice turned and walked down the stairway, a blank look on her face.

Chris Colt and Shirley were both wrestling with Brenna and Joseph on the grass in front of the porch when the buggy came down the driveway. Colt wore a badge on his left breast. Joshua, Tex, and Muley were in the branding chutes, branding new spring calves, but stopped and watched.

The buggy stopped, and Man Killer stepped out, then helped Jennifer down. They walked forward, holding hands. Shirley and Jennifer now both had tears in their eyes and smiles on their faces.

Man Killer said, "You wear a badge, Great Scout."

Colt said, "Not much scouting to do anymore. I'm a deputy U.S. marshal, full time now, and so are you if you want to."

Man Killer smiled and looked at Jennifer, then back at the Colts. He said, "Yes, I have a wife to support now. The ship's captain married us."

Jennifer ran forward to be hugged by Shirley and Chris. Colt and Man Killer shook hands and Shirley grabbed him in a bear hug. Tex slipped unseen over to the barn.

Man Killer looked at Chris and said, "The Apache Kid?"

"He came here to the ranch and blew up at me and left quickly."

Man Killer figured there was a lot more to that statement than just the words and chuckled.

Colt said, "Uncle Horace?"

Man Killer replied, "He is now good for something: fertilizer."

Colt said, "Remember the gang of gunfighters? They were hired by him to steal an Army payroll before he left. Guess we can tear up the warrant for him. Money's gone though."

Jennifer said, "No, it's not. I have the addresses and names of his banks and business accounts. We thought they might come in handy."

Joshua came forward and said, "Hey, haven't you gotten out of enough ranch work around here? You sure filled out. You can do a man's work now."

Laughing, he shook hands as Man Killer said, "Always could. Tell me, Joshua, is—"

His words were cut off by a commotion in the barn as Hawk raced out the door and ran up to his master, whinnying.

A large animal appeared across the pasture, and Tex ran to his Winchester.

Jennifer yelled, "Wait!"

Everyone watched as it got closer and closer. It was a great gray timber wolf, and it walked up to Jennifer and sniffed her, wagging its tail.

Tears rolled down her cheeks, as she petted him and simply said, "Wolf."

Man Killer explained, "Beaver and Chancy Banta were brothers. They both fell in love with the same woman, Jennifer's mother.

She chose Chancy, and Beaver went off into the mountains and never came back."

Man Killer squeezed Jennifer's hand, and they stared up at Spread Eagle Peak. Two eagles swept down from the heights and soared in the bright Colorado sunshine. A large wisp of snow blew off one of the jagged peaks and sharply contrasted against the deep blue sky. Man Killer looked into his wife's eyes and thought they had come from that sky. He looked at his friends, the wolf, his horse. The warrior had returned home. It was the only place to be.

DON BENDELL BRINGS YOU
FRONTIER ADVENTURE AND DRAMA
IN THE COLT FAMILY SAGA,
A HISTORICAL WESTERN SERIES
FROM SIGNET

CHIEF OF SCOUTS

Here is the first of the books which started
the series.

Christopher Columbus Colt, Chief of Scouts,
and nephew of gun maker Sam Colt, was always
the best man for the job. His skill with weapons
was legendary, his service to the Seventh Cavalry invaluable. But as a friend to the Lakota
Sioux and Chief Crazy Horse, Colt's loyalty to
the Indians ran dangerously high. At Little Big
Horn, by the side of General George Custer,
Colt faced the hardest choice of his life: fight
for a tyrant against overwhelming odds, or side
with the warriors who planned a killing field
that would live forever in infamy. Rich with the
passion and adventure of real history, this is
the roaring saga of frontier military life and of
a hero who had to work above the law to up-
hold justice.

COYOTE RUN

The legendary Chief of Scouts, Chris Colt, his
brother Joshua, and the proud young Indian
brave Man Killer are about to begin a battle
with the mining company that would do anything and kill anyone to take over Coyote Run,
the ranch that the Colts had carved out of the
Sangre Cristo Mountains with their sweat and
their blood. In a battle which moves to the
courtrooms, the savagery mounts, the stakes
rise higher and higher, and every weapon from
gun and knife to a brave lawyer's eloquent
tongue to the lure of two beautiful women become fair play.

HORSE SOLDIERS

In the embattled Oregon Territory, Christopher Columbus Colt was a wanted man. General O. O. "One-Armed" Howard, commanding the U. S. Cavalry, wanted this legendary scout to guide his forces in his campaign to break the power and take the lands of the proud Nez Perce. The tactical genius Nez Perce Chief Joseph needed Colt as an ally in this last ditch face-off. Rich, ruthless Rufus Potter wanted Colt out of his greedy way and six feet under the rich Oregon soil. And only Colt could decide which side to fight on in the most stirring and savage struggle the frontier ever knew....

COLT

Christpoher Columbus Colt, legendary chief of calvary scouts, was in for the biggest fight of his life. Forced to lead an all-black U. S. Cavalry unit on a suicide mission into the very heart of the explosive Apache wars, Colt would have to overcome million-to-one odds—and his own prejudice—to come out of this one alive. And even if the Chief of Scouts could conquer his own doubts, he would still have to reckon with two names that struck fear into the heart of every frontier man: Victorio and Geronimo, renegade Apache chiefs who led their warriors on a bloody trail that any scout could follow—but few dared to do.